Kingdom of Men
Sister Worlds Book 1

TIFFANY NICOLE TERRY

DEDICATION

This book is dedicated to a brown-haired warrior and a blonde-haired princess.

I started writing this book before you were born, and like a calling to the Universe, you came to be just as you were always meant to be.

You inspired me to finish my story.

CONTENTS

ACKNOWLEDGMENTS

I would like to thank my brother, a voracious fantasy reader, for reading my drafts and providing his input and encouragement. Sword-fighting with me in our college living room was also super helpful.

GLOSSARY AND MAPS

Places	Pronunciation	Description
Naldash	Nahl-dash	The planet where the story takes place
Denlerack	Den-ler-ahk	The sister planet, thought to be dead, that can be seen from Naldash.
Belarone	Bel-la-rohn	One of the three kingdoms. Surrounded by mountains and forests.
Extelli	Ex-tell-ee	One of the three kingdoms. On the cliffs over the coastline.
Lisodanya	Lis-oh-day-nyuh	One of the three kingdoms. In the plains, lots of farmland.
Erion	Err-ee-on	Village in Belarone Kingdom.

People	Pronunciation	Description
KaLeah Trapper	Kuh-lee-uh	Brown-haired girl from Erion village.
Clegg Trapper	Kleg	KaLeah's father.
Princess Amirra	Ah-meer-rah	Blonde-haired princess, daughter of King Erazus.
Prince Bylex	By-lex	Son of King Erazus.
Prince Nikolat	Nik-o-lot	Son of King Erazus

	Pronunciation	Description
King Erazus	Err-ay-zuss	Belarone King
King Mikroth	Mik-roth	Lisodanyan King
King Sarzoe	Sahr-zoh	Extellan King
General Zoseff Array	Zoh-sef Ay-ray	General of the Belarone army.
Captain Hilip Daven	Hil-lip Day-ven	One of the captains of the Belarone army.

Animals	**Pronunciation**	**Description**
Dirlin	Durr-lin	Dear-like.
Draggot	Dra-guht	Horse-like, covered in scales and fur, main, talons and hooves.
Doquer	Doh-kər	Wolf-like.
Juliebee	Joo-lee-bee	Bird-like, scales and feathers. Long talons.
Wuvat	Woo-vat	Cow-like but has dragon scales.

Dragons	**Pronunciation**	**Description**
Klackire	Klak-ire	Mythical dragon.
Anissa La Alani	An-ih-sah Lah Ah-lah-an-ee	Mythical dragon's real name.
Nala	Nah-lah	Race of flying dragons, extinct.
Dynack	Dy-nak	Race of land dragons, extinct.

Catelli Kingdom
ruled by King Sarzoe

Orion Village
Belarone Kindom
ruled by King Erazus
Lisodanya Kingdom
ruled by King Mikroth

1 PHANTOM DRAGON

KaLeah took a slow, silent breath and docked her arrow, pointing her nose in the direction of the sound. After a long day of hunting for big game without luck, she was glad to have finally locked onto an easy shot.

She could tell from the grunting and shuffling sounds that it was big, but she didn't care. KaLeah had carried home large forest beasts before, and she wasn't afraid of a little exercise.

KaLeah stalked closer to the sounds coming from a clearing up ahead. She knew the woods well and could picture the grassy clearing. She moved carefully through the thick forest foliage, using only her hearing to guide her to her target.

It was rare for animals to make so much noise, but she assumed it was most likely injured. Since it was in the clearing, it would be a quick shot straight to the heart, wrap it up with some vines, and then home before dark.

She readied her bow, took one step toward the edge of the trees, and froze. Crouched in the clearing beyond her was a monster with glistening emerald scales. It gracefully lifted its long, slender neck, and turned its jet-black eyes to hers.

Every muscle ached to run, but KaLeah couldn't connect the thoughts to the motion. Her eyes widened to take in the creature's massive body and muscular arms as it rose higher on its back legs. She saw the beast's muscular arms ended in long, black talons that were coated in grass and clumps of mud.

It had thin, dagger-like spikes along the side of its green scaly head. The long, pointed snout was shut but revealed sharp teeth poking out through each side.

A bead of sweat started to roll down the side of KaLeah's head.

The creature blew a chunk of mud from its snout. The noise was so sudden KaLeah jolted and released the arrow she'd been holding tightly docked. It flew and hit the beast right in the chest, bouncing off its scales and landing on the ground.

She quickly jerked herself back and dove behind the nearest tree, dropping her bow to the ground. Her breath came heavy and uneven as she tried to keep from making any noise.

Is that a dragon? she asked herself. *That cannot be a dragon. Dragons are extinct. I'm dreaming. I must have fallen along the path and hit my head on a rock.* KaLeah made an involuntary whimper, knowing she was most certainly not dreaming.

Most of the animals on Naldash had evolved from dragons, but dragons themselves had been extinct for many lifetimes.

She clenched her eyelids shut and reminded herself to breathe. Her father had taught her in any sort of panic-inducing situation, she must keep breathing steadily to keep her mind clear. A clear mind is more likely to survive in any situation.

But how do I survive a non-existent dragon? Is it a ghost? A phantom?

She took another deep breath, smoothed a loose strand of brown hair behind her ear, and then cautiously leaned out around the tree trunk for another view.

The monstrous beast was still standing there in the small clearing. Its long neck trailed down to a spine-lined back, past a set of silvery transparent wings, and ended in a tail. It beat open the two wings, stirring up the dirt around it, then pulled them back close to its body and continued digging furiously at a small hill in the middle of the clearing.

KaLeah tilted her head curiously, realizing the sound she had followed was the sound of the dragon clawing into the ground. It had seen her and yet was much more interested in what it was doing.

Is it trying to get at an animal or digging out a burrow? Did dragons even live in burrows? She shook her head violently, what was she thinking? *Dragons. Are. Not. Real.*

This is crazy, she said to herself. She realized it didn't matter what it was or what it was doing. It was still a dangerous-looking, beast-like creature, mere steps away.

I need to get away, now. I'll grab my bow and quickly head back through the thicker part of the woods where it will be too big to follow; unless it can break trees, of course.

KaLeah visualized the plan in her head, building up the courage to move. She began to prepare for a stealthy escape through the woods, bending first to reclaim her bow when…

Wait.

She froze mid-bend, fingers on the bow. She had heard the word as if placed inside her mind.

Wait.

Again, the word penetrated her mind, moving her own thoughts aside. Had the dragon just spoken to her? She formed the question in her mind. *Are you talking to me?*

Yes.

This isn't happening, she told herself. But she couldn't resist. *Are you real? Are you a dragon?*

Yes.

KaLeah knew she needed to run.

Look.

I must be crazy, she thought as she peeked back around the tree trunk. The dragon tore away a large section of mud with its claws, roots dangling in the air, and tossed the clump aside. With its other claw, it smoothed away more mud to reveal something shimmering beneath the mound.

Look.

KaLeah was still quite a distance away from the dragon, so she could only catch a slight reflection of light on the spot the dragon had cleared away. Regardless of whether it was her imagination or a real flesh-eating dragon, she wasn't about to step one foot out from the security of the dense forest.

As if sensing her fear, or hearing it in her mind, the dragon expanded its wings and began to lift itself into the sky, one slow beat of its silvery translucent wings at a time.

She watched the emerald creature gleam in the sunlight as it passed across the dead planet hanging in the sky. The dragon eclipsed the dark sphere called Denlerack, rising in the late afternoon sky, and then disappeared beyond her sight.

KaLeah pressed herself against the tree and held perfectly still, her breathing shallow, listening for any hint that the dragon was returning.

Long moments passed and her back started to ache from holding herself steady against the hard bark.

I should go home, she said to herself. But she knew she had just seen and experienced something important. Either dragons still existed in hiding, or their ghosts were around and strong enough to impact the physical world.

It had spoken to her. It had called to her.

When she was sure it wasn't coming back, and with her curiosity getting the better of her, she left the safety of the thick wood and walked out cautiously into the clearing. She took soft steps across the grass, looking up, around, and listened intently to the forest sounds.

She walked up a slight incline leading toward a large mound in the center of the clearing. When she reached the spot where the dragon had been digging, she leaned closer and brushed away more mud clinging to an object beneath.

There was something hard, smooth, and cool to the touch just beneath the large mound of caked dirt. It seemed to be almost shaped like a boulder, but it was abnormally smooth and there were no grooves.

She pulled out her dagger and began to tear at the clumps of dirt and grass around the edge, cutting and pulling off sections where the roots had tried to take hold. She worked until the sky began to darken.

It wasn't entirely uncovered, but what she had revealed resembled a sphere, which had been slightly pressed down upon from the top. The material was as hard as iron, black as a moonless night, and half the size of her two-bedroom house. She had no explanation for it, or for the dragon that had appeared to her.

She stood in wonder and noticed she could make out her own image quite well, similar to her reflection on the surface of water or glass. The object mirrored her curious gaze, her stormy blue eyes, ivory skin, and dark brown hair right back at her.

KaLeah stretched out her hand and ran it along the black surface. The object responded to her touch, and she jerked her hand back quickly. Rows of lights began to appear, flashing different colors at seemingly random intervals.

This is some sort of craft, KaLeah realized intuitively.

It was a metallic craft that had no name on her planet. The longer she stood in its now living presence, the more nervous she became. The sun was setting, and she didn't want to be here with the strange thing in the dark.

She grabbed her bow and arrows and slowly backed away, watching the lights trace patterns along the black reflective surface.

KaLeah turned and ran back through the woods, her long legs making fast work of the journey. She knew the woods and the trails well enough to soar through, even in the faintest of light.

She'd been to the clearing with the grassy mound hundreds of times throughout her childhood. But she'd never given it much thought. She'd scouted around it and perhaps climbed it a time or two, but only to gain the upper ground on whatever she was hunting. She felt completely dumb founded that a mysterious object had been hidden beneath the dirt for her entire life.

She burst from the edge of the forest and headed for the hut she shared with her father. It was the one he had built close to the trees and far from the center of the village.

Over the years, the village had grown and so had the huts that encroached upon their own. It soured her father to no end. He spoke often of building a new one in the middle of the forest where the village could not reach.

Her father was the wisest person she knew. The village children feared the large and stoically silent man who had trained her to hunt and fight, although girls were never supposed to learn these things. Not even the boys knew how to fight, stalk prey, and then skin it for proper cooking as well as she did. KaLeah had been doing things at six that most boys learned at ten.

All the children regarded her as an odd thing because of this, and yet, she cherished the time her father spent teaching her. His congratulations on a good kill was the only affection she ever received.

The village girls would sit together and braid each other's dark black hair into long, elaborate designs. KaLeah stood out with her unkempt brown hair that would show hues of red or golden depending on the time of day and how heavily the sun was shining on her.

She had strong cheekbones, a petite nose, and stormy blue, almond-shaped eyes. She would tan deeply in the summer sun, matching the skin tone of the villagers, but lose the tan every winter. She was the only one in the village who didn't have brown eyes.

When she was younger, the girls would sneak up on her and pull strands of her hair out, running off as if they had slayed a dragon and stolen its treasure. They regarded her as some wild animal in pants, where they were groomed and dressed in proper dresses. Once she learned how to punch, they stopped trying to pull her hair out.

The girls in the village had never been friendly and so, eventually, she accepted the distance and focused on learning all she could from her father.

Young girls her age were supposed to focus only on which boys they were going to wed while they learned skills like mending fabrics, cooking, and cleaning.

She had learned how to do all the same chores as the girls, but without a mother around to encourage her to be more feminine, she didn't see the need. She wasn't interested in the conversations the young girls in the village were having. She would rather spar with the boys than figure out if she could tolerate one long enough to wed someday.

The girls mostly saw her as a dirty boy, while the boys saw her as a strange and unkempt girl who was better than them at swordplay and archery. They had grown tired of teasing her and eventually knew by fighting with her, they may lose, but at least they would learn a new trick or two. Their tolerant acceptance made the girls like her even less, and the adults disapproved, but dared not say anything to her father.

Most days, she was proud to be so strong, fast, and skilled at combat. But loneliness carved scars into her heart.

Some days when she watched the other children playing, laughing, and holding hands, her heart ached in isolation. She reminded herself that the thing missing in her life was the loving embrace of a mother after a long day of hunting; someone to help remove her shoes and wash her face and hands before dinner.

She knew what other mothers did for their children. She watched other families and saw fathers were mostly aloof and unaffectionate. Her father was only playing his part accordingly. He wasn't supposed to figure out how to play the mother role as well. And so, she would sigh away her feelings as being nothing but childish.

She knew she was lucky to have a father who was so capable, who had been willing to teach her all he knew from such a young age. She could survive completely on her own in the middle of the woods thanks to him. Come what may, he had created a survivor, and she intended to put those skills to use someday.

But not today.

Today, she needed his wisdom. Her father knew the woods better than she did. He would either immediately be able to explain the black glittering object buried under a mound of dirt, or she would take him back to see it, and he would know for sure then.

Since dragons were supposed to be extinct, she decided she would leave that little bit of information out of the story for now as she reached the front door. She had a feeling he would dismiss the entire story if he knew she had been led into the clearing by a phantom dragon.

Their home was similar to the others in the village; small, built with interlocking pieces of wood that had been sealed with dried mud, and a thatched roof on top of it all. Theirs was cozy with a large kitchen and two straw-stuffed chairs in front of an iron stove used for cooking and heating. Furs were draped over the chairs, and woven rugs covered the wood floors.

When she opened the door, she was greeted with warmth, and the smell of cooked dirlin meat mixed with pipe smoke. The warmth was too much for her and she immediately began shedding her coat and boots. The run home had left her breathless, and nerves were starting to clench her stomach.

Her father was sitting near the fire, smoking a pipe. He was not the type to offer greetings, pleasantries, or smiles. He just sat with his brown eyes on his daughter. His skin was sun-worn, and his face was covered in a thick brown beard.

"Where's your kill?" he asked, looking her over.

Her hands and forearms were still covered in mud, and

she was sure she'd rubbed her face during her trek home. She looked more like a child who had spent all day playing in the dirt and not the hunter he had sent out earlier that morning.

"I'm sorry, father, but I didn't have a good hunt today. Something happened out in the woods."

She went to sit on the chair opposite him, and he lowered his pipe in interest. "I saw," she started and then stopped, remembering her decision to keep the phantom dragon out of the story. "I found something sticking out of the ground in a clearing. You know the clearing toward the north with the large grassy hill in the middle? I saw something shining beneath it and I started digging. I know it sounds silly, but there was something beneath the hill. It was solid, like a knife blade, but shiny black, and when I hit it, it made a sort of echoing noise, or a hollow sound."

KaLeah jumped up, and with a closed fist, rapped her knuckles against the kettle hanging above the fireplace. "Like this. But it wasn't this dingy; it was shiny and beautiful. And then lights, like fire bugs or lamp lights, just started twinkling all throughout the surface. It was glorious, father. What could it be?"

Her father turned his face to watch the flames, a brief look of concern crossing over his features before flashing away.

After a long pause, he asked, "Why would you waste valuable hunting time digging around in the ground? You know we need to eat, KaLeah."

"I was distracted," she said. She knew instantly he was irritated and was glad she hadn't mentioned the dragon. He would have accused her of making up childish stories instead of working.

"I wanted to know what it was in case it was something of value," she said, trying to defend herself.

"If we can't eat it, then it is nothing of value to us." His voice started to rise, and she looked down at her dirty hands, shamefully, absently flicking the mud out from underneath her fingernails.

He pushed himself heavily up from the chair and headed for the door. She watched him grab his coat, boots, his bow, and a quiver of arrows from beside the door, not once daring to ask him what he was doing. He opened the door and called back to her as he started to leave.

"You should have stayed on the path." Then he left, closing the door behind him.

KaLeah waited for a few breaths before jumping up and running to peek out of the window. She looked toward the village center, but seeing nothing, turned to just catch him disappearing into the woods.

They had enough food to last at least another day or two, and they could easily trade wares for extra meat in the village if necessary. She assumed it was his anger that drove him to go hunting this late, perhaps to prove a point. She felt terrible for letting him down, and a small ache filled her chest.

She went to the kitchen to scrub her hands in the basin and then grabbed a couple slices of bread to toast over the fire while she ate the meat her father had left out.

After eating, she washed the dirt off her arms and face and changed out of her hunting clothes. She slipped into a long sleeping shirt, then ran her hands through her hair to clear out any leaves or dirt.

Her bedroom was large enough for a small bed and a chest of drawers. She crawled under the layers of animal fur and fell asleep quickly, still seeing the phantom dragon in her mind.

The next morning, KaLeah woke up to find her father had not yet returned. Or perhaps, he'd come home to collect his things for the market and then left again before she'd woken. If he'd brought home any game, he would have taken it to the cellar for her to clean.

She dressed in a fresh pair of brown pants and a loose-fitting green shirt. KaLeah had gotten used to dressing like a boy. She was comfortable that way.

Out in the living area, she lifted the corner of a rug to reveal the door to the cellar. She pulled on the latch and lifted the door, then lit the candle they kept on the ledge beside the stairs.

The cellar was half the size of the house above, dug out of the earth to maintain the moisture and coolness the dirt provided. It kept their meat fresh longer and was a good place to hide the valuables her father would take to the market to trade or sell.

She used her candle to light a few lanterns. There was no fresh game waiting for her on the ceiling hook in the center of the cellar. She also didn't see the quiver of arrows he took with him when he'd left the night before. The stack of market furs was still lying in the corner, along with some newer arrows and knives they had made.

There went her theory that he had taken some furs, arrows, and knives to sell at the market.

So, now what? she wondered.

She could go out hunting again, but if her father was still out hunting, they might end up with more meat than they could sell. Her father did not like wasting food. One large dirlin was enough to last them for many days, and any more than that, they would trade for goods in the town.

She looked at the empty sacks beside the shelves that ran along the back wall. There were some jars containing jams and pickles and other items they'd grown and stored, but they hadn't yet begun to dig up the potatoes. She supposed her father might get over his anger quicker if she began that grueling chore without his instruction.

KaLeah walked to the shelves to grab a couple of the empty potato sacks. She pulled at one and some jars that had been stacked on top of the corner began to spiral. She moved quickly to catch them, but one slipped and exploded on the hard dirt, sending red jam across the floor.

"Oh great," she said.

One more thing for her father to be upset about. Maybe he wouldn't notice one missing jar.

She adjusted the jars on the shelf, so they were no longer resting on any potato sacks, and then grabbed a thick cloth to clean her mess. The jam was starting to soak into the ground, and she knew she wouldn't be able to hide the evidence of the mess. She carefully picked up the glass and then began to rub soapy water onto the red stained dirt, realizing how ridiculous it was to try to clean a mess off a dirt floor.

As she scrubbed, she started to see something that wasn't dirt underneath her strokes. Curious, she scrubbed harder and poured more water onto the area until she cleared away enough dirt to reveal a small trap door, half the size of the one leading to the cellar.

"What is this?" she wondered out loud.

Instead of a latch, there was a hole in one of the boards. She stuck her finger through it and pulled up. The door didn't open easily, and she had to clear more caked mud away from the edges before it finally lifted.

She lowered one of the lanterns into the dark hole, expecting to see shiny pieces of silver or gold glittering back like some lost treasure. Instead, the light hit the edges of something reflective that didn't shimmer. KaLeah pulled back the lantern, set it down beside her, and reached into the hole with both hands.

Her fingers touched something hard and cold. She lifted out a bulky, black object and set it beside her.

She had never seen anything like it. It was a shiny metal object, with a long cylinder-shaped section as long as her forearm. On one side there was what seemed to be an awkwardly shaped handle more for holding than lifting. She gripped the handle, and although it was a fit for a hand, she could tell it was for larger hands than hers.

She lifted it up, pointing the end of the cylinder away from her, and peered through a tiny triangle sight, feeling familiarity.

This is how I aim my arrows, she realized. Her finger came into contact with a switch of some kind. When she pulled her finger toward her, the object made a hollow click.

She set it down beside her and stared at it for some time before going back to the cubby hole. She retrieved four more objects that looked like the first, but of varying sizes. Then she pulled out a contraption that looked like three belts woven together with multiple buckles. She tossed it aside with the other items and then pulled out the final object; a black box with two clasps.

Once she had unearthed all the mysterious treasures, she started to lift each one. Her instincts told her they were weapons of some sort, but unlike anything she'd ever seen.

She opened the black box and found a neat row of black blocks. Lifting one, she saw each rectangular block contained thousands of tiny beads. The beads were yellow, and when she pressed her finger to them, they were hot to the touch.

This is all dangerous, she realized. Not knowing what any of it was or how any of it worked, she was sure anything kept underground that felt hot to the touch couldn't be safe. Also, her father wouldn't have kept this stuff hidden if it wasn't dangerous.

He'd taught her how to use every kind of weapon on Naldash, how to hunt every kind of beast, and how to survive in the forest. To not teach her about this meant they must be even more dangerous than all the other weapons, beasts, and forests on the planet combined.

She gently placed them each back into the hole, closed the trap door, and covered the door with dirt, using some of the water to help it harden as if it had never been disturbed.

She sat back on the dirt and stared at the floor. She pulled her knees up to her chest and wrapped her arms around them. She and her father didn't talk much, but it was still odd for him to keep something like this a secret.

She had seen men carrying the usual bows, spears, axes, and other weapons, and hunting tools through the village, but had never seen items such as these.

The weapons in the ground appeared to be made from the same metal as the large object buried in the woods. They had weapons made of gray steel, and her arrow heads were made from a gray granite rock they mined in the mountains, but this black metal was too perfect and smooth to be natural.

Is this related to the craft I found? she wondered.

Her father had been irritated, but perhaps he wasn't irritated about the lack of food at all.

What if he knows something about the object in the woods? What if that is where he went?

She took the potato sacks from the ground and put out the lanterns. She spent the day digging up potatoes in the garden, looking out toward the woods again and again. Once that chore was completed, she stayed in the house and tried to busy herself with cleaning while she waited for her father to come home.

Days passed.

She ventured out into the village to ask if any of the traders had come across her father on the roads or if any hunters had seen evidence of him in the woods. No one had seen or heard from her father in days. With each passing moment, she grew more curious and more anxious.

Her father may not be affectionate, but he was all KaLeah had, and she was starting to worry.

Something could have happened to him, she realized one afternoon. She decided the time to sit around and wait was gone.

She packed a bag with food and water, grabbed arrows, her bow, sword, and a couple of daggers. She dressed in layers, prepared to sleep outside, and then closed up the house. She informed a few of the villagers that her father was missing, and she would be traveling to find him. She asked the men who routinely travel the roads between towns to keep a look out for him.

They all scrutinized her, a few mentioning how unheard of, dangerous, and even scandalous it was of her to be traveling alone, and yet, none of them offered to go in her place. Her father had not exactly made friends with the villagers over the years. She assumed it had to do with his past, but she had never asked.

KaLeah set off into the woods, taking the familiar paths. She would return to the clearing where she saw the phantom dragon first, and if she saw no signs of him, she would continue searching.

She looked for any indication of her father along the way, tracking him as she would any other beast. She looked for tracks, broken branches, and signs of a camp, or moss that had been cleared from a log or rock. However, after hours of searching, she found nothing. She located the spot where the dragon had led her off her usual path and went in the direction of the mound. She moved quickly and quietly, using her memory to guide her back to that place.

When she found the clearing, she checked for signs that a dragon, or another human, had been there. Instantly, she noticed something odd about the mound. It was no longer a mound. She walked closer and saw that the large object had been completely extracted from the dirt and was nowhere to be seen. In its place was a large, circular crater.

Had her father come here to dig it up? Had it been light enough for him to move? Or what if the dragon had come back and carried it to another location? What if her father had been surprised by the dragon and eaten?

She shook her head back and forth, refusing to believe her father was no longer living. It wasn't a possibility. He was too strong and too smart. Besides, she thought, the dragon hadn't made any attempt to harm her, and the more time that passed, the more she questioned if she had seen or simply imagined the beast.

She was disappointed the mystery object was gone. She would now never know what it was or why it was here in the middle of the woods behind her village. She was even more disappointed that her father wasn't there; it meant she had to keep looking and she would have to travel further from the village than she'd ever been.

Erion was the northernmost village in Belarone Kingdom, the mountains to the north being impassable. Some people visited from other nearby villages to trade goods, and sometimes people left to move to other areas of the kingdom; but for the most part, everyone she knew stayed in Erion.

She sat on a large stone and thought for a while about which direction to resume her search. Many types of men traveled the roads between villages to sell and trade, so if they were looking out for her father there, she needn't also travel the roads or search out the nearby villages.

Another issue with traveling the roads was that KaLeah never actually had heard of women traveling alone.

Perhaps, if a family was relocating to work farms, they would travel together in a carriage. But it was completely unheard of for girls or women to travel without male escorts. Someone could try to scoop her up and drag her back to Erion, or worse, try to take her back to their village as a wife. No one was fighting to marry her in Erion, so she was safe there. But she would not be protected if she were caught while wandering the kingdom alone.

As far as other men were concerned, without an escort, she was fair game. She would be strong and skilled enough to fight off one captor, but not too many more if they were to gang up on her.

At the absolute worst, if she proved to be disobedient or discourteous about marriage, she would be taken to a comfort house to appease the appetite of traveling men. KaLeah would've rather died.

Traveling through the woods and staying hidden was the best option. The men of her village hunted the same woods, but she could easily avoid them. There were mountains to the north, and then the sea beyond, but no villages and no reason for her father to have travelled north.

If her father had gone west, then he would run into men from her village who routinely fished the river there. They would surely inform him of her search. And if her father had gone to the east, the men who traveled regularly to trade with the farmers there would come across him.

Since the forest thinned out to both the east and west, if her father had traveled in either direction, he would eventually be met. Everyone else would take the roads south to the Belarone castle markets, the most populated area of the kingdom.

The woods that surrounded her village also stretched down south toward the main center. Though it wasn't technically the center of Belarone Kingdom, people referred to it as such. If her father had traveled that way, it would be the only path he could take unseen for days until he reached the Belarone Center.

So, she set her course; she would head south toward the Belarone castle in the center of Belarone Kingdom. She would travel through the forests, stay off the roads, and keep searching for any sign of her father.

She traveled for days, resting only to eat the small game she killed along the way with any edible plants she managed to gather. Plenty of streams ran through the forest from the mountains above Erion, so she never ran short of water. She took only short naps when she found a turned over log or a circle of pines to hide in. As for her father, there had been no signs.

In fact, she hadn't seen any sign of hunters or other travelers in the woods until she happened upon what appeared to be a deserted camp.

Some rocks had been circled as if to create a fire, but no fire had been set. Some of the area had been cleared and a few piles of leaves and thick branches were stacked in a bundle, but she hadn't seen or heard anyone nearby. She decided to make use of the prepared space and set down her pack.

Suddenly, she heard a rustling coming from the brush behind her. She froze, knowing instantly she had made a mistake.

KaLeah drew her sword and spun, turning to face the loud, unsettling rustling sound coming from the brush behind her. Even stranger, she thought she heard a low growling sound and thought doquers could be nearby.

She had never had to fight off the sharp-toothed, four-legged creatures, and wondered if her time had finally come after years of being able to avoid them in the wild.

Instead of furry beasts, three large men emerged from the thick forest and stepped into the prepared campground. The one at the front raised a thick lip over missing teeth.

"What do we have here?" he said with a sneer.

2 KIDNAPPERS

The three men were large: taller and thicker than her father. They had been moving quietly and without speaking a word. KaLeah only heard them moments before they entered the small clearing.

She stood with her feet planted and sword drawn, not sure if she could out-run them. She had dropped her pack a few paces in their direction, meaning she would have to go toward them to grab her pack before running away. Her other option was to dart back the way she had come and try to survive without her travel gear.

The man in the front of the trio took another step closer, a smirk on his face as he eyed her up and down.

"Do you always take other people's camps, little lady?" he asked, with a lisp due to the missing teeth. "Where's your escort?"

One of the men in the back of the trio gently set down a large sack he was carrying and all three drew out daggers, looking around for KaLeah's escort, as if he might jump out at any moment to defend her honor.

"He is coming up right behind me," she lied. "I was just leaving your camp to go meet up with him now. I will grab my pack and be out of your way."

She took a hesitant step toward them and toward her pack, gauging her chances at outrunning them once she grabbed it. The leader cocked his head and took another step toward her.

"Wait now, are you traveling without an escort? What a scandalous little waif you are. Well boys, looks like we'll have some extra company to keep us warm tonight."

The air filled with their raucous laughter and hot breath. KaLeah's stomach turned as the men fanned out to surround her.

"That sword though," said the man in the middle, who appeared to be the leader of the trio. "Are you actually planning on fighting with it, or did you just bring it along to look tough, little warrior?"

He was leaner than the other two, but still very large and muscular. His black hair was matted down on his head by sweat. "You don't think you stand a chance in this situation, do you? Let's just make this easy and hand it on over? We wouldn't want you to get hurt, now."

The leader took another step and reached out his hand toward her.

Something inside KaLeah snapped. Training, instinct, and pure stubbornness that refused to let her run from the fight clicked together and she suddenly leapt forward, raised her sword in a quick arch, then down and across the man's left hand, severing it from his body. She spun, grabbed her pack from the ground, and turned to head back the way she had come.

The leader dropped to his knees, screaming like an animal, and KaLeah, shocked at the sound, stumbled backward. She quickly tried to regain her footing. The other two men were momentarily frozen with their eyes on the leader.

"Dragon's spit," said the man who had been carrying the sack. Then both men broke from their trance and turned their eyes back to KaLeah. "You're going to wish you were never born, little warrior."

They began to move in closer, and their leader ripped apart his shirt to wrap around his bleeding arm. KaLeah felt unsettled by how quickly the man seemed to recover and resolve himself to his situation.

These are not just poor bandits hiding out in the woods, she realized.

Her breath stuck inside her lungs like sap and her feet turned into two heavy logs. She was unable to turn away from them and unable to run. She knew she would have to stand her ground and fight.

Frozen to the spot, all she could do was look at them more clearly. They were dirty with scars across their faces, arms, and hands, as if they had seen many battles. The man to her right, who hadn't yet spoken, was missing an ear and had a scar that ran nearly the length of his face.

She noticed the one to her left was short a few fingers. The dirt on their clothing seemed more purposeful than happenstance. The clothing itself looked rather new and well-tailored, with a camouflage pattern of brown and green coloring.

Although they were quite large and muscular, they were stealth-like in their steps. She realized, had she run, these men would have easily caught her. They were in excellent shape.

KaLeah saw one small advantage in what could have been a desperate situation. The men only had daggers and did not appear to have swords. She could move faster than they could and reach them easier with her blade than they could reach her with theirs.

While the leader wrapped his arm, one man closed in on her from her left and one flanked her right.

She didn't think; she just quickly lunged to her right and thrust her sword into the gut of the man with the face scar and missing ear.

To her own surprise, her sword went into him easily, slicing up his middle with her upward thrust. She wasn't sure if it was her strength or just a testament to the hours she had spent sharpening the sword. As he fell forward, she spun around behind him, both whipping her sword free and ensuring she kept the two remaining men in front of her.

Their smirks faded as if suddenly realizing this wouldn't be as easy a fight as they had hoped.

The man with the missing fingers also had blood stains down the right side of his shirt and she noticed a cloth bandage tied around his upper bicep. He was carrying a knife in his right hand, which meant his dominant arm was vulnerable from the recent wound.

She moved her sword to her left hand and pulled out her dagger with her right. She planned her move on him in her mind and then executed it.

She pulled her sword up and when he moved to block her attack, she whipped it against his bandaged wound. He yelled in pain and anger. She quickly moved behind him and drove her dagger into his back. He coughed, staggered, and then fell near the feet of their leader, who had just finished wrapping his arm.

"What are you?" the leader asked, looking at her hard as he got to his feet. "Some kind of woodland warrior?" He gripped his dagger tightly in his remaining hand.

Her father had practiced fencing with her daily and had drawn onto his chest to show her where the vital organs lay beneath.

He told her no one would expect a girl to be able to use a sword, and yet, it was important to strike a vital organ quickly before they realized her skill and attempted to overpower her. He had drilled into her again and again to never hesitate.

She had killed countless beasts, skinning them, and then cutting them up to store, cook, or trade. She had never hesitated. But these were not animals.

One of the men groaned and the leader looked down hopefully, but KaLeah knew she'd struck both of his men in vital organs; they would not get up. They would die where they lay.

She knew she had to kill the third man before he tried to run. Even if he ran or said he'd surrender and walk away, he would come back to kill her in her sleep or when he was fresh and not stunned at how easily she'd dispatched his men. He would not be the type to admit defeat, especially by a girl.

He moved toward her with the knife in his right hand outstretched and the stump of his left hand against his chest. He moved his arm quickly at her, and she met each of his knife blows with her sword, easily knocking him away, moving faster than him.

She wondered if he was testing her reaction speed, trying to wear her down, or attempting to back her into a corner.

As he kept trying to find a way in to stab her, she stepped backward over rocks and branches, as limber as a mountain doquer.

Following her, he stumbled and kept losing his focus as his footing became more unstable. She swung her sword back and forth behind her as she walked backward, trying to find a tree.

Once she hit one, she jumped quickly around it, rolling her back against the trunk. She spun fast around the tree, spinning around to face his back before he realized where she was.

She drove the blade of her sword home, and for good measure, pulled the dagger blade across his thick neck. She kicked him forward as she pulled out her sword and watched as he toppled down into a pile of leaves.

She breathed fast and heavy, watching to make sure he was not getting up. She looked back to the two dead men behind her where they had fallen.

"Woah," she said in a whoosh of breath. "Dragon's blood, I killed you all," she whispered into the woods, surprised as the event played back in her mind.

She staggered slightly as she saw the sword going through the bodies again, the blood dripping, and she looked down at her own hands.

The world started to spin, and she realized she was breathing too fast. An invisible fist clutched her heart inside her chest, and she lost her grip on her sword and dagger, barely hearing the sound as they fell to the rocky ground.

Stars filled her eyes so thickly she didn't know if her eyes were still open or if she'd closed them. *Calm down, slow down, breathe in, breathe out, calm down.*

She had expected a little bit of trouble along the way, but nothing like this. KaLeah had never killed a man. She tried to reconcile in her mind that these were dangerous men determined to either harm or kill her.

I killed people, I killed people, she said as images of her blades slicing flesh filled her mind.

No, stop, just breathe.

Because of her training, she hadn't hesitated. Everything came naturally, just as her father had intended. And she had saved her own life because of it.

This is exactly what her father had trained her for, she realized, regaining control of her breath. The stars began to dissipate, and her vision cleared.

My father would be proud of me. But what if I never find him, she thought, nervous worry gripping the insides of her gut once again.

KaLeah looked around the blood-splattered camp and knew she could not stay there for much longer. She needed to worry about her feelings later and act on her survival instincts now.

The wild doquers would come for the meat. The four-legged hunters with fur and patches of scales, fierce claws, and fangs. She had heard their barks and howls throughout the nights as she traveled, but they had mercifully stayed away from her.

She knew they could smell her, but as long as she cleaned the small game animals she ate far enough away from where she set up camp every night, the doquers stayed clear of her.

Before leaving, she shook off the nerves and intensity of what had just occurred so she could inspect the men's loot for potential supplies.

KaLeah walked over to the sack the leaner man had dropped near the camp. She spun it around on the ground so all three of the dead men were still in her line of sight.

She was surprised by the sack's heaviness. She unwound a rope from the mouth of the sack and pulled it slightly open.

A tuft of wavy, silvery-blonde mane spilled out of the sack's opening. The first thought that came to her was of a young dirlin.

Dirlins, although graceful and beautiful, were often hunted for their meat. She and her father had hunted many for food, kept their skins for blankets, and made tools from their antlers.

She hoped this one wasn't dead.

As if in response, it moved. KaLeah jumped back to her knees and began to carefully pull the sack down over whatever was inside.

Big green hazel eyes stared up at her wide in shock and fear. They were the eyes of a child maybe half her age. There was a bundle of rags shoved into her mouth.

KaLeah stumbled back in shock at what she saw inside.

She quickly regained her composure and leaned forward to loosen the bag's opening.

"It's alright. I killed the men. You're safe," KaLeah said.

She pulled the tiny girl free of the bag, and then went to work, gingerly removing the rags from her mouth.

The girl's lips were dry and white. KaLeah pulled out her water pouch and held it to the girl's mouth. "It's water," she said.

The girl opened her mouth and let KaLeah pour the water.

KaLeah had never had to care for anyone or anything in her life, but giving the child water, knowing she was bringing this child back to life, filled her with a strange sense of fulfillment.

"Let me get your wrists."

She gently cut the ropes that were bound around the little girl's tiny wrists and then handed her the water pouch.

She took a quick sip and then drank the entire thing. Tears were streaming down her face as if the water was coming back out as quickly as she'd taken it in.

There was a pinch and tingle in her own eyes, but she blinked hard and took a deep breath to ward off emotion.

This is a time for strength, she said to herself, repeating the words her father had said often whenever she'd been close to tears.

"Are you alright?" KaLeah asked.

The girl nodded, tears still falling.

"Are you hurt?"

She shook her head that she was not.

"Are you hungry?

She nodded vigorously.

"OK, let's see what we have."

KaLeah had caught a tree rodent before she had found the camp but decided to give the girl some berries she'd found until they could relocate to a safer place. She handed a pouch of berries to the girl and took back her empty water pouch.

"Can you walk?"

The girl nodded.

"Let's move away from here and find a better place to cook up some food."

The girl's eyes scanned over the three men lying in their own blood and then nodded in agreement.

The girl stood up on shaky legs and the two girls headed off toward a stream KaLeah had passed earlier. She remembered seeing a bundle of closely growing trees they could make shelter in for the night. She was back-tracking, but only a little.

After reaching the spot she remembered, KaLeah squeezed in between the circle of trees to confirm it was empty of creatures and secure enough to huddle in for the night. The copse of trees was filled with a natural pillow of leaves and no obvious signs of a burrow or nest.

She slinked back out and found the girl sitting beside the narrow stream. The girl seemed to be looking longingly at the water but hadn't tried to drink.

"The water is fresh and cool," KaLeah said, reassuringly.

She reached out and refilled her water pouch in the stream, drank, refilled it again, and offered it to the girl, who took it gratefully.

KaLeah washed the blood from her hands and arms like she'd done hundreds of times before, reflecting that this was the first time the blood had not belonged to animals.

She closed her eyes tightly and reminded herself that they had been terrible men.

The girls settled in next to the trees and KaLeah started a small fire to cook the rodent she had captured and cleaned earlier. They ate in silence until finally, KaLeah couldn't help her curiosity.

"My name is KaLeah, what's yours?"

"Amirra," the little girl said, almost reluctantly.

Her voice was high and thin, as any child's voice might be, but it also held a sense of something she couldn't quite place. It was as if she had a slightly different accent than her own.

"Amirra, why did those men have you?"

"I was taken while I was out riding," Amirra said. Her tears had finally dried up, and she seemed to be shaking less. She looked at KaLeah.

"Are you going to hurt me?"

"Spirits, no," KaLeah said. "I just saved you."

"Are you going to take me home?"

KaLeah thought for a moment. If the girl lived in the opposite direction than the direction she was headed, it would definitely be inconvenient.

But to desert the girl would mean she'd saved her for nothing. Not only was she young and delicate, but she was dressed in the nicest riding gear KaLeah had ever seen.

Nothing like this existed in her village. The light gray

material seemed to shimmer in the fading daylight and was intricately sewn and beaded. Her boots were black and yet feminine with a slightly lifted heel. The pants and shirt were the same light gray color with what must have once been very white ruffles around the edges of the sleeves and neck.

A girl dressed like this was not an expert in survival, hunting, or anything besides perhaps riding fledgling draggots.

KaLeah felt a stab of jealousy. The draggots of Naldash were beautiful creatures, and she'd always wanted one. Like most of the animals on Naldash, they had evolved from dragons. Draggots stood taller than a man, on long, muscular legs that ended in thick hooves. The fronts of their legs were covered in scales in order to traverse rough terrain.

They had long, strong backs that would support a rider after they'd reached a year in age. They had powerful shoulders, a long neck, wise, round eyes, sharp, pointy ears, a long nose, and surprisingly sharp teeth. Scales also ran the length of their nose and up the fronts of their necks.

Draggots' manes and tails were long, soft, and beautiful, flowing gracefully as they ran. Their coats ranged in color but always seemed to shine. They were a rare sight in outlying villages like hers, but she assumed this young child had seen and ridden many. She swallowed back the resentment.

"Yes, of course I will take you home. Where do you live?"

"Belarone Castle," Amirra said.

KaLeah smiled. The girl must have meant Belarone Center, which was exactly where KaLeah was headed. She sighed in relief that her journey would not be diverted.

"I'm on my way to Belarone Center, myself."

"Belarone Castle," Amirra corrected.

"Yes, but you don't live in the castle, obviously," KaLeah said, smiling.

"I do. Those men took me because I am Princess

Amirra of Belarone."

The little girl looked up at KaLeah again but with an unspoken question in her eyes this time. KaLeah slowly lowered the piece of meat she was eating and looked Amirra in the eyes.

"You are not."

"I am, and there will be a reward for you if you return me safely."

"Of course, I'll return you safely. I'm not the kind of person who would leave a little girl alone in the woods. I'm just a bit surprised. If you say you are the princess, then I believe you. Am I supposed to bow or something?"

Amirra produced a faint smile and KaLeah was glad to see the girl's mood lifted.

"No. At least, not here. But you must know, in front of other people, you would be required to curtsy, like a lady. I wouldn't want you to get in trouble later."

"Well, thank you very much. Do I call you princess, or your highness?"

Again, she smiled. "Princess Amirra."

"OK, Princess Amirra. It's nice to meet you."

"Lovely to meet you. And thank you for saving me."

"Who were those men? Do you know why they kidnapped you?" KaLeah asked, resuming her small meal.

Princess Amirra wrung her hands, rubbing her fingers over the lines the ropes had left behind on her wrists.

"They took me while I was out riding on the castle grounds," she said. "They didn't talk much, but a few times they argued over payment, and I heard the word 'war', I think. I don't know where they were taking me, or why. Why are you out here in the woods, KaLeah? Do you live in the Center?"

"No. I am from the Village of Erion, north of here. My father has gone missing, and I am searching for him."

"You are searching in the woods?" she asked. The corner of her lip lifted curiously.

"Yes. Others from my village may cross his path on the

roads and let him know I'm looking for him. I figured I would search the woods along the way to Belarone Center, just in case he walked this way himself. He is a bit of a woodsman, and a loner."

"I see. Do you know at all why he went missing? Does he usually disappear like this?"

KaLeah shook her head in response, not wishing to discuss the details.

"What about your mother? Is she looking for him too?"

"My mother is dead," KaLeah said.

Amirra looked away into the woods. "So is mine, but I'm not allowed to speak of it," the princess said.

"Why are you not allowed to speak of it?" KaLeah asked, hoping she wasn't being too bold. She had never interacted with royalty before. It wasn't something anyone from Erion ever planned on experiencing.

"I don't really know," Amirra said. "My father and brothers just never speak of her and always ignore me when I ask questions; so, I assumed it isn't allowed. I have no memories of her. Did you know your mother?"

"No," KaLeah said. "And my father never speaks of her either, so I don't know much about her."

The girls sat in silence for a while, listening to the juliebees sing their mating songs, the insects clicking against the coming darkness, and night animals preparing to wake and hunt.

"We'd better move into the trees and out of sight," KaLeah said. KaLeah began to slip into the copse and felt Amirra's small hand clasp her own. She jolted at first but then relaxed and helped guide the child into the circle of trees. It was darker and slightly cooler, and the leaves were soft below their feet.

She sat down on them and began to fashion herself a small pillow of leaves and nettles. The princess stood in the entrance, looking lost, and so KaLeah scooped up a bundle of leaves for her, and motioned for her to lie down.

"It's alright, child. You'll be safe here. Try to rest. We

have a lot of walking to do tomorrow."

Amirra held her light blonde locks back while she kneeled, slowly sat, and even more carefully lied down.

After a few moments, she gave up trying to hold her hair and let it cascade around her and into the dirty leaves.

"I'm nine, but I'll be turning ten soon," she said, in apparent response to KaLeah calling her a child. "How old are you?"

"Sixteen years," KaLeah answered.

"I have two brothers. One is seventeen and one is nineteen. Do you have any siblings?"

"No, I don't." KaLeah said. "I'm sure your family misses you, and I'd guess the entire kingdom, if they know you have been kidnapped. Let's get some sleep and I'll return you to them soon. We can't be but a few days travel away."

"I can't wait to be home," Amirra said as she curled up on the bed KaLeah had arranged for her. "I really want to take a bath."

⊱⊰

It only took a couple of days to reach the outskirts of Belarone Center. Amirra had proven to be good company, assisting KaLeah in arranging sleeping pallets and cooking food. She also spoke very little, which pleased KaLeah, who was not used to talking much.

When they finally emerged from the thick forest, farmlands stretched out before them, and the familiar sight of Denlerack, the dead planet, hung above them in the afternoon sky.

KaLeah could see the rooftops of the Market Center. High upon a hill beyond the markets, but lower than the surrounding mountains, she could see the sunlight glittering off the many white towers of Belarone Castle.

There were mountains beyond the forests of KaLeah's village, but they were covered by thick trees, and being so close, it was hard to get the full view of them. Standing on the edge of flat farmland, the mountains seemed to tower in the distance like great sleeping dragons.

They were varying shades of green and gray, and black in the shadows. The sun glistened off the snow caps and KaLeah held her breath.

Belarone castle was nestled in the foothills, high enough to seem like a mountain itself with many peaks cutting into the sky. "Is that the castle? I have heard people in my village describe it, and I must say, they were rather accurate. It is quite beautiful."

"Wait until you see it up close. It is magnificent." Amirra beamed and seemed to pick up her pace as they headed out across the farmland. KaLeah squinted in the sunlight and tried to locate the edge of the farm and a possible road.

A wave of anxious frustration overcame her as she realized she'd made it this far without so much as seeing a hint of her father.

She considered, for a moment, just letting Amirra make her own way, so she could run to the market center and look for her father there. But, of course, she knew that was no way to treat a princess; especially one so young who had been nothing but cordial throughout the journey.

"Let us keep an eye out for a road to travel, so we aren't traipsing through loose, soiled dirt the rest of the way," KaLeah suggested.

Looking out beyond the farmland, she noticed a planned line of trees she thought might be framing a road. As she tried to make out the road from a distance, she thought she heard the faint sound of drums. She trailed her eyes up the line of trees and thought she saw movement there.

"Princess, are those soldiers from the castle, by chance?"

The little girl turned to look.

"Oh yes. Good, I am tired of walking. They will let us ride back with them."

"Well, there's no need for me to ride to the castle. They

can drop me at the market," KaLeah said, beginning to smile.

The band of draggots being ridden by Belarone soldiers suddenly turned direction and increased their speed. They were headed in a hurry across the farmland, having spotted the two girls. Amirra sat down to rest and wait, but KaLeah stayed on her feet, watching the hooves tear through the dirt and plants.

Did they really have to send the entire army across the field? she wondered, shaking her head.

They closed the distance rapidly and came upon her with swords drawn. A few men dismounted and scooped Amirra up from the ground before either girl had a moment to speak.

"Lay down your weapons." Two men wearing metal chest plates over red and white tunics pointed their swords at KaLeah. Their breast plates had the Belarone house sigil painted on them of a white dragon curled around a red ball of fire.

KaLeah squinted at the men, realizing their interpretation of the situation. "Of course," she said, very loudly. "I will gladly lay down the weapons I used to kill Princess Amirra's kidnappers."

"You?" A large, dark-skinned man with a prominent nose and hairless head rode his black draggot through the group of soldiers and pulled to a stop behind the men holding her at sword point.

Despite his size and volume, his eyes appeared kind.

"You expect me to believe you found the princess who was kidnapped a few nights ago, then killed the men who took her, and brought her back here when the King's own soldiers have been unable to find any trace of her until now?"

He didn't say it doubtfully, only as if he was stating the facts.

"No trace at all until she was out in the middle of a field on her way back to the castle, yes. I suspect you don't have very good trackers among your soldiers," KaLeah responded.

She had puffed-up her chest, pulled her shoulders back, not flinched at the swords pointed at her nose, and not making any move to remove her sword, dagger, or bow and arrows.

"General Zoseff Array," Amirra called out.

The girl had been carried back many feet from KaLeah and seemed to have kicked her way free by the sour look on the soldiers' faces.

Amirra marched up to KaLeah and spun on her heal to face the man. "General."

"Princess Amirra, are you hurt?"

She rolled her eyes. "This is KaLeah. She is traveling in search of her father and did indeed come across my captors in the woods. She killed them and offered to safely escort me home. I'd like to be getting home now, if you would be so kind. KaLeah is coming with us as my rescuer, and I want her treated with the honor she deserves. We'd like two draggots. Two of your men shall walk back."

KaLeah expected the general to be upset, but instead, he let out a raucous laugh and sheathed his sword.

"Gitton, Arren, bring your draggots here," he ordered.

Two men emerged from the center of the group, riding their draggots.

"Give them to the girls. We'll meet you in the center drink houses later. You're dismissed for the day."

The men dismounted and handed the reins to the two girls. The one closest to Amirra assisted her in her mount, but KaLeah brushed the other's assistance away with a quick wave.

KaLeah looked up at the tall draggot mare in astonishment. The creatures were too expensive for most villagers, and so she rarely saw them. Her father had given her instructions on how to ride, but she'd never actually ridden one.

Their necks were covered in scales that trailed down to

their legs, ending in hooves with sharp dragon-like talons. Their teeth were sharp, and they ate a combination of raw wuvat meat and grass. Their tales were long with plumes of colorful hair, depending on their dominate color. Some were pure white, some black as night, many were all shades of reds and browns, and there were rare golden ones, from what she'd heard.

Their manes were long and wavy and did little to conceal the two giant horns protruding from their heads. She found her mare to be exquisite, and it gave her a look as if to say she was bored by KaLeah's admiration.

She pulled herself up onto the mare and gave the golden brown draggot a reassuring pat along the furry part of her neck. When the draggot started trotting along with the others, KaLeah's heart raced, and she closed her eyes into the wind that brushed intensely against her cheeks.

She wondered if she would be out of line to ask for a draggot as a reward for rescuing the princess. It seemed like a very small reward, in light of the situation, that surely, they may consider it. But how would she ask?

She could start by saying how tiring the journey had been and how wonderful it was to ride on a draggot. She'd mention the journey back home in addition to the quest to find her father. She wondered about whom and how to ask for such a reward as the white towers around the keep grew taller in front of them.

Suddenly squeamish, her insides began to twist uncomfortably as she rode. She had never stepped foot into anything larger than her own home. She was intimately aware of how poorly she smelled and how unsuitable her village traveling attire was for visiting royalty. She hoped they sent her into the stables, fed her, and then sent her on her way with a draggot. That would be more than enough thanks for her.

She could not believe her fortune and the turn of events. The villagers back in Erion would never believe her, but she was sure her dad would be proud.

Her mood suddenly dropped remembering her dad and her quest to find him.

She looked at the faces of the people shopping in the Center Market as they passed through, but her father was not among them. She needed to go into each shop, each drink house, down alleys and into the neighborhoods. She needed to talk to people and describe him to anyone who would listen.

KaLeah realized the weight of how much time she was wasting here. What if he moved to another town before she was able to make it back to the Center?

"Princess," she said in a lowered tone.

"Yes, KaLeah?"

"I can't stay long at the castle. I must continue looking for my father."

"I understand. I do wish you'd stay, though. There are so many things to show you, and I'm sure the kitchen can make you things to eat you've never even heard of before."

Amirra's hazel eyes lit up with excitement, looking blue-green in the sunshine. KaLeah could see it would be hard to shake her.

The castle was magnificent. The small troop of soldiers rode the draggots up a long ramp and through two large wooden gates standing open in wait.

The gates were built into walls as thick as a man is tall. KaLeah noticed the same white dragon emblem was repeated in carvings along the wall.

There were more soldiers inside, along with servants who took the reins when the men dismounted. Guards wearing significantly less armor marched around the tops of the walls and the edges of the interior courtyard.

Inside the courtyard, the ground was made of polished stone, and the draggot hooves made a musical clanking sound when they crossed it. Once inside the gates, everyone began to dismount, and servants appeared from every corner to take away the draggots.

KaLeah tried to follow closely behind Amirra while

absorbing all the details around her.

Ahead of them, there was another thick stone wall and two smaller gates. Guards opened those gates and KaLeah noticed some of the soldiers that had ridden in with them had gone off in different directions.

Only the general, Amirra, KaLeah, and a few soldiers continued through the second set of gates. They went inside a stone tunnel, brightly lit by two long, narrow troughs that stretched the length of the tunnel. Sweet smelling oil inside the troughs provided fuel for the flames.

They came to a staircase that led into a grand room. It was three stories tall with columns holding up a balcony walkway above them. Tall windows on the second story let in the sunlight, which highlighted the marble floors and rich, colorful tapestries along the walls.

KaLeah never knew something this beautiful existed. She had to force herself to keep moving forward with the group. A soldier ran up quickly and said something to the general.

"Princess, your father has been informed of our arrival and wants to see you at once," General Array said. "He is in the study. I can have one of the soldiers show this girl to a room, if you'd like."

"No, she comes with me." Amirra turned back sharply to KaLeah and grabbed her hand. "Come along."

KaLeah followed at the princess' pace through long halls and up more staircases. The general and soldiers followed close behind. For someone who never got lost in the woods, the new world of the castle left her feeling disoriented.

They approached a guarded door. The guards standing on each side of the double doors were dressed in white tunics embossed with the same white dragon wrapped around a red ball of fire emblem across their chests.

The men opened the doors wide before Amirra reached them. She never slowed her pace as she pulled KaLeah into the room with her.

Amirra released KaLeah's hand and ran to her father, who was reading over papers at a large desk in the center of the room.

A smile spread across the king's face. The man looked much older than KaLeah's father, with deep circles under his eyes. His skin was pale with the lack of sun and his black hair and beard were lightly peppered with gray.

He stood up and moved gingerly around the large desk to receive Amirra. Despite his age, he lifted Amirra up easily and held her tightly for a moment before setting her back down.

Jealousy quivered through her. It was a familiar feeling she got anytime she saw a father hugging his daughter. She tried to bury the emotion, as she always had.

"My beautiful child. Amirra, are you all in one piece?" he said, placing his hands on the sides of her head and thoughtfully looking her over for any sign of damage.

"I am. I wasn't hurt. My friend KaLeah saved me. She is the most fascinating girl I have ever met. She killed three men, gave me water and food, and brought me safely home through the forest."

"A girl did all that?" The king looked at KaLeah, his brows drawing tight across his face. He seemed to scan her clothing and her hair, carefully considering whether or not she really was a girl and not just a lovely young man.

"Well now, that is quite something," he said after an uncomfortably long pause. "Come forward, girl."

KaLeah had never thought much about how the kingdom was run. She lived in a far-off region and cared only for the woods and for her father.

She walked forward toward the princess and king, surrounded by the most comfortable furniture she'd ever seen, and more books than she knew existed. Listening to her boots cross the marble floor, she suddenly felt immeasurably small in a world she knew absolutely nothing about.

"I am King Erazus, and I offer my infinite gratitude, dear

one," the king said.

KaLeah bowed, hoping she did it correctly. When she stood back up straight, he was smiling slightly. He reached out and took her hands in his.

"Where are you from, child?"

"The village of Erion, Your Highness."

"Ah, that might explain how you could traverse the woods, I suppose. But a girl with the ability to fight men? Amirra, was it swordplay?"

"Yes, father."

The king still studied KaLeah's face doubtfully, and rubbed the callouses on her palms, as if seeking some proof to reconcile the image of a girl with a sword in his mind.

KaLeah somehow knew to keep quiet and wait for a direct question from the king. She didn't feel like defending her father's decision to train her against traditions and norms would be the smartest thing to do in this moment. She wanted to leave the castle as soon as possible and didn't want to say or do anything that would elongate her stay.

"Well, it seems my daughter is quite fond of you, and we must see to it you are amply rewarded for bringing her back to us. You shall stay here with us a while so I may get to know you better and determine a suitable reward. I'm sure my daughter would love the company."

Amirra squealed her excitement and hugged her father. "Thank you, thank you," she said.

KaLeah's heart sank. She had never stood up to her dad, and standing before the king, she felt as small as ever. She knew there was no way to refuse the king.

Her palms were sweaty, and everyone looked at her with expectation, as if she would jump around with excitement like the princess just had.

This was not what she wanted, but she was too afraid to say no to the king, his daughter, and all of the guards in the room.

After a few moments of silence, KaLeah dropped her eyes to the floor. She bowed again, since it was the only way

she knew how to show respect to royalty.
  "I would be honored to stay," she said, lying.

3 BELARONE CASTLE

I can't stay here, KaLeah thought as she was shown into her room.

The room was as large as her entire house back in Erion, the bed itself bigger than her bedroom. The floors were a beautiful dark wood with thick, richly colored rugs spread about. There were two large chairs with wooden carved arms facing a fireplace across from the bed.

The bed had four posts on each of the corners that almost reached up to the ceiling. The bedposts, along with most of the wood furniture in the room, had depictions of dragons intricately carved throughout.

The fabrics and pillows on the bed looked as if they had come from a dream. Gold, crimson red, and stark white covered every inch of the room.

She unlatched her belt and removed the quiver of arrows from her shoulder. She set all her weapons on the bench at the foot of the bed, then took off her boots. She ran her fingers across the blanket on the bed and slowly crawled onto it.

The massive bed was more comfortable than anything she'd ever slept on.

Well, maybe I could stay a night or two, she reconsidered.

Her eyes closed and all her senses were acutely aware of the way the bed melted around her body, how she sank down in slow motion, how the silks and furs tickled and soothed her hands and arms as she spread herself across the bed. She slipped into a light nap before realizing it.

"Nice, isn't it?" Amirra asked, giggling. "Much better than a bed of tree needles and leaves."

KaLeah bolted upright on the bed, embarrassed to be caught so enamored with bed linens.

"Princess," KaLeah said, edging herself off the bed.

"Don't worry," said Princess Amirra. She moved closer and jumped up onto the bed, her skirts spreading out around her. She had changed from her riding gear and now wore an empire-waisted, light green dress with white piping.

Her hair had been brushed free of dirt and leaves and pinned back along the sides and shimmery-blonde ringlets fell down her back. The princess smelled as if she'd bathed in rose oils.

KaLeah admired the dress, never having seen anything so beautiful, and yet, she had a feeling this was nothing compared to other dresses the little princess probably owned.

"I'm glad you like the bed. You're going to have a lot of fun here. We'll go riding together. Maybe you can teach me how to hunt. Father doesn't like it when I act, well, unlike a princess should."

Amirra rolled her eyes and continued, "But I really like to learn new things; whether or not they are things a princess should learn. It isn't fair my brothers can do things I am not allowed to do. Will you teach me how to hunt and fight with a sword?"

Her eyes, which seemed to be greener now that she was wearing a green dress, sparkled up at KaLeah. Teaching someone to hunt and fight could take months. She knew she couldn't refuse the king, but she needed to make it clear to Amirra that she wasn't planning on staying long.

"Princess Amirra," KaLeah said. "I must keep searching for my father. I cannot stay here. I can teach you a few skills in a few days, but after that, I must leave. My father could be out there in the Market Center right now."

Amirra lowered her eyes in a pout. "I understand. At least you will be here for my birthday celebration. You will be an honored guest; a hero."

"I don't think—" KaLeah started.

The child princess immediately puffed up. "You must and you *will*, KaLeah. Let us go meet with Felair and Dohori. They are going to help me choose dresses for you."

Amirra jumped down from the bed and headed for the bedroom door.

"Why do I need dresses?" KaLeah looked down at her traveling clothes. They were covered in dirt stains and splatters of blood. Her boots were so stiff with mud, she wasn't sure if she could even get them back on without a thorough scrubbing.

"Leave those things. The maids will clean them for you. For now, we will get you cleaned up and then transform you into someone fancy." The little girl looked as mischievous as she was excited, as if KaLeah were some sort of life-sized doll.

KaLeah left her weapons and boots in the room and followed Amirra through corridors that seemed to become more and more lavish. Large tapestries hung on the walls, illustrating the creation stories of Naldash. She had heard the legends but had never seen them illustrated.

The tapestries told the story of two dragon species, one of land and one of air, that feuded for thousands of years. A dragon was born from a forbidden union of both species, the first and only mixed-species dragon.

Men named the mixed-species dragon of their legends, Klackire. It is said that when his mother was killed by her tribe as punishment, he became so angry, he let out a stream of magic so powerful it sent his mother's entire tribe to the barren planet Denlerack.

All the dragons eventually died off, and other animals, including humans, began to evolve on Naldash. According to the stories, Denlerack became known as the dead planet.

It hangs in the sky above Naldash as a dark and desolate orb. It is said that Klackire continues to send the souls of the dead to Denlerack.

KaLeah paused in front of a tapestry depicting the immortal dragon. He stood on two legs with his silvery wings spread out behind him. His scales were dark green and his eyes menacing.

He didn't resemble the phantom dragon she'd seen in the woods, but for a moment, she wondered if maybe the legends were true.

Had she seen the immortal dragon?

Princess Amirra cleared her throat impatiently at the end of the hall, snapping KaLeah out of her trance.

She followed the princess into a massive dressing room where two women were waiting with selections already dangling from their arms.

The room was a giant closet. Every wall had shelves stacked with boxes and hundreds of shoes arranged by color and size. There were racks draped with rows and rows of dresses, silks, linens, and scarves.

Hats lined the top rows of every shelf. Dresses hung from rods that connected one set of shelves to another. A tall panel of three mirrors stood off to one side, near a row of windows, and in the center of the room was a round, velvet blue, tufted ottoman, the size of the bed back in her guest quarters.

The room was a paradise of silk and cotton, robes, and gowns. There were tables strewn about with various jewels, necklaces, bracelets, and other glittery items laid out neatly, hanging from small hangers in the shapes of trees, horns, and dragon talons.

"KaLeah, these are my nurses, Dohori and Felair. They've taken care of me since I was a baby." The princess led KaLeah to where the lady nurses were standing to view their selection. She nodded and the ladies carried the clothing over to the large, round ottoman.

Dohori, the oldest nurse, was plump with short gray hair that seemed to perfectly match the long gray dress she wore. Her face was wrinkled around her eyes and mouth as if she had spent many years worrying.

After laying her selections on the ottoman, she returned to searching the racks for more dresses.

The other nurse, Felair, was much younger and very pretty. Her nose was sharply pointed and somehow, even though she also wore an ugly gray dress, hers seemed to hang in a way that flattered every curve of her body.

Felair had manicured eyebrows and strawberry blonde hair hung in a loose braid over her right shoulder. She was picking through accessories and ignored KaLeah entirely. Felair lifted a diamond and ruby necklace.

"Dear, Princess," Felair said. "Nothing catches the eyes of strangers quite like red. This piece would look very mature with a red dress."

Amirra looked over at the necklace Felair was holding and then shrugged. She went back to searching the racks.

Dohori shot Felair a nasty glance and then said, "Pink is much better for 10-year-olds. Honestly, Felair, can't you find something more appropriate for her age?"

Felair huffed and set the piece down, reluctantly moving toward the jewels that were lighter in weight and color.

KaLeah managed to slowly back away from the women and lean against the door to the room, watching the women fluttering around the racks and shelves.

She shuddered uncomfortably. She was accustomed to dark pants and green or brown shirts. The ladies of Erion wore dresses, but their dresses more closely resembled the long, gray dresses worn by the nurses. KaLeah had never desired to wear anything other than pants her entire life.

"Found it," Dohori cried from behind a row of racks.

She scurried around to face the other ladies. In her hands, she held out a dress for all the women to see. Amirra began clapping and laughing.

The dress was long and dark pink. The shoulders were tiny straps that came down to meet a high, empire waist. From the top of the dress there was a sheer, lighter pink fabric that hung down over the darker pink.

"It is perfect," Amirra exclaimed.

The ladies proceeded to dress Amirra in her birthday gown.

"But what will your rescuer wear, Princess Amirra?" Felair asked, mischievously raising one eyebrow.

Amirra whispered something to Felair. The tall, thin woman smiled wide and then laughed as both girls turned their gazes toward KaLeah.

"You will wear a red one," Amirra commanded.

KaLeah's stomach knotted.

Felair came out from behind a rack holding a very mature looking red dress. It had a slit on its right side that extended from mid-thigh to the ground, and it was lined with diamonds.

KaLeah gulped.

"I will not wear that," she said with shock.

Then, feeling a bit disrespectful, she changed her tone to one of modesty.

"It is much too expensive and glamorous for me, princess," KaLeah said, bowing slightly for good measure.

Before she knew it, there were four hands peeling her dirty clothes away from her. KaLeah felt as if her very skin was being removed.

And then, she was in a dark red cave as the ladies pulled the dress over her head. When it was all over, KaLeah was escorted to a mirror.

"You look beautiful," Amirra said, gleefully clapping her hands together again.

"And I don't know why you bowed earlier when we saw my father, but you cannot bow in this dress. Ladies curtsy. You are a lady in that dress."

She lifted the corner of her lip, not bothering to ask what

a curtsy was. It sounded ladylike and she wasn't interested.

KaLeah brushed oily dark strands of hair away from her face and looked at herself in the mirror. She no longer looked sixteen.

She looked as mature as any of the women in her village.

It was laughable, silly, and yet, she couldn't quite help but feel a little different.

She was still dirty, a hunter, and a farmer, but standing there with a princess, wearing a dress that was worth more than her house, maybe more than her whole village, she wondered if she could be more than just a hunter and farmer from Erion.

What would her father think? He had always been fine with her dressing like a boy. *But would he be upset seeing me in a dress?*

Princess Amirra came up to stand beside her in front of the mirror.

"A curtsy is like this," she said. Amirra took up two edges of her skirt, pushed one foot back behind the other, then lowered her head and torso.

KaLeah scrunched her face up. She was right, it was very ladylike, like the dress, but she didn't want to hurt the little girl's feelings.

She pinched the silky red fabric between her fingers, pulled it up slightly, then bowed down, without tucking one foot behind the other. She felt ridiculous. The princess chuckled sweetly.

"We'll practice," she said.

Two days later, KaLeah was standing in the same dress in front of the same mirror. She had spent those two days eating, bathing, napping, and walking around the castle grounds with the young Princess Amirra who told KaLeah stories and gave history lessons on Belarone Kingdom and her royal family.

KaLeah had admittedly taken more baths in the last two days than she had in a month back in Erion village. Being in the castle was like being in a dream where all her worldly concerns melted away into nothing.

She hoped that her father had started to head back to their village, and she told herself that she would start back there soon after the party.

Looking at herself now, pampered, powdered, and polished, and seeing how her long brown hair fell in waves across the dark red dress, she felt as if she were no longer KaLeah at all. At least, she was no longer the version she'd known all her life.

The red dress was sleeveless and tight, lifting her small breasts up. It hugged her slight curves, traveling down her body from breasts to ankles.

The shimmery red was accentuated by a trail of diamonds lining the edges and the slit. The slit started mid-thigh and opened only slightly down the length of the dress where it finally pooled out at the floor.

Felair had spent hours expertly curling and pinning her and Amirra's hair and painted their faces with powders and lip stain. She stepped back to admire her work. "Everyone at the party will think you're a noble," Felair said. "No one would believe from looking at you now that you are just a village farmer."

KaLeah could hear the disdain and jealousy in Felair's voice, but she ignored it because her words were true. She did not look like herself at all.

"Are you ready, my friend?" Amirra bounced up and down excitedly behind the ladies.

She was wearing the pink dress they had chosen two days prior, and her light blonde hair hung in ringlets around her petite face.

She smiled brightly. KaLeah smiled back, finding herself entranced by the princess' excitement.

Even though the woman in the mirror looked like a

stranger, the little princess was about to lead her into a room full of noble and royal families for the first time in her life. She was surrounded by luxuries she never imagined existed, and her trepidation was slowly turning over to excitement.

For one night, she didn't have to be a poor farmer, a hunter, or a girl who skinned animals and slept wrapped in their fur.

She looked again at herself and pulled her shoulders back, holding her head higher. She looked at Felair, feeling grateful for the opportunity to be someone different for a night.

"If they all think that I am a noble, maybe that will not be such a bad thing."

❧Nikolat☙

Prince Nikolat hated parties at the castle. He would have to feign charm, meet, and talk to people he had no interest in, and try to keep himself entertained by stumping strangers with dry wit and sarcasm.

He made it a point to enter the ballroom late and to slip in unnoticed.

He entered through a side servant door, coming out behind a long table stacked high with various food and drinks that did nothing to interest him.

Servers were busily handing guests tiny cakes on saucers or teacups filled halfway with warm juices. They didn't notice him passing behind them and beyond the table, which rounded inward to complete an illusion of separation between the guests and servants.

The long ballroom had been divided into sections, establishing areas for eating, lounging, mingling, and dancing. It was sometimes also called the throne room, depending upon how the room was being used at the time.

Nikolat stayed close to the tapestried walls, trying to go unnoticed as he looked past the dance floor toward his father's table.

His father sat on his throne and the table had been placed horizontally so that his father, the king, was squarely in the middle of not only the table, but the centerpiece of the party as well.

The room was loud with scattered conversations. Nikolat tried to focus on the sound his heels made against the shiny marble floor; a calming sound that was unfortunately lost before it reached his ears. Instead, he was submerged in the sounds of hubris, nobles bragging about their newest this or that, a child's accomplishments, successes, and other such menial things.

It was the laughter that he found the most excruciating. He wondered why the people with the most terrible laughs always seemed to laugh the loudest.

Candle chandeliers the size of small tables hung from the ceiling, and candelabras a head taller than Nikolat were strewn about the edges of the ballroom. The light from the flames made the figures in the tapestries appear to be dancing.

Doing well, he thought, *I've managed a few moments in here without anyone noticing me so far.* He didn't feel particularly like smiling, shaking hands, or being praised for doing absolutely nothing all day long except preparing to be the backup king, in case by some miracle, his older brother, Bylex, were to get trampled by a draggot.

Nikolat clenched his fists and turned his glare to his older brother, sitting obediently at his father's side. Anger slowly rippled through him, as it always did, when he looked upon the "rightful" heir.

It was ludicrous.

Not only was Bylex slower and simpler, but he hadn't excelled at his lessons, as Nikolat had, or bested all the kingdom's swordsmen, as Nikolat had.

He lacked charm and even lacked the good looks that Nikolat and Amirra had been graced with.

Sure, they were both olive-skinned, dark-haired, and blue-eyed, but Nikolat's features were more chiseled and refined. He also kept his form in top shape, where his brother had always been soft and weak.

Nikolat turned his attention back to the ballroom. It was the largest room in the palace, and he thought it an amazing room despite the absurd decorations. Tonight, the ballroom was decorated with pink silk ribbons, pink roses, hydrangeas, and fragrant lilies.

His father's royal rejects, wealthy, and yet not quite lucky enough to be royalty, meandered about, dressed in their finest, newest clothing and jewelry.

Nikolat knew that most of the young ladies in the room hoped that one day, as the daughters of wealthy men, they'd be married to a prince. They didn't care if that prince were to ever become a king; it was the *"prince"* part that really got them excited. The rich Favor families were bred to marry royalty.

He cringed at the sight of some of the women. Most tried to hide their age beneath dark makeup, while the younger ones batted their eyes and flirted relentlessly.

The men stood around, hoping the princes wouldn't notice the women they had already chosen for themselves. A smile spread across Nikolat's face thinking about the satisfaction of stealing some other man's fantasy girl.

What no one except Nikolat and his father knew was that he wouldn't be marrying one of the favors' daughters.

The kingdom of Lisodanya, to the southeast, was ruled by a king with too many daughters. In order to ensure peace between the two kingdoms, Nikolat would marry one of those daughters, regardless of looks or intelligence.

Although, a tiny part of him was enticed by the idea of moving out of the castle, he did not like the idea of being pleasant to a princess and her father until the father died. It was hard enough being pleasant in his own father's castle.

He'd have to pretend to love her until that fateful day, which may not come for a very, very long time. Nikolat wanted to be king sooner than later.

He continued to slink along the edges of the walls and

let his mind drift back to his own tenth birthday ceremony.

It had been exhilarating, walking out of the double doors and into the ballroom. He had caught his father's eyes first and then cast his glance over a hundred other smiling faces, all apparently happy to see him, and yet all as blank and empty as Bylex behind their pleasant expressions.

He looked out now over the same smiling faces as they eagerly awaited his sister's arrival. He rolled his eyes to himself and grabbed a glass of wine from a nearby table.

A cold chill gripped his spine, and he shuddered. He turned and sure enough, Favor Lamone was making his way over to him. He loved the man about as intensely as one loved the blade of a knife at one's throat.

Lamone knew Nikolat's darkest secrets, which was unfortunate since Lamone was the last man Nikolat would ever want to trust. However, there was no man better for plotting and scheming.

"Good evening, my Prince," Lamone said in a high pitched, thickly nasal voice. Lamone, who was nineteen, a couple of years older than Nikolat, was tall like him, but much thinner and paler in the face with a sharp nose and sunken eyes.

"Lamone," Nikolat said. He glanced around to make it look as if he was snarling because of the party and not because of Lamone's arrival.

"Why so down?" Lamone asked. "None of the women catch your eye, yet? There's a tight butt on the far wall in a light blue dress. Wonder who helped her squeeze into that one?"

"For dragons' sake, don't you ever do anything besides gawk?" Nikolat said, nonchalantly turning an eye in the direction Lamone was looking. But then, after seeing the girl, he added, "Not bad."

Just then, a few of the king's attendants clanged their silverware against their glasses. The talking and laughing instantly died down and everyone turned to face the king.

King Erazus had been sitting on his throne watching his

guests. Now he stood.

Nikolat's eyes took in the golden trimmed throne. The arms were made of carved dragon heads, and the back was a great oval covered in brilliant red silk. Nik often dreamed of sitting on that throne.

Everyone grew quiet and faced the king.

"Loyal friends and favors, welcome to Belarone Castle," King Erazus bellowed. "Today is my daughter's tenth birthday. Amirra Belarone came into this world on a day the sun didn't rise. We lost her mother, my beloved Queen Sorara, and for the first time in a hundred years, the sun was eclipsed by Denlerack. Both events cast our world into darkness. But from that darkness came my daughter, whose cheerful spirit seemed to bring back the light. We will no longer mourn on this day. From this moment on, this day is to be celebrated across the kingdom as Princess Amirra's birthday. May I present my daughter, Princess Amirra Belarone."

All eyes moved with the king as he raised his hands toward the doors directly behind and to the left of the throne.

The enormous double doors were etched with dragons, like most everything else in the castle. Not only had most of the animals on Naldash evolved from dragons, but dragon spirits were believed to linger and influence every aspect of daily life.

It was in the best interest of humans to ensure their surroundings were adorned with respectful depictions of the strength and beauty of those lingering spirits.

Nik had grown up surrounded by them and the legend but had found no influence in his life. At least, not enough to put any faith in them.

Royal rooms reserved for family and special guests lay beyond the doors. There were lounges with mirrors, water basins, chambers, and refreshments for last-minute needs.

Nikolat reluctantly turned with everyone else to look upon the doors and tried to smile as if he hadn't seen his sister a million times.

The doors were opened, slowly and theatrically, by two house guards. Amirra stood in the threshold, wearing a classically pink princess dress, high-waisted, and bowed out. Her smile was so wide that it seemed as if her face might split in two.

She was wearing at least five different jeweled necklaces, and her tiny wrists were weighed down with bracelets. He knew she had picked them all out herself. No one would dare tell her not to overdo her jewelry.

Lamone let out a sudden gasp beside him. "Dragon's blood," Lamone said.

Nikolat was just about to tell Lamone that Amirra was just a child when he saw her, a young woman in a red dress, walking through the doors behind Amirra.

Brown hair with hints of red rolled across her shoulders and with every other step, a long, ivory leg peeked out from a delicate slit cut into the side of the dress. She was glowing without smiling, and it was that lack of a smile that really got to Nikolat.

His heart started to pound harder as he moved his eyes down her body. She was wrapped from head to toe in a bright red dress that seemed to squeeze her in all the right places.

That's no woman, he thought. The leg, that he could see, had the most defined calf muscle he'd ever seen on a woman. Her arm muscles were more rounded than most soldiers he knew. Her long neck went straight up to piercing eyes that seemed to scan everything. She was fierce. She was strong. *That's a killer.*

"Who is she?" Lamone asked. "One of the favors?"

"No, I've never seen her before. It must be the girl rumored to have saved Amirra from the kidnappers. She is supposed to be just some young village girl. She is definitely not as I pictured her."

"That girl saved the princess?" Lamone asked with a scoff. "What did she do, sex the kidnappers to death?

Maybe not such a bad way to go." Lamone chuckled at his own joke and stood so close to Nikolat that he could smell the mead on his breath. "I've got to have her, prince" Lamone said. "With your permission, of course?"

Nikolat could feel his neck get hot. The first interesting new woman in a long while and Lamone instantly tries to claim her. It irritated him to no end, but he bit his tongue.

Nikolat couldn't take his eyes off the woman. Her hair fell in soft curly waves and seemed to reflect the candlelight. At one moment it looked like burnt gold and the next like crimson blood.

Her eyes never seemed to leave Amirra, but he knew she was scanning everyone in the room. He could sense her, feel her from across the expanse, and he was enticed.

Princess Amirra sat down, and the girl in the red dress stood directly behind her. She was beautiful. He tried to tear his thoughts away from her and instead gritted his teeth. He did require more of Lamone's services, after all.

"Prince?"

"Fine," he said to Lamone, who lightly clasped his wiry fingers together. "She's all yours."

He could have sworn the little rodent squealed.

❦KaLeah❧

"Thank you, friends, for the warm welcome," the king said. "We have many reasons to celebrate today. Not only is it the celebration of the birth of my beloved daughter, but as many of you know, her life was recently in great danger." The king looked lovingly at the princess, sitting in her chair. KaLeah stood directly behind her, not knowing what else to do.

"Men kidnapped her while she was riding," the king told the story with grand inflection and drama. "General Zoseff Array and his captains are still trying to uncover the reasons and the criminals responsible. We were lucky that the dragon spirits intervened and sent an accidental rescuer along her path. I would like to introduce and honor the woman who found and rescued her. Please welcome the lady KaLeah from Erion."

KaLeah's face flushed with heat, and she wished that the absurdly long table could be just as equally tall. She looked out over the elegant crowd as they clapped with gloved hands.

Some women had tears in their eyes, and some of the men just looked stunned. Standing in her diamond encrusted red dress, she did not look capable of defeating a cute little animal, let alone kidnappers in the woods that had eluded the king's soldiers for days. Of course, to most of the king's men, no woman looked capable of such a feat. To say it was out of the ordinary was an understatement.

"We are most grateful to the lady for returning our princess to us," the king continued.

He took a couple steps to stand beside KaLeah, then lightly lifted and kissed the back of KaLeah's hand. She was surprised and found herself smiling up at him. He gave her a quick wink and turned to face the patrons, placing his hands on his daughter's shoulders. KaLeah stepped to the side and Amirra beamed up at her father.

"Thank you all for coming this evening to celebrate the long life of our royal daughter, Princess Amirra. Please enjoy the birthday festivities."

The king returned to his throne in the center of the table. Amirra was seated to the king's right, with a chair beside her reserved for KaLeah. She felt more than a little out of place when Amirra finally asked her to sit.

"Am I not a servant, your highness?" KaLeah asked.

Amirra chuckled. "You are a hero today, KaLeah. Please sit and eat beside me."

One of the servants quickly pulled the chair out for KaLeah, who realized that sitting in a tight dress would be the first challenge she hadn't prepared for.

Her leg seemed to dive out from the slit, and she felt embarrassingly exposed. She overcompensated by sliding into her chair too quickly.

The bright smile never left Amirra's rosy cheeks. The young girl patted KaLeah's arm, reassuringly. "You will get used to all of this," she said. "That is my brother, Prince Bylex, sitting on the other side of my father."

KaLeah leaned forward a bit to see the handsome man to the left of the king. Prince Bylex was talking with his father with a drink in his hand, which seemed to be adorned with more jewels than KaLeah had ever seen on a man.

He was of average build, not muscular, with black hair that hung slightly below his ears. The chair to the left of Bylex was empty.

The long table stretched the width of the ballroom, but there were no other chairs. KaLeah had the impression that the honor of an extra presence at the table was not one that others enjoyed often.

Swarms of servers were suddenly flitting about the table, lightly moving to stand near various food options laid out on the table, waiting for a royal to nod in approval of a selection. They would then quickly select a modest portion and move to the next option.

The server responsible for KaLeah cleared her throat. She didn't even recognize most of the options as food. Everything was so pretty.

Slabs of meat were surrounded with potatoes and other vegetables cut into decorative shapes. She made eye-contact with her server and leaned toward her. The girl was about her size with dark hair cut short behind her ears.

"You choose," KaLeah whispered. KaLeah widened her eyes, trying to wordlessly communicate her need for someone with a little more experience to make the selection.

The girl seemed to understand perfectly, and she gave a slight smile in response. She and the other servers moved in a dance around one another as they interpreted nods and made selections.

When the girl returned with two full plates to present to KaLeah, she laid them down and whispered, "A few of my favorites, miss."

KaLeah was relieved and thanked the girl. She suddenly realized how hungry she was and began to eat.

"My brother, Prince Nikolat, doesn't like these sorts of parties," Amirra said. She had made her selections and was eating, using very delicate silverware. She nodded toward the crowd in the ballroom. "He is out there in the crowd somewhere, I'm sure. You may meet him eventually."

She rolled her eyes, insinuating that her brother was difficult to intercept.

KaLeah took a bite of a richly colorful fruit salad and looked out across the crowd. She was startled to notice several eyes on her, quickly darting away to continue discussing her, she assumed. She was not used to people looking upon her, curious and admiring.

"KaLeah, I dare say, you've taken on quite a transformation," the king boomed from his place at the table. "I'm guessing my daughter was responsible for the dress and hair?" he laughed heartily. "Never fear. Her punishment shall be harsh and swift, and you will be restored to your comfortable self soon enough. Shall I call the guards?"

Amirra's cheeks turned pink with embarrassment.

"Father," she said proudly. "The ladies have done a marvelous job with KaLeah."

"I do not disagree, dearest," the king said. He smiled at them both and then left the table to mingle with his guests.

Everyone who passed by the table to wish Happy Birthday to Amirra couldn't help but let their eyes pass across her humble savior as well. KaLeah felt like a thick slice of wuvat steak hanging over starving, salivating dragons.

The men were especially gawky. She tried to ignore them, and instead, tried to admire the ballroom and the colorful spectacle of the decorations and dresses, twirling about the room like paint brushes.

She suddenly felt as if she were being intensely watched

and turned to see two young men staring at her from across the room.

One of the men was very thin and pasty white. He looked as if he was ill or lost in treacherous thoughts. He was giving her a grimacing smile, and a tingle crawled up her spine.

The other was leaning against a wall and looking at her without any expression on his face. His hair was dark black, and he was lean but muscular. He was wearing a long, dark gray cape connected to a sleeveless black vest that buttoned from his waist to his neck. He had cuffs from his elbows to his wrists, but his upper arms were exposed. They were strong and defined, and even though he was handsome, her first inclination was to fear him.

"Oh yes, that's him there, my brother Nikolat," Amirra said from beside her.

Nikolat turned away from her and she watched him walk into a small group of women. He moved with the grace of a prince, but the caution of a fighter.

KaLeah had to look away when one of the ladies reached up to touch his arm. She knew she could knock them all down in three seconds, she told herself with a smirk. But maybe 'delicate' is what this prince wanted in a girl. Delicate, precious, and eager to please; all the things KaLeah was not.

Just then, a boy about Amirra's age approached the table. He had soft blond hair, a sweet smile, and beautiful blue eyes. He bowed and Amirra blushed slightly.

"Happy Birthday, princess," he said. "I am Jeron, son of Favor Bisar. My father is ill, and could not make it, but from our entire family, we wish you much merriment and many presents."

He winked and then bowed again. Amirra let out a tiny giggle at this and shot a quick glance at KaLeah.

"Thank you, Jeron," Amirra said to the boy. "And it is nice to meet you. Send your father my well wishes."

"That's very kind," Jeron replied. "As gracious as she is

beautiful."

KaLeah fought the urge to roll her eyes at their flirting. Amirra was smiling from ear to ear and KaLeah realized that the poor child probably didn't stand a chance.

No doubt, King Erazus had already chosen her future husband. He had probably made the arrangement when she was born. Amirra had probably already been sold to the highest bidder.

KaLeah let her thoughts go back to Nikolat. When her eyes finally found him again, she was relieved to see that he was talking with a few men and most of the women had dispersed.

His fate would be similar to his sister's, KaLeah imagined. Some poor girl is out there right now, just waiting to be forced into a marriage with the most beautiful man KaLeah had ever seen.

His smile turned into a laugh as the small group of men broke out into laughter. He turned that laugh toward KaLeah and caught her eyes. For some reason, he held them there even after the laughing faded.

Why is he looking at me again? she wondered. *It must be the dress. Or maybe he is just looking at his sister to see she is having a good time.*

As her heart picked up the pace in her chest, she wasn't sure which one she preferred.

Reluctantly, she forced herself to look at the food on her plate. *I must get out of here soon,* she told herself.

4 ATTACKED

KaLeah finished eating the celebratory dinner and then sat quietly with her hands in her lap, nervously rubbing the smooth red fabric of her dress.

Princess Amirra finished eating a strawberry tart with chocolate flakes and then gently dabbed her mouth with a napkin, turned, and smiled vibrantly at KaLeah.

"Follow me, dear KaLeah," she said, bouncing up from her chair.

A servant standing almost directly behind her pulled out her chair in one fluid motion as Amirra stood. KaLeah was left to scoot her chair out on her own.

Princess Amirra placed her hand gently on KaLeah's lower arm and led her down from the table and into the ballroom.

KaLeah shadowed the little lady in pink, nodding, and smiling politely when the princess introduced her to group after group of polished people.

As they moved from one small party to another, Amirra took the time to quietly inform KaLeah of details concerning the guests. Some were wealthy families, shop owners, family members of generals, captains, and others who ran in the more affluent circles.

Amirra told her about a smaller selection of friends and confidants to the royal family who were more like distant relatives and referred to as Favors, or the Favor families. They had been gifted with the title for certain favors they and their families had performed for the royal family over the years.

KaLeah didn't see Prince Nikolat again that evening. She was exhausted and relieved when the night finally came to an end.

Back in the room-sized closet, the nurse maids were waiting to help the girls disrobe. When the nurses finally pulled the dress off her, KaLeah felt like a snake shedding its skin.

The ladies then dressed KaLeah in a comfortable, long ivory nightgown. She felt silly at first, but then decided it was better than the red dress and would be more comfortable to sleep in than her hunting clothes.

With a household full of guards, it wasn't likely that she would need to jump out of bed fully dressed and prepared for danger. The ivory gown would have to do for now, at least, while she slept at the castle for another night or two.

Once her feet were slipped into comfortable slippers, she excused herself from the company of the ladies and found her way back to her room.

She noticed immediately that the doors of her wooden armoire were open and hanging inside was an assortment of dresses and riding outfits. She moved the pieces from side to side, realizing that there were more articles in front of her than she had possessed throughout her entire life.

A knock on her door startled her. Her first thought was that it was a mistake.

"Who is it?" she called out.

"Servant to Prince Nikolat, with a letter for the lady KaLeah."

She was at the door in two steps.

"I am KaLeah," she said, swinging open the thick door.

The servant's eyes were downcast and red, his hair and

shirt disheveled as if he'd just been pulled out of a deep sleep. She took the letter from his scrawny hand, thanked him, and retreated into her room to read it.

She walked to a small table and held it beneath the light of a candle flame.

Lady KaLeah,

Prince Nikolat requests your presence at his chambers.

KaLeah read it a few more times, and a strange sensation filled her stomach, as if she might be sick. She didn't know what the Prince of Belarone could possibly need to see her about, but she knew better than to keep standing there dumbfounded.

She assumed that her night dress was more for sleeping and perhaps inappropriate to wear for a meeting with a prince. She reached into the closet and selected what she hoped to be a more comfortable dress than the one she'd worn earlier. It was one of the less vibrantly colored ones, at least; a pale shade of blue.

She shook her head at herself while she changed, surprised she even had to think such things about garments. She changed quickly, leaving the night slippers on her feet, and then left her room.

She asked a guard at the end of her corridor for instructions on finding the prince's chamber. She expected a look of judgment, but he didn't even look at her as he gave her directions.

Her mind started to wonder about why Prince Nikolat would request to see her. Perhaps, since he'd stayed hidden all night, he wanted to formally thank her for saving his sister. Maybe he was suspicious of her and wanted to confirm her reasons for being here.

Of course, KaLeah thought, I don't want to be here. That would be an easy answer for her.

The prince was a rather attractive man and had looked

at her very intensely that evening. *What if he wants to see me because he likes me,* KaLeah wondered, and then quickly pushed the thought aside, saying to herself out loud, "Don't be ridiculous."

She had known many boys and men who had courted women back in her village. Though never directly involved, KaLeah had seen flowers given, kisses stolen, and smiles so big it must have made their cheeks hurt.

She had seen the love pass between couples' eyes back in her village. But she had never known it herself, and was sure she never would.

Admittedly, she had probably watched the exchanges of affection a little too closely. Hugs, kisses, and the words "I love you," were all unknown experiences.

She thought back to when Princess Amirra had first hugged her, and the strange sensation. It was so unfamiliar that it had been a shock to her. Her father had never hugged her or even kissed her as a child, as she had seen some fathers do.

She wondered if there was something about her that all men, including her father, disliked enough to keep from ever hugging her.

After seeing Nikolat earlier, she partly hoped that this was some sort of formal request and tried to keep herself from getting her hopes up about a boy, a young man, actually being attracted to her.

KaLeah had almost reached Nikolat's door when she heard footsteps behind her in the hall. She grabbed for her dagger and then remembered that she hadn't thought to bring it. She hadn't needed any weapons since her arrival at the castle.

Back at her home in the village, there had always been weapons within easy reach. Her father was very aware, and always watched out windows, as if a threat were continually lurking.

She had adopted that cautious energy as her own, but being in the castle the last few days had started to lull her into a calm sense of security.

She spun around to face her intruder, hands out in front, ready to grab, claw, or choke.

"Calm down, old girl." The man's voice was thin and high. She recognized him as the man who had been standing with Nikolat in the ballroom. He looked even more ghastly up close.

"Who are you?" KaLeah asked.

"I am Favor Lamone, a friend of Prince Nikolat and the entire royal family, of course," he said, bowing slightly.

"The prince has requested my presence. Please excuse me." KaLeah lowered her hands.

"Tut, tut, girl," Lamone said, taking a few steps closer. "The prince did request you, but only as a special favor to me. After I saw you this evening, I just had to meet you and well, get to know you better."

His intentions slid with his eyes down the length of her body. Lamone reached out a hand to touch her cheek and she pulled back fast, slapping his hand away.

He looked stricken and grabbed his spindly fingers as if they had been broken. Then he narrowed his eyes and squared up his shoulders.

"You have no choice, girl," he said. "By order of Prince Nikolat, you are to be mine for tonight; maybe every night from this one on."

KaLeah's stomach muscles tightened. She wasn't sure which was worse, that this disgusting man was propositioning her, or that Nikolat hadn't wanted to see her after all.

If she had been in possession of a blade, it would have found its way into this man's heart. She figured that it would be possible to seriously injure him with one swift kick to his groin, but logic overcame her fighting response.

She knew that she was a guest, and he was a favor. Whatever that status truly meant, she was sure she was below it.

So, instead of kicking him, she turned and stormed to

Nikolat's door. She pounded on the door, eyeing the guards that stood passively to either side.

After a few moments she heard more footsteps, and assumed they belonged to Nikolat. Lamone was still talking but her ears were burning so hot she couldn't hear him. The door opened and soft candlelight flooded into the hallway from Nikolat's room.

Nikolat eyed her with a hint of humor on his face. He crossed his arms over his chest and leaned all his weight on one foot. "The famous lady KaLeah. I wondered if I might see you tonight," he said smoothly, as if everything were alright.

Now KaLeah squared up her own shoulders. Lamone squeezed up behind her.

"Your Highness," she said and narrowed her eyes into a glare. "Favor Lamone has come to me tonight as a buyer of property. Unfortunately for him, I am not owned by anyone. I am here as a guest of your sister. I am not a slave or a concubine for this kingdom or anyone residing within its walls. With all due respect, I am the sole owner of my body, and it is not for sale."

The moments passed painfully slow. KaLeah became increasingly embarrassed and a little frightened for speaking so directly to a prince. The thought of discussing her body sexually also made her a little dizzy.

She watched Nikolat carefully. His face turned from humored to thoughtful. He unlocked his arms and reached out to grab KaLeah's shoulders.

She jumped but didn't resist when he pulled her into his room. Lamone followed. Nikolat spoke to Lamone without taking his eyes or hands off KaLeah.

"She's right, Lamone. Your request is denied by the owner. And I deny it. Return to your chambers."

"But prince, you—"

"Silence. I am revoking my permission. I believe my brother keeps concubines in the castle. See him about fulfilling your request."

"But you've already filled my request, sire," Lamone said, tightening his jaw. "She's just a villager, and she must obey your command."

Nikolat turned sharply then and looked Lamone squarely in the eye.

"And so do you," he said, emphasizing each word.

Lamone held the prince's glare for a moment and then dropped his head, pushed past them, and stormed out of Nikolat's doors. The guards standing in the hallway watched him leave and then shut the doors behind him.

"Forgive me, KaLeah," Nikolat said, squeezing her shoulders affectionately. He finally released her, and she just stood there, frozen.

KaLeah stared up into his glassy gray-blue eyes. Her stomach started to spin, and she suddenly wished his hands were back on her shoulders to steady her.

"Why did you promise me to him?" she asked, her voice cracking slightly as she regained her composure.

He turned from her and walked toward his window. "Because he asked," he answered, simply. "What am I to do? Deny my friend something he wants?"

"Yes," she said. She was feeling braver with his back to her. "You absolutely deny him what he wants when what he wants is me or any girl for that matter."

He scoffed.

"Well, aren't you noble?" he said. "You must be a lonely girl, so far from home."

KaLeah couldn't believe he was attempting to justify his actions.

He moved to sit down in an oversized chair.

"I thought you might enjoy a little male company."

"Well, I don't, and you shouldn't make assumptions about a person you don't know," KaLeah shot back, not containing her anger.

"Whatever you say," he said. He laced his fingers together in front of his face and stared intensely into her eyes.

Unspoken questions began to swirl in her head. *Why did he pull me into his room? Why hasn't he dismissed me? Why is he holding eye contact so intensely? Why did he change his mind?*

She told herself that it didn't matter. She did not know this person, and prince or not, she owed him nothing.

She gave a slight bow and headed to the door.

"Goodnight, prince."

He said nothing, and she let herself out.

৶৹৶

That night, KaLeah had a dream. In her dream, she was standing on the top of a rocky mountain, overlooking a kingdom she had never seen before. In fact, she'd never seen or heard of towers like these stacked so closely together and spread across the land. Lights much brighter than candlelight seemed to light up every corner of each tower.

Above her, the sky was filled with flying dragons. There were dragons all around and they were screaming at her. She couldn't put the sounds together into sensible words. Then, a large dragon flew straight at her, chomping its jaws, and she woke up.

The dream stayed with her as she washed her face and selected a riding outfit from the closet. She dressed in a gray pair of riding pants and a light green tunic. She was pleased to see various sets of riding boots in her size. She selected a black pair.

As she headed to the door, the dream stayed with her like a fog. She could see the dragon's jaws and hear them clamping together repeatedly.

The way the dream stayed with her gave her an eerie feeling that it had been more of a premonition than a dream. The mood of the dream made her grab her sword on her way out, as if to protect herself from the dragon spirits themselves.

Princess Amirra was in a particularly cheery mood that morning as they headed toward the dining hall. She was in a pink and white riding outfit and was chattering about the day ahead, but KaLeah wasn't really listening.

Her eyes absently scanned the dragon murals that decorated almost every wall in the castle as if she was looking for something. Then she saw one that made her freeze in mid-stride. Amirra stopped too.

"What's wrong?" Amirra asked. "What are you looking at?"

KaLeah stared at a mural depicting a scene similar to the one in her dream.

A warrior was standing on top of a mountain. He was surrounded by dragons, flying around him, as if he commanded them.

"I think I dreamt about this tapestry last night. It seems so familiar to me."

Amirra stepped closer to the mural. She took a deep breath and then raised one eyebrow.

"Huh, I wonder what she is doing? I've never paid much attention to these tapestries."

"She?" KaLeah asked. She stepped closer and looked at what she thought was a man with long hair. But Amirra was right. The figure was a woman on the mountain, surrounded by dragons.

Just like she had dreamed.

"You must have seen this walking through the castle and then dreamt about it," Amirra said. She reached for KaLeah's hand and pulled her down the hallway.

Much to KaLeah's dismay, Prince Nikolat was in the dining room waiting for them.

"Good morning, ladies," he said.

He was dressed in varying shades of black. A long, black, sleeveless vest hung over tight black pants, secured with a black belt. He had on a V-neck shirt that hung so loosely that most of his chest was exposed. He wore long black arm guards on both arms.

His biceps bulged out and KaLeah couldn't help but notice his bare arms and chest.

She felt dumb for looking, especially once she noticed that Nikolat was staring just as intensely at her. Her cheeks flushed with heat.

"I was hoping you two would accompany me riding this morning after breakfast," Nikolat said.

"Of course, we will, brother," Amirra said. "Won't that be fun, KaLeah? We were planning on riding anyway."

KaLeah pulled her hard gaze away from Nikolat and gave Amirra a soft look. She smiled at the little girl and said nothing.

I am just spending a few days here to make her happy, and then I am leaving, she reminded herself. She was not about to give up the chance to ride a draggot again.

After they finished their large breakfast, they walked together through the castle and out into the sunshine. The planet Denlerack hung heavy in the sky above, with hints of gray and brown streaming across its face.

KaLeah tried to avoid Nikolat by keeping Amirra between them, but it wasn't easy. He snuck closer every chance he got.

"Lamone's pretty angry with me," Nikolat said as they followed Amirra across the lawn to the stables. Amirra was running ahead of them and KaLeah just didn't have the energy to run after her. "I may have to find a new best friend."

"You shouldn't have promised him something that wasn't yours to give," KaLeah said.

"That's right," he said. "I guess he should have gone to my sister. He'll have to ask her for you from now on, I guess."

KaLeah resisted the urge to punch the prince in the nose. She clenched her fists together and spoke through gritted teeth.

"I am the only one who will ever give myself to anyone, Your Highness," KaLeah said.

She put some effort into walking faster. When he tried to keep up, she took off into a run, although the food in her stomach protested.

She was used to punching boys in the village. She was used to standing her ground and speaking her mind. But she knew that in this castle, she was far from her village in more ways than one. If a prince could so casually offer to sell her to a stranger, she could only imagine the punishment for standing up to him.

In the stable, a boy younger than KaLeah was putting a saddle on Amirra's tall, white draggot while she stood by and rung her hands impatiently.

"Hurry and saddle up the golden mare, KaLeah," she said. "Her name is Maze."

KaLeah didn't need to be told to hurry. She wanted to get back out of the stable and away from Nikolat, hopefully outrunning him on her draggot.

Maze kicked the stall door with her hoof excitedly as she approached.

"I'm coming, girl," KaLeah said as she let the draggot out and threw the saddle over her.

Nikolat entered the stable and KaLeah heard Amirra yell at him to hurry up. She smiled at the child's lack of patience.

KaLeah lifted herself up and saw that Amirra had also mounted her draggot. The girls tore out of the stable, leaving Nikolat in their dust.

For someone with no experience riding draggots, KaLeah found it came naturally.

They had only trotted slowly that day she had emerged from the woods with Amirra. Moving now at a much faster pace, she stood up slightly in her stirrups, easing the bumpiness until she reached a rhythm with the draggot where she was almost gliding across the grass.

The castle grounds were quiet. A few fat wuvats were grazing on the lawn. The scales along their backs, inherited from their dragon ancestors, glistened in the sunlight.

The wuvats lifted their big lazy eyeballs up at KaLeah and Amirra as they ran by on their draggots. The only sound was the rhythmic beating of the clawed hooves on the ground below her and the princess' draggots.

In the distance, KaLeah could hear the flying juliebees singing from the border of the woods. There was a great field that stretched out for miles in front of the castle. To the east were farmlands and a road leading to the towns that surrounded the southeast side of the castle.

To the north and west were thick forests and then mountains beyond that. The mountains to the very south of the castle were visible from some of the rooms, including her own.

Although she yearned to run off for miles with the draggot, she knew that the lawn would be all the ground they would cover today.

KaLeah heard draggot hooves approaching. She turned her head around and saw Nikolat gaining on them. She was annoyed by his presence and rolled her eyes.

"KaLeah," he yelled.

She pretended not to hear him.

"KaLeah, I just thought you'd want to know that you were in my dream last night."

That got her attention, but she didn't slow her draggot down. He caught up to her anyway and the three of them all slowed down.

"Don't you want to know about it?" he asked.

She tried hard not to look at him. Anytime she did, she found herself immobilized by his gaze and confounded by a mix of conflicting emotions.

"I do," Amirra said, circling her draggot back toward them.

Nikolat took that as his cue and started to tell them the dream. "KaLeah, you were riding on top of a large dragon and wearing ancient warrior garb like the warriors in the tapestry murals."

KaLeah's heart started to flutter nervously. A tightness clenched her chest. It was the same feeling she had when she had realized her father was missing. The same feeling she had before the men had come upon her in the woods.

Danger.

She said nothing and saw Amirra crinkle up her nose. "That's it?" Amirra asked. "That was the dream?"

Nikolat looked stricken. "Well, yes," he said. He turned back to look at KaLeah. "Maybe you don't know this, since you're from a village, but here in the kingdom, we grow up hearing stories about the dragon spirits helping warriors win battles hundreds of years ago. It's said that the spirits would take physical form and the warriors could ride them into battle. Of course, only men are warriors, so you being in the dream doesn't really make sense."

He kept his eyes locked tightly on KaLeah while he told her, and she tried her best to keep her eyes on the back of her draggot's neck while she stroked its furry mane.

"I don't normally have dreams, let alone remember the details like this," he continued after a brief pause. "But there you were, riding on the back of one as it flew over the kingdom grounds, its green scales shimmering in the light of the sun."

KaLeah's eyes shot up and met his involuntarily. She could picture that dragon because she'd seen it before… the phantom dragon from the field.

Maybe it was a coincidence, she told herself. She tried to remember the colors of the dragons depicted in the tapestries. *Were there a lot of green ones,* she wondered? Maybe they were all green.

While her mind tried to work things out, a slow grin started to stretch across Nikolat's face. He was looking at her intently now and she realized he and his draggot had come much closer to her over the last few moments.

What if he had just overheard her telling Princess Amirra about her own dream that morning, and he was just trying to use that to win her over?

Her eyes narrowed as this realization set in, and a low growl sounded in the back of her mind like a warning.

KaLeah was just about to tell him that she wasn't interested in hearing about any more of his dreams when a shrill scream filled the air, accompanied by the sound of hooves.

KaLeah knew instantly that there were many sets of hooves. Her eyes darted around the castle grounds, and she saw that Amirra was gone; she had trotted toward the direction of the forest.

Amirra's draggot galloped back toward them fast with Amirra tucked low and leaning forward against her draggot's neck.

Good girl, KaLeah thought as she kicked Maze into a full gallop toward Amirra.

There were three men on draggots following close behind Amirra. They didn't appear to be running at full speed, and they had their swords drawn. They probably hadn't expected Amirra to run off so quickly when they emerged from behind the trees.

KaLeah was fuming. These men had caught them all off guard. KaLeah passed Amirra and then brought Maze to a stop to face the attackers.

She pulled out her sword and turned Maze so the men could see the sword in her right hand. KaLeah saw their faces. They showed no signs of concern.

The three men were running almost perfectly parallel to each other. All three were dressed in blue and green uniforms of the Lisodanyan army. She stared hard at the man in the middle, keeping the man to the left of him in her peripheral view.

Just as they were about to plow into KaLeah, she kicked Maze into action, and with her sword extended she ran around the men and sliced her sword down across the chest of the man on the end. He groaned and fell off his draggot.

The man in the middle of the group spun his draggot around to face KaLeah, while the third kept on course for Amirra. KaLeah charged the second attacker, but he held his ground, waiting for her.

She leaned over toward the right with her sword extended. He was waiting with his own sword extended on the right side of his draggot. It would be a clean duel, but she had a trick planned.

She lined up Maze's nose with the assassin's draggot so that it appeared she would run into him head-on. At the last second, she veered to the right, threw her sword over to her left hand, and then stabbed the gawking assassin in the side.

KaLeah held onto her sword tightly. As Maze kept moving forward, KaLeah pulled the sword out of the attacker, causing him to spin around and fall off his draggot.

She kicked Maze lightly, realizing the draggot responded almost instinctively with KaLeah's plans, as if trained for battle.

Maze must be used to having a fighter on her back, she thought as the draggot kept running full speed back toward Amirra.

Up ahead, Nikolat and the last assassin were sword fighting from the tops of their draggots, and Nikolat was doing well. The attempted assassin, or kidnapper, kept trying to break free and get around to Amirra, who was scowling from her draggot behind Nikolat.

"Get back to the castle, Princess," KaLeah yelled, annoyed to see the child lingering there.

Amirra only casually directed her draggot backward as KaLeah turned to help Nikolat dispatch the attacker.

The kidnapper must have known he was beaten because he started to lash out with his sword chaotically. KaLeah and Nikolat had him pinned between them and he tried frantically to maneuver his draggot out of the trap.

The man widened his eyes, and his features softened. He stopped fighting as if he were preparing to surrender. He turned his dark eyes to KaLeah.

He opened his mouth to speak, but instead of words, Nikolat's sword struck him through his back and out his chest. He bent over without making a sound and then fell from his draggot. His sword landed on the ground beside him.

The expression on Nikolat's face was serious when he

looked up at KaLeah.

"We were going to win, you didn't have to kill him," KaLeah said. "Now we won't find out why they came or who sent them."

"He attacked my sister," he said, nonchalantly as he wiped the blood off his sword onto his pant leg. "Besides, did you let the men live who attacked you the day you rescued Amirra?"

"That was different. I was alone."

She turned to the sound of guards on draggots coming from the castle. "I didn't have an entire army just a few moments away to assist me in taking them captive," she continued.

Amirra came up beside KaLeah on her draggot.

"And why are you still here?" KaLeah asked incredulously. "You were in a full run! You should have kept going until you were behind the castle portcullis."

"I knew you and my brother would protect me," Amirra responded. "You are so good sword-fighting on a draggot"

KaLeah's jaw was hanging open. No wonder the child had been previously abducted. She was careless.

"How did you learn to fight like that?" Prince Nikolat asked her. "Did you have draggots in your village?"

KaLeah shut her jaw and shook her head. "My father taught me to sword fight, but I've never had a draggot. It's obvious that Maze knows how to respond to my slightest suggestions, which made my movements effortless. It all seemed very... natural to me, I suppose."

"Like a warrior on a dragon," Nikolat said, smiling wryly again.

"Warrior KaLeah has saved me again," the princess chirped.

The castle guards were almost upon them, and KaLeah didn't feel like being either praised or questioned. She had an unsettling feeling in the pit of her stomach that something was amiss.

KaLeah lightly nudged Maze into a gallop, past the

assassins lying on the ground, and toward the edge of the forest.

She saw something glimmer between the trees. Her adrenaline began pumping hard through her veins and she ducked her head as they shot straight for the forest.

She thought she heard Nikolat yell something from behind her, but his words died before they reached her ears. KaLeah plunged into the dense forest, looking for her prey.

If there was someone hiding there, she was going to find him.

5 FAVOR

The air was moist inside the forest and the light trickled down on her through tiny holes in the treetops. The trees were not as thick as she thought they would be and before long, she found herself on an animal-beaten path.

She kept stopping Maze briefly, holding them both still as she tried to catch a glimpse or the sound of another draggot. A man would be quiet and hide in silence. She knew that it would be easier to track the draggot.

After a short trek into the woods, she spotted a man standing beside a tree without a draggot. He appeared to be dressed in dark colors instead of the bright blue, green, and white of Lisodanya.

He had not noticed her and appeared fixated on a black, metal object he was twirling around in his hand.

"Hey," she yelled out. "Surrender now and your life will be spared."

She maneuvered Maze carefully forward, not knowing if he was armed. But when she reached the area where he had been standing, he was gone.

She turned her head, searching, and saw him again, deeper in the forest, but he appeared to be strolling casually.

KaLeah directed Maze toward the man, wondering how

he had moved away from her so quickly.

She drew closer and could see that he was wearing armor. Attached to the back of his armor looked like a pair of dragon wings.

She kicked Maze and charged at him, sword raised slightly above her head, but he stepped behind another tree and was gone.

She was suddenly dizzy, and tiny stars began to cloud the edges of her vision. She was confused about the feeling, since she wasn't holding her breath, had just eaten, and had drunk plenty of water.

She wasn't one to just feel light-headed for no reason. She shook off the strange physical sensation and tried to focus on locating her target.

She couldn't tell how he was moving around so quickly, and he seemed to vanish every time she turned around.

Suddenly she heard a familiar sound. It was faint but she was certain it was the same sound the dragons had made in her dream. It was like thunder rolling over words, pushing them out toward her, desperate for her to understand.

KaLeah's head began to ache slightly at her temples, the stars growing bright across her eyes, blinding her. She dropped her sword and pressed her fingers to her head, trying to rub away the pain.

More growling sounds entered her mind, rolling in and out of her eardrums, so loud they seemed to pound the inside of her forehead. She heard strange words mixed into the growls that she couldn't understand.

She closed her eyes tightly and fought back the urge to scream.

Suddenly the voices stopped, and the pain vanished, as if it had never been there. She opened her eyes and heard Nikolat's voice through the woods.

"KaLeah is in here, be careful. KaLeah, make yourself known! The soldiers will take it from here! KaLeah," Nikolat said as he came into view. He sounded exasperated, and immediately dropped his eyes to her sword, laying at her draggot's feet.

Her cheeks flushed with embarrassment, and she slid quickly down from the draggot to pick up her sword.

"The soldiers will deal with anyone left alive, KaLeah. We need to go report to the king. Amirra is asking for you."

KaLeah re-mounted and nudged her draggot onward as she tried to maintain focus on her original objective.

The soldiers were all around her now, coming into the forest. Nikolat rode up beside her and grabbed Maze's reins. He pulled hard enough to turn her draggot's head.

KaLeah's frustration at not being able to capture the rogue man was turning into anger toward Nikolat.

"Let go of my draggot," she snapped, trying to yank the reins back. A layer of ice passed across Nikolat's face, and for a moment, she feared him. He bared his teeth like a beast and narrowed his eyes at her.

"Maze is not your draggot; she belongs to the royal family." He spoke slow and deliberately, enunciating every word. "I am your prince and I order you to go back to the princess," he said. "I will let this insolence slide only once, as you clearly are just some wild village girl with no concept of hierarchy."

KaLeah suddenly felt like a child being scolded. She ripped the reins loose from his grip and turned Maze around fast, coming side-by-side with Nicolat.

"After you, Your Highness," she said, not taking her eyes off his. He looked away and headed back to the castle lawns. KaLeah reluctantly followed.

Back on the lawn, there were twenty or so Belarone soldiers standing guard around the princess, who had been coerced down from her draggot, and was standing stubbornly with her hands on her hips. When she saw her brother approaching, she pushed her way through the blockade of armor.

"KaLeah, thank the spirits, where did you go?" Amirra asked. Amirra stood beside Maze and ran her hands over the mare's golden coat, looking up sweetly at KaLeah. She felt momentarily guilty for leaving the princess behind.

"I saw a fourth man in the woods," KaLeah explained. "I followed him for a few moments but lost him. I'm sorry."

"Don't worry, KaLeah. The soldiers will track him down. You were wonderful. I've never seen a woman fight like that before."

The child princess seemed so small standing beside the draggot. KaLeah had never had a sibling, but the protective instinct for this princess was growing stronger by the moment.

How had those men snuck up on them? How could anyone want to harm this child? And why did they keep coming for her? Questions filled her mind as the young girl smiled up at her with a look of pride.

KaLeah smiled back, suddenly overcome by just how out of place she was here among soldiers and royalty, chasing assassins on a draggot.

She had now saved this tiny, blonde-haired princess twice. Maybe there was something to this strange new place. Maybe she needed to be here.

She looked over to Nikolat, who was discussing something with a soldier. He turned toward her absently and their eyes met.

Even after their exchange in the woods, his eyes seemed to carry more curiosity than animosity. Her heart rate increased, and she dismounted in order to walk alongside Amirra back to the castle. She hoped that the young girl wouldn't be able to pick up on the tensions rising between herself and Nikolat.

The soldiers formed a moving cocoon around the girls as they headed back to the castle. At the castle gates, the soldiers were replaced by a dozen royal guards who led them safely through the courtyard.

Once inside the walls, they were escorted to the king's study. They could hear the king yelling from behind his closed doors.

"Do not tell me you don't know where they came from," he yelled. "Then find out if this was Sarzoe, or Mikroth, and find out why they are after my children."

The doors opened and General Zoseff Array walked out, followed by two captains.

The first was a thin, muscular man with sharp features and a long scar that ran the length of his face. The second man was young and handsome with blond hair and kind, blue eyes. He glanced at KaLeah and held her gaze as he passed them. Both men were dressed in red and white tunics, armor emblazoned with the dragon symbol of Belarone Kingdom.

The swarm of guards moved aside to let the general and soldiers pass, and then a few took the lead into the study.

Princess Amirra, holding KaLeah's hand, pulled her into the study behind her, leaving the rest of the guards in the hallway.

King Erazus was on his feet and moved quickly out from behind his desk.

"Amirra," he said, wrapping his arms around her. The hug was brief and so was the friendly tone in his voice. "What were you thinking going near that forest? You shouldn't have left your brother's side. You had to run from the assassins. Do you realize what could have happened if you hadn't seen them coming?"

"Sire," KaLeah said, feeling protective. "She responded swiftly, and Prince Nikolat and I took care of the assassins."

The king spun his angry face on KaLeah, his cheeks red behind his gray and black beard. She gulped back any more defensive statements.

"And how could you let her leave your side?" he asked, taking a step closer to her. "Do you think it was prudent to kill those that might have been questioned so we could have found out who keeps attacking my daughter?"

He held eye contact for a few moments and KaLeah wanted to tell him that it was Nikolat who had killed the last assassin, not her, but she kept frozen in place, barely breathing instead.

"Sit down, child," he ordered.

KaLeah lowered her eyes to look for the nearest chair, and then quickly dove into it, grasping the wooden arms firmly for a sense of security.

The king walked back to the far side of his large desk but did not sit. His desk was bulky and unadorned; covered in papers, scrolls, and ink quills.

The walls held overflowing bookshelves and hanging maps of Belarone, Lisodanya, and Extelli, all the kingdoms of Naldash. It was obviously just a room for working and never for entertaining.

"KaLeah," he said, "I am amazed to find myself once again in your debt for saving my daughter." He put his hands on the desk and leaned forward, looking at her.

"How did you come to know sword fighting, especially on draggot-back? We do not train women to do these things."

"My father taught me, Your Highness," KaLeah said.

The king drew his eyebrows closer together, considering that. "Who is your father?"

"Clegg Trapper, Your Highness."

"I do not know that family name, Trapper. How would he have come by these skills? Was he a soldier?"

"I do not know."

KaLeah spoke the words slowly, realizing that she did not know how her father had come by those skills because she had never thought to ask.

"And you had draggots? Did you breed them?" he asked.

"No, Your Highness. I had never seen one until I arrived in Belarone. Riding her, Maze, just seemed very natural." She didn't realize until that moment how easy it had been to knock down those assassins while riding a draggot at a full run.

Surely, those assassins had been trained at not only sword fighting but also fighting on draggots. How had she dispatched the men so easily? She was a third of their size, a young girl, and had not had the same type of training those men had surely received.

Her eyes rose to meet the kings, and she realized he too was having these same thoughts. She hoped that he did not suspect her of somehow being a part of the assassination and kidnapping attempts.

Her palms started to sweat.

"I am an old man, and I have seen a lot of things," he said, much calmer and quieter now. I have learned not to question everything because some things go beyond our understanding. One thing I know I don't need to question is your loyalty to my daughter, young KaLeah."

An overwhelming sense of relief flowed through her.

Just then, the doors swung open and Prince Nikolat sauntered in. He gave a short bow to his father then stood behind Princess Amirra's chair, placing his hands on it.

The king stood back up straight and looked at each of them before turning to look out the window behind him. The bright afternoon light cast him into silhouette while he spoke.

"Apparently, the first kidnapping attempt was not the last. I am concerned for the princess' safety and require that she and KaLeah both stay inside the castle until we can determine who is behind this and why."

A small sigh escaped Amirra's lips, and the king turned to her with a stern expression on his face.

"You are not to leave the interior of these walls, with or without escort. Do you understand?"

"Yes, father," she said, nodding with a mix of fear, obedience, and disappointment. She looked down at her hands, fidgeting with them in her lap.

"Guards, take the girls back to their rooms," he called loudly to the men behind the doors. KaLeah flinched involuntarily at the sudden volume.

The girls stood and KaLeah followed closely behind the princess, making very brief eye-contact with Nikolat as she passed him.

His expression was blank, so she tried her best to keep her face from revealing her emotions.

Her heart was racing, and when she looked down and saw the blood on her clothing, her mind began to replay the assassins' attacks.

She could still hear the king's booming voice reverberating in her mind as she followed the guards down the corridors.

This was far more than KaLeah had ever expected when she had packed a small sack and headed out into the woods in search of her father. *How have I gotten here?* she wondered.

Three guards escorted the girls to Amirra's room. They opened the doors and Amirra went in. KaLeah hesitated in the threshold.

"I would like to be alone for a little while," KaLeah said. "Will you be okay without me?"

Amirra nodded silently. KaLeah gave her a reassuring smile, a quick bow, and then headed down the hallway to her own room. Two guards remained outside of Amirra's door, while the third followed her to stand outside of her own.

KaLeah closed the heavy door, kicked off her boots, and shed off all the blood-stained clothing as quickly as she could. She slipped into a robe, walked to the giant bed, and fell onto it, face-first.

She curled up into a ball, wrapping the covers all around her.

What am I still doing here? she wondered.

It wasn't her responsibility to keep an eye on the princess or argue with the prince. This wasn't her life. She had to leave and find her father, and then they could return to the normalcy of her village.

She pictured her father going back to the village, into their home, and not finding her. He'd be furious. She meant to find him and maybe save him from something, but instead she'd found and saved a child.

She felt lost and hopeless.

Although the sun was coming through her windows, she was overcome with exhaustion and fell into a light sleep.

Her dreams kept taking her back to the attack on the lawn and the mysterious armored man in the trees.

She was walking in circles, around tree after tree, in endless spirals through the woods. She heard a sound she knew was a dragon call, it was deep and low, reverberating all around her in the dark forest.

Instead of a dragon, she caught glimpses of the armored man. KaLeah couldn't recognize any colors, there were no crests to identify which kingdom he was from.

The glimpses she caught grew longer and longer, until she saw the man's armor was bronze in color with two metal wings that seemed to sprout from the backside of the armor.

She couldn't tell if the wings were moving or if it was just the movements of the man wearing them.

The closer she got to him, the louder the dragon calls grew. She was covering her ears now, running in circles in the woods, zigging and zagging around tree trunks. She was getting dizzy, and the sound was painful, like a beating in her head.

A strange feeling began to overcome her, as if she was running toward safety instead of toward someone dangerous.

Had she misjudged something? she wondered. *Had she missed something?*

KaLeah awoke to an incessant tapping at her door. She hadn't moved much during her sleep, but she noticed that the dragon calls were instantly quieted.

She scrambled out of the bed, wrapping the robe tighter around her, and opened the door to find Felair with her arms full of dresses, jewelry, and other items.

"You look a mess; this is going to take longer than I thought." Felair moved as if falling into KaLeah's room. She dumped her armload onto a small sofa and spun toward KaLeah.

"You'll first need to wash up. You have a big night ahead of you." The young woman smiled and clapped her hands together.

"A big night? Did something happen?" KaLeah didn't move from the door just in case she needed to make a hasty escape.

"KaLeah, you have saved the life of the princess twice, you are a friend to her, she enjoys your company, and you are, well, a woman instead of a man.

"The king would much rather have a female guard protecting his daughter at every moment than a male guard, especially as she gets older."

"I don't understand, Felair," KaLeah said, sighing and leaning into the heavy door.

The woman walked back toward her, pulled her off the door, and shut it heavily.

KaLeah was unsteady on her own feet. Her head was still clouded from sleep and every muscle in her body ached.

Felair huffed and walked back toward the clothing.

"The decision has been made. Tonight, the king will raise you to the status of a Belarone Favor and assign you as the personal guard to the princess. It is the highest appointment a non-royal woman has ever received."

"No, no, no." KaLeah took a step back and waved her hands. "I need to find my father and return home. I have to leave. I need to speak to… who do I need to speak to?"

Felair lifted her already sharply pointed eyebrows even higher.

"There is no one you can speak to. The king will make his appointment tonight. Riders are already out calling the Favor families in to attend. You will be honored with a ceremony binding you to the royal family forever."

KaLeah's legs begin to weaken.

"I am a prisoner? Will I ever be allowed to return to my home? How can they do this to me?"

Her eyes began to burn with the threat of tears.

"You should be happy," Felair said.

"It's better than being a dress maid, or any kind of maid. You were just a villager, a farmer, and now you will be able to live in the castle and have whatever you desire. You'll be put into a much more lavish room next to Princess Amirra's, living in complete luxury."

"But I love the woods, the outdoors, my home in Erion."

"Once the king allows it, you can teach the princess all about the outdoors. I had a home once too, with my family. But this is our home now. It is an honor to your family to be selected to serve the kingdom. And you will have the highest honor bestowed on you. From farmer to favor, you should be grateful. Now come on, we need to start getting you ready."

KaLeah just kept shaking her head back and forth in disbelief. Finally, Felair stormed over to KaLeah, grabbed her shoulders, and shook her fiercely.

"Listen, if you do not accept this appointment, you will be seen as a traitor and will find yourself in a real prison."

Though Felair had not shown much kindness to KaLeah, she could hear the concern behind her warning.

But her heart still pounded in her chest. This was so far from what she ever wanted.

"Maybe I can plead with Amirra, explain. She knows I do not want to stay here," KaLeah said, taking short, quick breaths.

"The princess is only ten-years-old. This decision is not hers. She can do nothing."

"Then I'll run away." Tears of desperation trickled down KaLeah's cheeks.

Felair released KaLeah's shoulders and crossed her arms, seeming to grow tired of the argument. KaLeah had to steady herself, feeling weak.

"Yes, KaLeah, you may run away. But you will be tracked, brought back, imprisoned, and executed. Who knows, you may even be blamed for the previous attacks on the princess. Your desertion will be seen as traitorous. I have been a servant here for many years and I have seen terrible things and heard terrible things."

Felair kept her arms crossed and walked toward a window, peering down and then out across the land.

"This is not our world, KaLeah," Felair continued. "This world belongs to the king, his sons, and his soldiers. For your life, you must do as they say. For any woman born in Belarone, any woman born on Naldash, marriage to or a servant of the royal family is the best any woman can hope for. To you, it may feel like being a servant after growing up free in a farming village. But here, in this castle, you will at least be one of the highest forms of servant."

KaLeah was silent for a long time, letting the few tears that had fallen evaporate from her cheeks. Felair returned to stand in front of her and then took her hands gently and guided her to the wash basin.

She chattered on about the room she would be moving into, and how instead of basins, there were large baths filled with warm water.

KaLeah let the young woman clean, dress, and style her.

When Felair was finished, KaLeah looked at herself in the mirror, but all she could see was a very lovely prisoner.

҈

Hours later, KaLeah had finished picking at a small plate of food that had been brought to her in the early evening.

No one other than Felair had seen her, but she'd been given precise instructions not to leave the room until she was escorted to the ceremony that night.

KaLeah paced her room, watching her reflection in the mirror as she passed each time.

She was in another red dress that flared out beneath the waist and had a slight train that trailed behind her. Instead of diamonds, white pearl beading ran down the back and sleeves.

Felair had chosen the dress, and she couldn't help

wonder if the red was starting to represent the blood on her hands.

Five men. Dead.

"I had to," she said to her reflection.

The sides of her hair were pinned back, simulating a thin crown, while the rest of her brown hair hung long down her back. Felair had clipped an ornate pearl clip to her hair, and a simple silver necklace with a single diamond trinket hung around her neck.

KaLeah looked more like a princess than a personal guard, in every way except for the blood red of the dress reminding her that she was not delicate.

There was a knock on her door, and she took a deep breath before opening it.

She followed the house guard wordlessly through the halls until they reached a corridor that led to two large double doors she knew opened into the throne room.

The guard nodded and she walked the length of the corridor to the doors alone.

The massive wooden doors were carved with ferocious depictions of dragons wrapped in battle, claws digging into tough hides, pointy teeth bared.

She suddenly felt faint and had to put her hand against a nearby wall to keep from falling over.

"My Lady, are you unwell?"

The voice was a soft whisper. KaLeah slowly opened her eyes and looked up into gentle blue eyes that seemed familiar.

She realized that it was the young, handsome captain she'd passed going into the king's study after the assassination attempt.

He had his arm outstretched, as if preparing to catch her should she faint. The gesture made her want to give into that feeling, faint, and let him catch her. The thought surprised her.

"I am very unwell, sir," she replied.

He moved swiftly, putting an arm around her shoulders,

while holding her forearm with his other arm. Then he took her weight onto him and led her to an ornately carved wooden bench, gently sitting her down on a tufted red cushion. He sat beside her, leaving his arm around her, and she laid her head against him.

"Are you alright?" he asked.

Tears begin to sting her eyes, and a hollow cramp filled her stomach. Her forehead ached with the strain of holding back tears.

With everything going on around her, no one had asked how she was feeling. No one cared who she was or what she needed.

"I don't want to be here," she whispered. "I want to find my father and go home. I have to leave."

KaLeah didn't dare look up at this stranger. She was embarrassed and couldn't believe she was telling all this to a Belarone captain. But he squeezed her shoulder reassuringly.

"I understand, and I am truly sorry," he said gently. "I don't know you or anything about the village where you are from, but it seems like you are here completely by accident."

He sighed and gave her a moment to respond. When she said nothing, he continued. "It may not seem fair to you that you are now being required to stay when you didn't come here seeking out this appointment. But you must accept this appointment of favor. If you refuse..." he paused.

"I know," KaLeah said, lifting her head and straightening her shoulders. "If I refuse, I am choosing death."

He turned his eyes to hers and squeezed her hand before letting it go and taking his arm from her shoulders.

She felt the sudden loss of his comfort but knew that it was time.

He stood up and extended his hand to her.

"I know that you will never be ready, so I won't ask you if you are. But will you allow me to escort you?"

She nodded her reply, and he helped her to her feet. He guided her arm into his and slowly began to lead her toward the doors.

"What is your name?" she whispered.

"I am Captain Hilip Daven," he replied, just as quietly.

"Thank you for your kindness, Captain Daven."

He smiled in response.

The guards on the other side of the doors opened them as they approached, and the captain escorted her into the throne room.

KaLeah was surprised by how many people were there. Everyone was lined up into neat rows on either side of a main aisle.

They stared at her and put their fists to their chests as she passed. Felair had told her ahead of time that they would do this as a sign of respect and solidarity.

Each of the favor families had gone through a similar ceremony, but none of them were assigned to guard a member of the royal family.

There were house guards and there were soldiers. The favor families ran businesses to suit the kingdom's needs, provided a bloodline for heirs, and were wealthy landowners.

It was unheard of for an outsider, especially a poor villager, to be appointed to favor.

Once she was within ten steps of the royal family, she stopped as previously instructed. Captain Daven bowed, released her arm, and moved to stand along with the crowd of favors.

The royal family sat in front of her on their thrones. The king was in the middle, his two sons to his right, an empty throne for his deceased queen to his left, and Amirra on the other side of her mother's empty throne.

The chairs were encrusted with gold, but the fabric was a deep red. The backs were tall and covered with etchings of dragons in combat.

KaLeah took five more steps forward and directed her

gaze to Amirra. She curtsied toward the princess as Felair had instructed, which made her feel very feminine and awkward.

Then she rose and turned to Nikolat. His eyes seemed to penetrate her, and she feared for a moment all the instructions would vanish from her mind. But she peeled her eyes from his and curtsied, then moved again to curtsy to Prince Bylex.

She took one more step forward and then curtsied deeply toward the king, spreading her skirts around her as she crouched. She held the position and kept her eyes and head focused on the marble floor.

"Loyal Belarone Kingdom Favors," King Erazus boomed across the throne room. "Today we honor KaLeah of Erion. She has twice proven herself not only loyal to the Kingdom of Belarone by saving the life of its princess, but she has also shown tremendous skills in fighting." The king scanned the throne room on these words, as if daring the audience to be shocked with the revelation of a female fighter. When no one uttered a sound, he continued.

"It is my wish, and my command, that she be appointed a favor of this kingdom, and the personal guard to Princess Amirra. If anyone here has just cause for why this honor should not be bestowed, please come forward."

KaLeah waited silently for the speech to end. She tried to hear the king over the sounds of herself screaming inside her own mind, yelling out how much she wanted to go home. She dared not move for fear the yelling would spill out of her.

"These witnesses have confirmed that KaLeah is known to be honorable, loyal, and deserving of the title and duties she receives today. Rise, Favor KaLeah of Belarone. May no man stand in the way of your duty to protect the life of the princess from this day forward."

KaLeah rose and remained in place so Captain Daven could approach and pin a round pendant to her dress. It was the pendant that all favors wore; a silver dragon encircling a red flame made from rubies.

A respectfully subdued clapping filled the room.

Captain Daven took her arm and escorted her out.

"That wasn't so terrible," he whispered, trying to give her a smile.

She didn't return his smile, but she was thankful for his arm. It seemed to be the only thing keeping her from falling to the marble floor.

6 NIKOLAT

Nikolat managed to maintain his composure throughout the brief event. The favor ceremony required that he sit in the chair beside his obnoxious brother, Bylex.

His mother's throne was empty, and Amirra was sitting in the throne beside hers. The royal family sat together, facing the crowd of favors with their families.

When KaLeah walked in, he was captivated by her beauty and unable to take his eyes off the way her hips rocked from side to side as she walked toward him in that red dress.

When she made eye contact, he imagined what it would be like if she were walking straight to him in an empty room.

The vision was interrupted by his father's voice, and then Nikolat felt a surprising tinge of jealousy when that captain pinned the favor pendant onto KaLeah's dress.

The ceremony was over quickly, and as soon as KaLeah's back was turned, he slipped out of his chair and out the back door of the throne room. He was never in the mood to stick around and talk to his family or their entitled friends.

Walking through the corridors, his mind kept replaying KaLeah's walk down the aisle. She had looked pale and didn't have her usual confident air. It seemed to him that KaLeah wasn't excited at all, in fact, maybe even a little upset, about her royal appointment to the favor position.

Of course, that would be absurd. Since she was only a village girl, maybe she just didn't understand what was being gifted to her. Everyone in the kingdom wanted to be a favor, or part of a favor family, at least. It was the next best thing to royalty.

Her trepidation intrigued him.

Why would anyone not be happy about this? he wondered.

For him, it simply meant that he'd be seeing a lot more of KaLeah, which he liked.

Nik made it to his room and removed his sword. He walked to his favorite chair near the fireplace and poured himself a drink. It had been a long day, and the castle servants and guards had been going full force since the events of the morning ride.

A sinister smile crept across his face as he remembered how he had taunted KaLeah and then watched her slice through men like paper. Although, he knew that she'd killed his sister's kidnappers just days ago, seeing her actually in battle was both enticing and unsettling.

For one, he'd never seen a woman use a sword before. And second, she was capable of complicating his plans more than he'd anticipated.

Not only would this girl be around his sister now more than ever, but she was lethal. He knew that most men would underestimate her after what he'd seen.

Nikolat ran his fingers through his hair and pulled his hands down across his face. He was running out of ideas.

He heard a knock, and the guards announced that Favor Lamone was waiting.

"Enter," Nikolat called out.

He did not want to see the wormy man, but he thought perhaps yelling at him might improve his mood in the long run.

"Quite an interesting turn of events, wouldn't you agree

my prince?" Lamone said as he helped himself to a drink and a seat in a plush, oversized chair opposite his own.

"But don't worry," Lamone continued. "I'm sure Sarzoe will think of something else. We obviously can't try a third kidnapping at this point; especially with that woodland warrior girl shadowing the princess."

Nikolat stood up and began pacing across the room.

Sarzoe's name sent an angry tingle down his spine.

Lamone kept talking about how ravishing KaLeah had looked, but Nik couldn't hear the rest. The anger had bubbled up into his inner ear, blurring out sound.

He saw his sword where he'd laid it on a small table, grabbed it, and then walked back toward Lamone with the blade extended.

"Whoa," Lamone said, putting his hands out in front of him. His drink fell to the floor.

"Tell Sarzoe that he can do it on his own next time, without my help," Nikolat said.

He swung the sword down across Lamone's left arm. It made a sound like a clap and Lamone yelled, jumped up from the chair, and pulled his own sword from his belt.

"I don't think you'll want me to tell Sarzoe that," Lamone said, fending off another blow.

"Tell him what you want," Nikolat said, trying to jab Lamone in the belly.

"You don't know what you're saying," Lamone argued. "You're just mad that the plan was unsuccessful. The kidnappers failed and now King Sarzoe will be angry. Sarzoe thought Amirra would be an easy target. He may think differently now and come up with another strategy."

"Why didn't they go after my father or Bylex first?" Nikolat asked. "The spirits know it would be easy to kill my lazy brother, as long as we could pull him away from kissing father's boots."

"It was easy the first time when Amirra was out riding alone," Lamone said. "No one expected her to be rescued by a traveler. And this second time, well, we didn't realize that farm girl would still be around. Now that she's a favor, we may never be rid of her."

Nikolat could taste blood and realized he'd bitten his tongue. Lamone had told Nikolat all of King Sarzoe's promises a year ago, and they had sounded great.

King Sarzoe of Extelli wanted an alliance with Belarone in order to ease trade between the two kingdoms. His land was on the rocky edge of the sea and not as fertile as Belarone lands.

His plan was to orchestrate a kidnapping.

King Sarzoe's men would kidnap Amirra, and the blame would fall on Lisodanya because of the colors worn by the men. While everyone focused on finding Amirra, Nikolat would let assassins into the castle to kill Bylex.

Sarzoe's men would then 'rescue' Amirra from Lisodanya and return her to King Erazus.

Grateful, King Erazus would then join alliances with King Sarzoe instead of King Mikroth of Lisodanya. Then Nikolat would be the sole heir to the throne of Belarone as the kingdom prepared for war with Lisodanya. Once Lisodanya was conquered, the lands would be divided between Belarone and Extelli.

Nikolat had zero guilt about having his brother killed for the greater good of him becoming king. He told himself that a Belarone led by his brother would be a travesty.

And now that the plan had not worked out, Nikolat didn't know if he could trust King Sarzoe or Lamone. He didn't know if either man would keep any of their promises.

This was all Lamone's fault, he thought.

Nikolat ran at Lamone again with his sword. His sword met Lamone's, and they fought.

"What is this?" Lamone asked. "You're still on our side, right?"

Nikolat didn't answer.

"Sarzoe won't try another attack like that," Lamone said. "The royal family is too well guarded, even against me. He'll have another plan soon and then you'll be the only male heir."

Nikolat tripped Lamone and he fell to the floor. Nikolat kicked Lamone's sword away and pointed his own at Lamone's throat. Lamone squealed.

"What's the matter with you?" Lamone asked.

Nikolat was sick to his stomach. Deep inside, he wanted to just kill the sniveling man, but he knew he couldn't. Not now. Not like this. There would be too many questions.

He pulled his sword away and sheathed it. He walked to the bookshelf that concealed the entrance to a secret passageway.

"Tell King Sarzoe what you want," Nikolat said. "I'm still on his side, but I'm limiting my involvement. I'm not sure how I feel about an alliance with a king whose best men are defeated by a young girl from Erion. Now get out."

Lamone scrambled up and out through the double doors.

Nikolat was fuming. He was angry with Lamone, angry at King Sarzoe and the failings of the kidnappers. He was attracted to and yet frustrated with the girl who had appeared out of nowhere to ruin his plans.

He couldn't sit still, but he didn't want to be seen by anyone out in the castle either. After a few moments, Nikolat walked to a tall bookshelf against his wall. He lifted a lever tucked behind a book. There was a sound of gears shifting to open a hidden doorway.

Nik slipped into a dark passageway to walk where he wouldn't be seen or disturbed.

❦KaLeah❧

Captain Daven escorted Favor KaLeah all the way back to her new bedroom suite. She froze in the hallway, confused.

"Ah, I'm guessing that nobody told you about this part," Hilip said. "It was discussed between the king and General Zoseff. Instead of a room down the hall, your chambers will now be adjoined to Princess Amirra's. You will have access to a passage directly connected to her room."

He opened the door for her.

"Felair did tell me," she said. Her head was foggy, and she felt like she was walking through mud. "I just…forgot."

"The nursemaids will have already moved your belongings and clothing to your new room. They should be along shortly to help you… um… change, miss."

He turned away from her and she saw his cheeks had flushed a light pink color. She walked by him into the candle-lit room.

Her new room was twice as large as her last, with a round tub, mirrors, bay windows, and a sofa, in addition to luxurious chairs, curtains, and linens.

All her new clothing was hanging in the tall wardrobe. She knew that the clothes she had arrived in were hanging there too, tucked in between the fancy new riding clothes. And beneath all the clothing she would find her boots cleaned but well worn.

She wondered what her father would think if he returned home to find her gone with no explanation and felt a sharp pang in her chest.

No one in the village would guess to look for her inside the Belarone Castle. She regretted not telling anyone, at least the direction she'd been heading.

"You'll find that you have more clothing befitting a bodyguard, now," Hilip said, coming up behind her. She realized that she was staring absently into the wardrobe.

"You won't have to wear dresses around the castle, if you do not wish to," he clarified. "You shall have considerably more access to weapons, also. I can show you to the armory later, if you'd like to choose additional swords, daggers, or anything else."

His kind eyes twinkled as he smiled at her. She realized that he was excited about her new position. Or at least, he was excited about something, maybe showing her the weapon selections. She watched him with more curiosity.

She took a breath, relieved that at least she'd be more comfortably dressed in her new role.

She pulled out a light gray tunic with a dark gray pattern that ran from the collar to the skirt, black pants over black boots, then pulled out a black double belt to secure the tunic. She laid it all over a nearby chair.

"I admit, this is all more familiar than… well, this." She motioned to the dress she wore. "I had never even worn a dress before coming here."

"If I may say so, you do look lovely in the dresses," Hilip said. He looked away quickly, seemingly embarrassed.

KaLeah was surprised to find yet another smile curling at the edges of her lips. Smiling was not something she had expected to be mixed in with her heart being torn between finding her father and protecting the princess.

"Before I leave you to change, Favor KaLeah, I do need to discuss your new position with you." Captain Daven's voice had changed to a more formal tone.

"So, what is it that I am to know, Captain Daven?"

"You may call me Hilip in private, if it pleases you, Favor KaLeah."

"Only if you call me KaLeah," she responded. "I'm not a formal lady. I… I don't know what I am right now."

"Well, KaLeah, you are the first woman bodyguard in the history of Belarone, maybe in all of Naldash. You have been charged to protect our princess. From what has transpired thus far, I'd say that you are the best person for this position."

"Do you know why anyone would want to hurt her?" KaLeah asked. "Why do these men keep coming after her?"

The captain shook his head.

"I wish that I did. We are all working to try and uncover the plot and purpose, I assure you."

A silence followed his words, and KaLeah realized how close they were standing. She quickly turned and walked to sit in front of the fireplace, which had been lit and well fed with wood. Hilip cleared his throat and then followed her, sitting in the companion chair beside her.

"First, these orders come directly from the king and are to be followed precisely, unless he instructs otherwise," Hilip said. "As a Favor and as a personal guard to the princess, your duty is to her safety in all things. You will be the first person she sees in the morning and the last in the evening. You will accompany her throughout the castle, and once it is again deemed safe enough, you will accompany her in the lawns and gardens."

Hilip had been looking at KaLeah, but he paused and let his eyes drift to the flames in the hearth.

"It is most unusual; however, you are also to begin training her to fight. This is not something to be discussed with anyone outside the royal family, the general, the other captains, and myself. Given the recent events, the king feels it may be necessary for her to learn how to defend herself, even while riding on a draggot."

"The king wants the princess to know how to fight," KaLeah repeated.

Hilip nodded.

She turned to him.

"But in secret?"

Again, Hilip nodded. "The king has always been traditional, but after losing his wife, he is genuinely scared of losing his daughter too. He is willing to break tradition with you. He trusts you. He trusts that you can help make the princess strong enough to defend herself, if it should come to that ever again."

KaLeah sighed long and deep and then fell back into the chair.

Oh, what a mess I've gotten myself into, she thought.

Unable to leave, tied to a new responsibility and a princess, when all she wanted was to find her father and go home.

Even growing up in the small village, she never longed for adventure beyond the woods. And yet, adventure found her.

"The nursemaids may be allowed in the princess' room, but no one else," Hilip continued. "There are to be guards stationed outside every room she is in. However, there are secret passageways built within the castle that only the royal family, the general, and some captains know about." His eyes darted to her wardrobe and back before he continued.

"You must learn these passageways and teach them to the princess. In case of attack, they lead to a secret chamber in the lower levels of the castle."

"How am I to learn these passageways? Is there a map?" KaLeah asked.

"No, lest it fall into the wrong hands," he replied. "A few times a week, I will come to you after you have seen the princess safely to bed. I shall guide you through the passageways bit by bit, until you know them by heart. There is a simple pattern, like following the left wall of a maze. The entrance from this room is behind your wardrobe. However, I wouldn't advise going in without me until you learn them thoroughly. There are still some areas deep in the castle that even I have never seen. I wouldn't want you to get lost."

The smile on his lips met his eyes as he looked away from KaLeah and to the wardrobe, then back to her.

"Captain, Hilip, why were you assigned to teach me? Is this something you normally do, as part of your role?"

Hilip smiled again and stood to leave. He nodded a slight bow to her and began to walk to the door.

"I wasn't assigned, Favor KaLeah. I volunteered."

KaLeah stood up more quickly than she'd intended, and she suddenly felt faint again.

"Thank you for the escort, and for the kindness," she managed to choke out. His cheeks flushed and he smiled wider.

"It was my pleasure," he said, and he pulled the doors closed behind him.

After Hilip left, the nursemaids came in and helped KaLeah slink out of the dress. They kindly put her into another sleeping gown and then left her alone in her new room.

In the sudden quiet, KaLeah found herself staring at her wardrobe. Hilip had warned her not to go in without his instruction, but she could at least look beyond the entrance.

She opened the tall wooden doors to her wardrobe, slid a pair of boots to the side, then pushed apart two rows of hanging clothes.

She could see a light peeking through a long vertical line in the back. Assuming it was the outline of a door, she felt for a latch. Once she found it, she pulled, and the door swung into the passageway beyond.

She was surprised to see that the path outside the door was candlelit. The soft light flickers invited her into the quiet hallway.

She climbed through her wardrobe and stepped into a stone tunnel that stretched to her left and right. The left was dark, but to her right, a small white candle sat flickering on the ground.

If she stretched out her arms, she could touch both tunnel walls at the same time. If she reached way up, she could touch the ceiling.

She decided to creep as far as the end of the light, checking behind her as she walked, to make sure she kept her wardrobe entrance in sight.

As she came nearer to the candle, she noticed another one flickering further down the tunnel.

Her first instinct was to turn back.

Someone has lit these candles recently, she realized. *Who would be in the passageway lighting candles?* It couldn't have been the captain because he had just been with her. Princess Amirra's room was in the other direction.

Could someone be trying to lead me somewhere? Could it be a trap?

The questions flooded her mind, and she knew that she should go back to her room, and yet, she was too curious at this point. She wanted answers to the questions.

KaLeah noticed how her body reacted to the small adventure. She was excited chasing the mystery, momentarily pushing all other cares from her mind.

Her mood lifted as she followed the pathway of lit candles.

The silence and solitude caused her mind to drift, and it took her inexplicably to thoughts of Nikolat.

Since Amirra's birthday, he'd been everywhere; watching her at the party, watching her at meals, and then suggesting the draggot ride.

She wondered then, but only for a moment, why he had suggested that ride? Had it been a coincidence?

She thought of the assassins and the attack. It had been the second attack on the princess and may not be the last.

How am I supposed to protect this little girl? What if there are traitors among us? What if they knew of the secret tunnels?

KaLeah's heart started to beat faster as her mind brought her back around to her new responsibilities; the responsibilities she never asked for.

Calm down, she told herself. She took a few steps and heard something behind her. Instead of turning around she froze, straining to hear the sound again.

Suddenly, there were two arms around her and a blade to her throat. The arms were strong and held her tightly.

KaLeah didn't try to struggle. The man's body was pressed up against hers and she felt him take a deep breath as if breathing her in.

Does he know who I am?

"What are you doing here?" he asked.

She instantly recognized the voice. Her heart started pounding and she wondered why he didn't just let her go. She wasn't armed.

"Prince Nikolat?" she asked. "It's just me, let go."

"What are you doing here outside my room?" he asked

again. His grip on her didn't slacken. She started to struggle and felt the prick of the blade.

Thoughts flooded her mind.

Was it really Nikolat? Or was he an assassin stalking the passageways looking for the princess? No, it must be the prince. Maybe he thinks that I'm an assassin.

"I was following the candles," she said. "I didn't know I was outside your room."

She could feel Nikolat's grip loosen, and he lowered the knife.

She took a deep breath, and he backed away from her. He still had hold of one of her arms.

For a moment, she was afraid to turn around, afraid that it wouldn't be Nikolat.

She turned around, slowly, and then stepped back.

He was standing there in the candlelight, every flame accentuating his high cheekbones and piercing eyes. She quickly composed herself.

"You were going to kill me," she said.

"Maybe, if you had been anyone else."

"What are you doing in here?" she asked.

"The damp air helps me clear my head, if you can believe it," he said with a smirk. "I can be alone here. Besides, I don't feel much like going outside after the attack on Amirra." He looked down at the knife in his hands remorsefully.

KaLeah noticed that his voice shook when he said the last part. She hadn't even thought about the attack bothering him.

She was ashamed for thinking he might have had a hand in it and embarrassed for raising her voice at him. He was a prince after all, and she should be somewhat respectful.

But then she remembered how he'd promised her to Lamone, and she narrowed her eyes at Prince Nikolat.

"I am going to say goodnight and return to my room now, Your Majesty," she said, starting to leave, taking a step around him.

He tightened his grip on her arm briefly and then let her go.

"I'm sorry about Lamone," he said.

She stopped dead in her tracks. She always had time for apologies.

"It's just," he started. "I hoped that if I knew you were with another man, then..."

He stopped and seemed to take a strained breath. "It would just be easier. Better."

"Easier for who? What in dragons' sake do you mean?" She turned to face him.

"Easier for me," he said. He raised his eyes and KaLeah's heart tightened in her chest. "It would be easier for me if you were with someone else, KaLeah."

KaLeah's thoughts couldn't keep up with his words. *Easier for him if she was with someone else? What wasn't being said?*

"Nikolat, I don't understand," she whispered.

Something inside her belly stirred. She tried to tell herself that she only felt an inkling of interest because someone was expressing interest in her, and that had never happened before.

KaLeah didn't know how to react. She had not been trained to ward off these kinds of enemies.

Seduction. Desire that blinds the senses. It clouds your reason, your mind, and distracts your body.

She could just leave, she knew, but then he reached out and ran his fingers down her arm.

He was slow and meticulous. Her skin pricked to life beneath each touch, and she wanted to surrender to him and run from him at the same time.

Her feet wouldn't make up their mind.

That hand was just holding a knife to my throat, she reminded herself, cursing the bumps beneath his touch that gave away her nerves.

"Nikolat," she said, but then as if her own voice had woken her up, she turned her head away from him, looking at the candles leading back to her room, and began to pull away.

But he stepped up behind her and she couldn't move.

He ran his fingers across the back of her shoulders to the nape of her neck. Then both hands moved down her arms.

She could feel the butt of the knife, still in his hand, rub against the skin of her right arm.

She was very aware of how thin her dressing gown was, and she could feel every movement as if he were pressed against her skin.

KaLeah had never been touched like this. She closed her eyes as he wrapped his arms around her waist. He leaned in and began to breathe against her skin, with warm, wet breath.

KaLeah felt dizzy and lightheaded. She tried to think about Amirra alone in her room. She tried to think about Lamone, slinking around and cackling.

Nikolat had almost given her away to Lamone. How could a man who wants you just give you away?

He couldn't ever really love me, she told herself.

She somehow managed to repeat that in her mind as she slowly pulled herself away from his hypnotic hold and forced herself to walk away.

He won't love me, he can't love me, he can't love me, he won't ever love me, she told herself over and over again to the rhythm of her steps as she followed the lit candles back to her room.

"KaLeah, please," he called after her, but she kept walking. She knew where she was now and where she was going.

She reached the passage door at the end of the candles and stopped suddenly, looking down at the candle on the floor.

Had the one outside Nikolat's room been the last? Or had she been too distracted to see that they continued down the corridor? She couldn't remember.

Why had the candlelit path begun outside of her door?

She climbed back through the secret door in the back of

the wardrobe and pulled it shut behind her. She found that the latch had a lever to lock the door, so she locked it.

She closed the carved wardrobe doors and then leaned forward, resting her forehead against the wood.

Closing her eyes, she could still picture Nikolat's face turned down to her with a longing expression, flames flickering reflections in his dark eyes.

That may be the toughest enemy I'll ever have to face, she told herself. Then she pulled herself up and went to lie down with shivers still running up and down her spine.

7 WAR

The following morning came too early for KaLeah. She tried to hide her face from the beams of sunlight streaming in through the windows, thoughts of Nikolat still clinging somewhere behind her eyes.

Had she dreamt of the encounter in the secret passageway? No, she remembered. It had been real.

"Are you awake, yet?"

"Holy dragons' ghosts!" KaLeah scrambled up and out of bed, nearly tripping on a blanket that she'd wrapped around her leg in her sleep. "Amirra, how did you get in here?"

Nonchalantly, Amirra raised her long, purple gown to her knees and climbed up onto the tall bed. She plopped down, folded her gown around her legs, and smiled up at KaLeah. "There is a door connecting our rooms behind one of the tapestries."

KaLeah calmed down her beating heart and unwrapped herself from the bedding.

"We have to find something fun to do today," Amirra said.

KaLeah moaned, closed her eyes, and fell back down face first onto the bed.

Amirra started to shake KaLeah.

"Come on, get up," she said. "I don't care what we do, but we can't just sit around. Let's start with breakfast. KAH LEE AH."

KaLeah groaned again at the combination of Amirra's whining and shaking. She finally rose to her feet and went to wash her face in the basin.

The water was cold, and as soon as the fogginess of sleep was gone, she saw Nikolat's face again.

KaLeah could still feel his hands on her, and she trembled. She smiled at Amirra and silently hoped that they wouldn't see him today.

The princess handed her the plain gray tunic, belt, and tight black pants that KaLeah had set out the night before. She decided to arm herself only with a knife in her belt, since they would be indoors and presumably out of harm's way.

Once she was dressed, Amirra handed her the silver and ruby dragon pendant she had placed on the table beside her bed after undressing the night before.

"You have to wear this at all times," Amirra ordered. KaLeah reluctantly took it from the child's small fingers and pinned it onto her tunic.

She followed Amirra down staircases and hallways, toward the dining room.

"KaLeah, have you had any more dragon dreams?" Amirra asked.

KaLeah hadn't thought about her dreams since becoming too preoccupied with Nikolat. She started to tell Amirra that she hadn't had any more dreams when she heard a faint voice.

KaLeah stopped suddenly and looked around the hallway.

"KaLeah," Amirra said. "Why did you stop?"

The whispers intensified, as if competing to be heard. KaLeah tried to focus but couldn't discern any words.

"Do you hear something?" KaLeah asked.

"Uh," Amirra started.

She looked at KaLeah carefully, as if it were a trick question.

"No," she finally answered. "Do you?"

KaLeah's ears were starting to ring, and she realized that the whispers were in her mind, just as the phantom dragon's words had been.

She put her hands over her ears in a futile attempt to respond to the rising volume. As quickly as the sounds started, her ears popped, and the whispers stopped.

"It's gone," KaLeah said, lowering her hands.

"What was it?" Amirra asked, deep concern furrowing her brow.

KaLeah looked thoughtfully at the young princess standing below her on the stairs.

"I don't know," she said. "But I'm sorry if I scared you."

"That's okay," Amirra said. "I know that you are special. You'll protect me."

Although it was true that KaLeah had already protected the princess, it still struck her as a curious comment. She had never thought of herself as a protector. This was still all so new to her.

Before she could consider the comment or the strange sounds that had permeated her head, she heard men's voices float up from the bottom of the stairs, and KaLeah motioned for Amirra to keep quiet so they could listen in.

"You hear those voices, right?" KaLeah whispered.

Amirra nodded up at her with a knowing grin.

"The assassins were wearing Lisodanyan colors," said a calm, smooth voice.

"But what motivation would King Mikroth have in harming Amirra or Nikolat?" The second voice was deeper.

"He stands to win more from an alliance with us if Nikolat is alive."

A third, softer voice added to the conversation. "The colors could have just been a ruse to trick us. They could be affiliated with either kingdom, or just bandits looking for a ransom."

The voices faded away and KaLeah's curiosity drove her to follow them. "Do you want to see what is going on?" she whispered to Amirra. "It'll be fun."

Amirra nodded her head and took KaLeah's hand. They crept silently down the hallway and then followed the voices to a stairwell. The girls reached the bottom of the stairs and stopped, peeking around a corner.

Down the hall, she could see General Zoseff Array standing outside two doors being held open by royal guards.

KaLeah watched as the three men she had overheard went through the doors along with other men coming from other areas of the castle.

She could tell something important was happening and wished that she could follow them into the room.

Instead, she and Amirra walked slowly and casually toward the general as if being in that hallway was perfectly natural.

Nikolat suddenly stepped out from behind a corner at the end of the hallway, Lamone following closely at his heels.

KaLeah's eyes met his and then she quickly looked away. It was too late to duck out of sight or turn around, so she held her head high and kept walking forward.

General Array acknowledged the girls as they passed with a slight nod and a kind smile.

KaLeah noticed that Nikolat made quick adjustments in his stride in order to nearly collide with her in the wide hallway.

"Good morning, little sister, Favor KaLeah," he said, smiling at them.

His sleeve was dangerously close to touching her shoulder as he passed them.

KaLeah nodded, not knowing exactly if she should stop and curtsy, but not wanting to, regardless.

"Good morning," Amirra chirped in reply. After a few steps, she asked KaLeah in a whisper, "What do you think they are doing?"

"I believe they are meeting to discuss what to do about the recent abduction and the second failed attempt. I wish I could be in there," KaLeah admitted.

"Well, you are not allowed," Amirra said, matter-of-factly. "You are the first woman to ever be named a bodyguard, but women are not allowed in the legion."

"Do you ever wonder why?" KaLeah asked as they continued on the longer route toward the dining hall.

Amirra shrugged. "We are not strong enough, I suppose."

"That isn't true. I could defeat all the boys and most of the men in my village at simple swordplay. I could outsmart them, out track, and hunt, and worked twice as hard as any at whatever task I took on. My father understood that and never limited me. Your father and brothers shouldn't limit you, either. Who knows what you could be capable of if only given the right instruction and encouragement."

Amirra was quiet, lost in thought, as they entered the dining hall and then sat at the long, wooden table. They were served a meal of eggs, meat, and sweet jam on toast.

"But what else would I do?" Amirra asked after the servers left them alone in the room. "I am a princess. I will learn things, marry into a partnership with a man, and have children of my own someday."

"Is that what you want to do?"

Amirra took a long time to answer. After they had both taken a few more bites of their breakfast, she finally responded.

"I do not know."

❧Nikolat☙

Nikolat tried hard not to think about KaLeah, but in refusing his advances in the passageway the night before, she had risen to a special place inside him.

He wanted her like a man would want to tame a wild draggot. He felt alive with the prospect of a challenge and walked a little taller than he had in years.

The best part was that he wouldn't tell Lamone about it until after he'd won KaLeah over.

Lamone would be furious with jealousy.

Nikolat tried not to smile as he met General Zoseff Array in the hall outside the war room.

"Good day, Prince Nikolat," General Array said loudly. People often cringed or jumped back in alarm when the general spoke. General Array would say, "I'm not loud. Weak people just have weak ears."

Nikolat tried not to react to the jolt of volume.

"Is it such a good day, general?" Nikolat asked. The large man, with skin much darker than his own, leaned forward to speak man-to-man. Nik wasn't a small man, but he looked tiny beside the general.

"There's talk of war, my prince," the general said. "It's always good when your father's men talk of war." He winked.

Lamone snickered behind Nikolat, and General Array's eyes went cold. He glared at Lamone for a moment and then looked away from them both as they entered the war room.

The war room was long and narrow, with a wooden table running the length of the windowless room. A line of lit candles down the center kept the room well lit.

The walls were covered with maps of the three kingdoms on Naldash. Some were new, but others were yellow and frayed, with holes depicting regime movements from previous wars and battles.

All ten captains were in the room already. Some were seated and some were standing along the walls, while soldiers and guards remained stationed outside the doors.

Two guards closed the doors after Nik, Lamone, and the general entered the room.

Nikolat and Lamone joined King Erazus and Prince Bylex at the table. The king looked old sitting at the end of the table with all the young, strong men before him. His dark black hair was more and more gray every day, and his beard was so thin, Nikolat could see his pale white skin through the whiskers.

He wondered how his father would be able to handle another war.

"Dear friends," King Erazus started. "We are here to discuss the recent attack on Prince Nikolat and Princess Amirra. General Array, I know your opinions. Would you start, please?"

"An honor, My Lord," General Array boomed. All heads backed an inch away from him as if he had shoved them away with his words.

"First, there are the assassination attempts to discuss. An attack on our beloved leaders calls for immediate retaliation. The problem is that we are unsure if the attacks came from King Sarzoe of Extelli or King Mikroth of Lisodanya. There is also a chance that the assassins were from another source entirely. To delay action would signify doubt and uncertainty, which is exactly what we are facing."

Nikolat had never considered that they would assume the assassination attempt was aimed at him as well as Amirra.

"The assassins wore the blue, green, and white Lisodanya colors, but it could be that King Sarzoe is trying to make us believe that our allies in Lisodanya orchestrated the attack," General Array continued. "King Mikroth has sent his concerns and blessings to our king, and he has sworn on his own children's lives that he has perpetrated no harm on our royal family."

The general began pacing the room and continued. "Of course, King Sarzoe has also sent his blessings for the health of our royal family, sworn allegiance, and claims that his men were in no way involved. Your Majesty, I am more inclined to believe King Mikroth, as you know. He has nothing to gain from the loss of your children. He has more to gain from a union by marrying one of his daughters to Prince Nikolat."

The king nodded in agreement with this theory.

A familiar sickness roiled in Nikolat's stomach; it was the concern that he was being used more for breeding than royal leadership.

"King Sarzoe routinely gives shelter to our Belarone criminals," the general continued. "There are reports that Extellans are looting coastal towns and sinking fishing boats. "Although we receive complaints from the fishing villages, it is never enough to start a war. However, if we suspect Extelli, as I do, even if we are wrong, taking over Extelli would solve multiple problems."

"I agree with the general, Your Majesty," Captain Schar said. He was the second in command due to his length of time in the service of the king. He was a lean man with a scar that ran the length of his face. He used a lightweight sword and sharpened it so much that he had to sheath it in a metal case.

"Extelli is small and would be easy to take," Schar continued. "We should hit them first. No one, not even King Mikroth, will mind. We hit quickly and cause minimal casualties. The way Sarzoe runs things, his people should welcome our rulership with open arms."

Nikolat's mind started to wonder as the men all congratulated themselves for agreeing with the general and his captain. What if they did take Extelli? Who would rule that country? They would have to send somebody over there.

A new advantage to the original scheme began to grow in his mind. Perhaps Nikolat could be a ruler after all. Sure, it wouldn't be Belarone, but far away in Extelli he wouldn't have to answer to anyone.

"Besides, each prince will have some land to rule," Captain Schar continued, practically reading Nikolat's mind.

Nik wanted to jump up and say, "Yes!" right then and there but he bit his tongue and put a calm and unassuming expression on his face.

The king turned his eyes to Captain Daven. "What do

you think?" he asked the newest and youngest captain.

Captain Daven was around the same age as Nikolat and always took a peaceful and thoughtful approach to situations. Nikolat wondered how such a man could be a captain. He was quiet and often wandered on the grounds alone, lost in thought.

But Nikolat had also seen the man in battle. Captain Daven was a master. He never missed. And his first blow was always a deadly one.

Captain Daven's eyes were sharp and crystal clear. If anyone could read the treason in Nikolat's eyes, it would be the young captain.

"Extelli is not a real threat," Captain Daven said in a voice so smooth you couldn't help but believe him. "They are smaller, their swordsmen are not as good, they feud amongst themselves. All we really need to do is heighten our security."

Nikolat wondered about the chance of more assassins and if King Sarzoe would want to use him again. Nik needed them to go to war in order to cover his true intentions and involvement in the schemes.

King Erazus let out a long sigh. "I too am against a war," the king said. "There are always lives lost. I wonder if such a battle is worth losing any of you."

Nikolat watched as his brother, Bylex, reached out and placed a comforting hand on his father's shoulder. "Captain Daven is right," Bylex said. "They probably aren't a big enough threat to risk the lives. We would look like angry savages striking without any real evidence."

The coward, Nikolat thought. He just doesn't want to get his pearly white fingers dirty.

Bylex wore more jewels than his sister, and Nikolat knew for a fact that he hadn't gone to the practice hall in over three years. He stayed close to Erazus because the old man would protect him with his life, and Bylex wouldn't have to lift a finger.

Nikolat and Bylex had never been close. Where Nikolat

stood back and observed, Bylex was a social know-it-all, always shaking hands, smiling, and laughing to please others.

Nikolat knew it was all just a front and that his older brother was simply afraid to look like a fool in front of his father. Nikolat was taller, stronger, and could defeat his brother in any kind of fight: fist, sword, even a draggot race.

Lamone stirred beside Nikolat and cleared his throat to speak. "Your Majesty," Lamone said, addressing the king.

Nikolat curled his lip in disgust at having someone as low as Lamone trying to talk to his father, throwing his opinion into the ring as if it mattered.

"I would like to agree with your decision against war with Extelli. Heightened security should be the first priority here."

Nikolat was surprised and wondered what Lamone's new agenda might be. Lamone was the one who recruited Nikolat to help King Sarzoe of Extelli instigate a war.

Nikolat didn't care anymore for King Sarzoe's agenda. All he ever wanted was to rule his own kingdom.

Since his mother had died, his father and brother had made it clear that Nikolat was the least important prince with no true purpose but to perhaps marry into the Lisodanyan kingdom or into a favor family.

Nikolat was ready to take over his own destiny. "Father," he said, standing to his feet. "I believe that if we do not strike down Sarzoe now and remove him from the throne of Extelli, that he will try to take the throne from you and from your children. Sarzoe will try to scheme his way into this castle, maybe with more assassinations, successful ones. We can heighten security for years and Sarzoe will just keep pounding on the castle doors, trying to get in."

Nikolat leaned forward and banged his fist onto the table for a dramatic effect. "He is an evil man ruling over criminals. If we do not act now, in time, the Kingdom of Belarone may come to regret it."

After a pause, the captains began to put in their support

for Nikolat. Soon, the only men still opposed to the war were the king and Captain Daven.

Erazus' eyes looked even more tired than they had at the beginning of the discussion. Nikolat thought he saw sadness there.

"I suppose you are all right," King Erazus said. "Putting a stop to Sarzoe now is probably the best plan."

For a moment, Nikolat felt guilty about pulling his father into a war. But then he looked at Bylex who had gone from his usual pearly white to a sickly ghost white.

Nikolat was sure that if he were to look under the table, Bylex's knees would be shaking.

The men discussed strategies for about an hour longer, and then everyone left the room, shaking hands, or bowing on their way out. Lamone vanished quickly, but Nikolat was feeling too victorious to care.

Back in his room, he wanted to talk to KaLeah, but he didn't know why. Nikolat wanted to celebrate, and in his rush of adrenaline, he found pen and paper and wrote a note to KaLeah.

He sealed the note closed with wax and then called to a servant.

"Take this to Favor KaLeah," he said to the shaking servant girl. She was maybe close to his sister's age, but she looked much older in the face. For good measure, he added, "And if the seal is broken before it reaches her, I shall throw you to the dragon spirits in the forest."

He laughed as her eyes popped open wide, and he shooed her on her way.

⸀KaLeah⸃

"Favor KaLeah?"

KaLeah nodded and then took the sealed note from the tiny servant girl. She looked relieved and quickly scampered away down the hall.

KaLeah returned to sit across from Amirra in the

princess' room, where Amirra was showing off her collection of porcelain dolls.

"Open it," Amirra said. "Who is it from? What does it say?"

KaLeah broke the seal, confused and curious.

"KaLeah," she read aloud, her own name sounding foreign on her lips. She saw the prince's name signed at the bottom. "It is from your brother. He says there will be war with Extelli. After a lengthy debate, my arguments for war won out over the others. I..."

KaLeah stopped. She scanned ahead in the note and then quickly tucked it away.

"That's it," KaLeah stated. "There's going to be a war."

Amirra's eyes lit up with both fear and excitement.

"Will there be danger? Is it going to be here?" Amirra asked, her voice shaking.

"Perhaps, but all you need to do is hide in the secret passageway until I come to get you." KaLeah stood up and headed to her own room through the door behind a tapestry woven with the image of a woman sitting near a pond.

"What else does the letter say?" Amirra asked, trying to follow KaLeah into her room.

"Nothing," KaLeah said.

"But there is more; you were about to read more. I want to hear everything that my brother said about the war. I am not afraid."

KaLeah didn't want to read the rest because it was not about the war. Nikolat wanted to see KaLeah in private.

KaLeah squared her shoulders and looked down at the whiney princess.

"I said there is nothing else and you may not read the note," KaLeah said forcefully.

Amirra's eyes went a little wide for a moment, then narrowed defiantly at KaLeah.

"You are hiding something," she said. "I know there is something you are not telling me." Amirra danced around to block KaLeah's escape, the princess' skirts flowing around her.

"Does it have something to do with Nikolat? What does he want? I may be younger than you, but I am not stupid, you know. "You have been acting strange lately, and now you get a personal note from my brother? Why would he send you a note?"

KaLeah looked at the note in her hands and ran a finger across the broken seal. Suddenly, feeling too exposed, she looked down at Amirra.

She assumed that the princess could order her to read the letter or call in the door guards to rip the note from her hands.

With a sigh, KaLeah unfolded the note and began to read.

"I cannot tell you what seeing you the other night meant to me," KaLeah read.

"You saw my brother?" Amirra interrupted. "Did you talk to him? Where were you?"

KaLeah looked up and lifted her eyebrows in irritation. Amirra sat back slightly.

"Sorry, read on," Amirra said.

"I wish to see you again," KaLeah kept reading. "We can talk of the war. Meet me in the ballroom at eleven. I will be waiting, Prince Nikolat."

"Do you love him? What if you marry him? Then we can be sisters, and you can be a princess. He must love you or something. I have never seen him with a girl. When did you talk to him? What did you talk about?"

Amirra kept rattling on, but KaLeah stopped listening. She didn't love Nikolat. At best, she hated him.

"I'm not going to see him tonight. I do not love him, and I most definitely will never be a princess," she blurted out, interrupting Amirra's cascade of questions.

Amirra looked stunned and her eyes began to sparkle with tears. "What's wrong with being a princess?" she asked.

KaLeah turn to look at the fire burning in the hearth.

The flames danced, distracting her for a moment from answering the question. She felt a little guilty that the princess had picked up on the snide tone in her comment. It wasn't as if Amirra had chosen to be a princess any more than KaLeah had chosen to be a village girl.

"There is nothing wrong with being a princess, Amirra, of course. It is just that you were born to be one, and I was not."

"Many women who are not born princesses marry into royal families," the little girl countered.

"Yes, but those women are born to be…" spoiled, elitist, entitled, rich snobs who love fancy dresses and jewelry, she thought to herself while she mulled over how to respond.

"They were not born farmers or villagers who learned how to fight, and plant, and hunt, and fish. They are different from me. They are born to be favors and friends to royalty."

"Well, you are a favor now," Amirra added smartly.

"I am merely a bodyguard who wears a fancy dress when commanded." KaLeah smiled at the princess warmly but felt the bitterness in her heart burning with the truth of the words.

"Well, then I command you to put on a dress and go meet with my brother." Princess Amirra stood up a little straighter. "You can gather more information from him regarding this war with Extelli. Should we be afraid? Is father going to leave the castle? Is it Extelli who have been trying to kidnap me? You must go and find these things out and report back to me."

Amirra's command gave KaLeah a mixed feeling of annoyance, curiosity, and nervous excitement. The longer she sat with those feelings, the harder it was for her to determine if she was more annoyed or more excited. KaLeah was curious about what war meant for the kingdom, the castle, the royal family, and especially for Nikolat. Would he be going to battle? Would the king leave KaLeah and the princess behind?

She finally nodded in agreement and Amira squealed, darting off toward KaLeah's wardrobe.

The princess chose a silky, long black dress for her to wear later that night. Trying it on, KaLeah refused to pin on the favor pendant, finding it unnecessary. Amirra brushed out KaLeah's long hair so that it flowed down the back of her dress and tickled her through the fabric.

Amirra giggled about the romantic nature of it all, and then KaLeah changed back into her gray tunic. "Let's go kill time in the armory throwing daggers," she said.

The girls enjoyed hours of practice and a large dinner before heading back to their room. KaLeah sat with Amirra until the girl fell asleep, and then she re-dressed herself in the black dress. She felt like one of Amirra's dolls as she walked to the ballroom later that night.

The ballroom was dark, and she drifted like a shadow across the expansive space. She stopped to wait by a large statue of a Nala dragon carved from black stone.

The Nala race of dragons had inhabited Naldash after the planet was divided. They were flying dragons with scales that changed between shades of blue, purple, and black, so they could fly camouflaged in the skies. The tapestries always depicted them with long dark wings.

The statue reminded her of her dreams. There had been both kinds of dragons in her dreams. The Dynack race had supposedly lived on the planet Denlerack. They were the land race, running and burrowing, with smaller wings.

The phantom dragon she had seen in the woods looked more like a combination of the two, or a race completely separate.

"Why do I see you?" she asked the statue. "Why do I dream of you and your extinct ancestors all the time?"

She realized that the dreams were probably the result of being surrounded by more depictions of dragons she had ever seen in her entire life.

She rolled her eyes at the statue and turned away from it, silently blaming it for her nightmares.

There were no tables or chairs in the great ballroom, just a big open floor and a high vaulted ceiling. Moonlight twinkled in from high windows, casting shadows across the floor and walls.

After a few minutes, she heard boot heels on the floor. She couldn't see him, but she knew it was Nikolat. He seemed to almost flow across the floor, like a dragon stalking a meal.

She watched as he went to the middle of the floor and spun on one heel in a full circle, as if dancing with himself. She heard him light a match, and soon, she saw the candle in his hand. The light made his features leap from his face and into the darkness again and again.

KaLeah took a deep breath, stood up straight, and slowly walked out from beside the dragon statue. Nikolat turned and watched her, but she couldn't tell what he was thinking by the look on his face. He seemed to be smiling slightly.

"You take my breath away," he said.

KaLeah stopped walking and just looked at him.

"I'm here to talk about the war," KaLeah said, crossing her arms. She wanted to be clear about being ordered to be there.

"Of course," Nikolat said. He looked over the dress she was wearing and said, "the war, of course."

He put the candle on the floor, and then walked to KaLeah, drawing nearer as if his words to her would be sacred.

"We are going to attack Extelli, take it over, and I will rule that kingdom," Nikolat said. "I am the one who convinced all of my father's men to pursue this war, and it will be an historic victory. There has not been a war this important in a long time."

She knew little about the wars that happened before she was born. Older men told stories from time-to-time back in her village, but she'd never paid them much attention.

"It is so good to see you," Nikolat said, sliding his eyes up and down her dress. "I'm excited about the war, and I knew that you would be the only one who could understand my… excitement."

He slowly reached out a hand and touched KaLeah's bare arm. His fingers were cold, and she shuddered, but didn't turn away.

"Please, don't touch me," she said, barely able to hear her own voice, as all Princess Amirra's questions vanished from her mind.

He looked hurt and pulled his hand back.

With more effort than she would want to admit to herself, she turned around toward the statue, dead set to leave him then and there. She didn't know what she'd been thinking answering his letter in person and dressed like she was. "Good luck, Prince," she said. "Thanks for the information."

"KaLeah, stop," Nikolat yelled. His voice bounced off the walls and echoed across the ballroom.

KaLeah froze, and for a moment, she was frightened. She instinctively thought of the dagger securely fastened to her inner thigh.

"If you do one thing for me, I will leave you alone," he said. "I will forget the way I feel about you."

He's lying, she told herself.

He sounded like an animal caught in a trap, calling for help, but only drawing another victim into the trap with him.

"You are disarmingly beautiful and a complete mystery to me," Nikolat said. He stepped up behind her and put his hands on her waist.

Her heart skipped and a thrill sparked up her spine. He moved one hand up to her ear and pushed back a few strands of hair. His fingers were soft against her skin, and she gulped back an involuntary verbal protest.

"Kiss me once and I'll leave you alone," he whispered.

He put his hands on her shoulders and began to slowly turn her around.

She found herself pushing and pulling at the same time;

her heart struggled against her mind as it tried to shout out warnings.

Hadn't he put a knife to my throat in the passageway? Hadn't he offered to give me to Lamone as a plaything? Is this man good or bad? she wondered.

There was strength and yet, a tender passion emanating from his fingertips and into her shoulders. There was an energy surging from him, and somehow, she knew he felt that same energy like a spiritual connection between them.

Face-to-face with Nikolat, KaLeah looked deep into his eyes, which seemed to be black in the dark ballroom.

He was a beautiful young man, with smooth creamy skin, and a smile that spread like a river across his face.

His hand tightly cupped around the back of her neck. He pulled her firmly and steered her mouth closer to his.

Her heart was on fire, beating so fast she felt the pulse in her throat and fingers. She had never been kissed, never even held a boy's hand, before this moment.

He lightly pressed his lips against hers. She kept her eyes open, distrusting the man she hardly knew. He started to kiss her harder, and she felt like she was falling. She lost control of her eyes, and they finally shut, giving into the swirl of emotions.

She was swimming in a dark pool of the most amazing excitement she'd ever experienced. Her bones ached with curiosity, and she knew her attempts to not get attached to him were over. Somehow, she had lost something; she would be vulnerable now. Her mind was only focused on Nikolat, and she realized her hands were raised and moving around his arms and his back.

She was kissing the prince back.

The whispers that had been haunting her came upon her again, creeping into her mind slowly, prodding the edges of her consciousness, and then getting louder until it was as if they were in the room and all around her.

The whispers and growls seemed to grow in numbers and volume until finally KaLeah's ears were hurting.

She didn't want the excitement of the kiss to end, but it seemed that the voices in her head had a different opinion.

She let Nikolat pull her in closer just as the sounds were becoming screams, and what she thought sounded like roaring, as if from animals or possibly... dragons.

Suddenly, a real sound rocked her back and away from Nikolat. The ringing in her ears was gone and replaced by a low-pitched ringing of bells all along the outside of the castle.

KaLeah looked at Nikolat, who looked just as stunned as she was.

"An attack," he said.

That was all he had to say. KaLeah was out of the ballroom and running through the candle-lit hallways, up the stairs to Amirra.

8 ASSASSIN

KaLeah ran fast, holding the dress up as high as she could manage.

When she got to Amirra's room, she found the doors unguarded. The men must have run off when the alarms sounded. Their duty was first to the castle, second to the princess.

It was KaLeah's job to protect Amirra, and nobody knew that she wasn't inside the room with the princess.

Once inside her room, KaLeah went straight to the secret passageway entrance. It was behind a mountain landscape tapestry hanging on the wall beside Amirra's bed.

"Amirra, it's KaLeah," she called out.

She moved the tapestry and opened the door. Amirra leapt out and threw her arms around KaLeah's mid-section, knocking the breath out of her.

She was dressed in a long silver nightgown, but her eyes were wide and alert as if she hadn't yet gone to bed.

"What's happening?" Amirra asked. "Are we being attacked?"

"I think so," KaLeah answered. "I wanted to make sure you were safe. Let's get you some warmer clothes, blankets, and some pillows so you can hide in the passageway."

"You mean so *we* can hide?"

KaLeah started to gather items and tossed them through the opening into the dark hallway.

"No, just you."

"But I don't want to stay here alone," Amirra said, her voice shooting up in pitch and volume. Where are you going? Why can't you hide with me?"

"Amirra, people are trying to get into the castle to hurt us," KaLeah said. "You're better off staying where they can't find you. And since I *can* fight, it's my duty to defend the castle."

She felt the resistance to her own words flooding up. She knew better than to run out into the night, but her body was shaking with adrenaline. Her hands ached to grab the sword and fight alongside the soldiers.

KaLeah knew that if she crawled into the passageway with Amirra, that she wouldn't be able to sit still for more than a few moments.

The battle called to her.

Amirra rolled her eyes.

"There are real soldiers out there, my father's soldiers, and it is their duty to protect the kingdom. You are supposed to protect me."

"I *am* protecting you by making sure you are safely hidden. Now take this blanket and climb back into the passageway."

"Why can't I go out and fight too?" Amirra asked.

"Because protecting yourself is one thing, throwing yourself into the mouths of your enemies is quite another. You've never had a sword go through your belly or daggers in your eyes. You've never seen blood flowing from an open wound, soaking the ground at your feet."

"You can stop talking now," Amirra said. "I'll stay." The princess reluctantly grabbed the blanket and tromped back into the passageway.

"Just relax and try to get some sleep. I'll be back soon."

It took every bit of patience KaLeah had to make sure

the secret door was closed, and the tapestry set back in place, smoothing it down, instead of running out of the door to join the fray.

She slid a chair over in front of the tapestry, hoping to conceal the passageway even further.

KaLeah left Amirra's room and made a quick stop in her own room to change out of the dress and arm herself. She didn't have any armor and wasn't sure if enemies were already in the castle or not, so in haste, she grabbed a thick book and shoved it into her brown shirt as a makeshift breastplate.

She pulled on her old hunting boots over black pants, then strapped two daggers to her belt and grabbed her sword. She ran as fast as she could down the halls and stairs to the castle entrance.

As she got closer, she could hear metal hitting metal, men calling out, and screams of pain. She got to the entrance of the castle and ran out toward the gates beyond the cobblestone.

She heard feet pounding damp grass as men ran and fought one another, draggots neighing and complaining, and what she imagined to be bodies thudding to the ground.

She was breathing fast and had to warn herself about the lack of oxygen and fainting. What kind of a soldier would she be if she only lasted two minutes from running too hard? KaLeah took one long, deep breath and held it, let it out, and took in another, slowly.

She was suddenly afraid of death, afraid of the faces of men beyond the large gates, afraid they would all charge her the moment she emerged.

Still, she kept moving forward.

Her ears popped and began to ring. The whispers sounded like individual voices this time, pushed into her mind, replacing her own thoughts, and they were telling her to go. She clearly heard the words *go fight* over and over.

The strange guttural voices seemed to be driving her on. She was becoming more comfortable with the mental intrusions. Running through the dark castle, listening to the men shouting orders to one another, knowing that she wouldn't be receiving any commands, hearing the voices made her feel less alone among all of the men. She felt more courageous.

Her heart was beating hard, but she told herself that she couldn't be afraid. She had to go into battle. She was a fighter, and fighters fight. They don't comfort little girls in their nightgowns.

She approached the gates, and the sound of metal crashing against metal was almost deafening.

The dark fields surrounding the castle were covered with tiny sparkles of twinkling silver armor over white uniforms. Her vision began to adjust to the darkness, and she could see the faces and thick bodies of soldiers beneath their armor.

Clusters of men were scattered and fighting across the fields between the front of the castle and the forest toward the horizon.

The dead planet, Denlerack, hung above silver in the moon's reflection.

She could see the purple Extellan colors mingling with the red and white of the Belarone army, but barely. It was easier to see the flashes of white in the moonlit night, giving the Extellan legion an advantage.

She made a mental note to tell someone later those white uniforms were not a good idea. At least she knew she wouldn't accidentally attack one of her own men.

She wondered briefly about her lightweight sword and whether it could withstand blows from much heavier swords, or if it would snap in half. It had survived hits so far, but she hadn't been in actual battles.

Instantly, she realized that it was foolish to be here without true armor or shields. She kicked herself for not going to the armory before heading into the fray.

KaLeah shook away her doubts and ran onto the battlefield anyway.

Before she'd made it twenty steps, something ice-cold grabbed her ankle and yanked her, slamming her face-down on the wet grass.

She propped herself up but couldn't move. KaLeah looked back across the ground and into the scarred face of an Extellan soldier. He grinned dangerously across her own body at her.

His fingers were wrapped around her ankle and squeezing tighter. He seemed to be reaching for something on the ground beside him, and KaLeah could see that he was unable to move from the waist down due to a very deep wound across the back of both legs.

KaLeah scrambled to sit and lifted her sword, bringing it down fast across the middle of his arm.

The man's scream made bumps crawl across her flesh, and when he jerked back, his arm didn't follow. KaLeah bounced up, and then went looking for another man to fight, hoping the next one would be standing.

She didn't have to go far. A man came rushing at her and she got a good look at the Extellan uniform. It was black, but she noticed his shirt didn't have sleeves. She wondered if it was supposed to make him look tough in the chilly night with bloodstains on his biceps.

The man had wild long black hair, and he raised his heavy sword above his head and kept coming. When he was near, he brought the sword down with a growl.

KaLeah ducked and swung around behind him, keeping an eye out for other attackers. She jabbed her sword into his side, angling upwards so it would be a deadly blow.

He hollered, staggered, and then spun around to whip her with his sword. KaLeah dodged him and stabbed him again, this time in the thigh.

The man kept trying to fight her for a time, but she grew tired of it, kicked the back of his legs, knocking him to the ground, before driving her sword in again.

Suddenly, there were warriors all around her with bare arms and shiny teeth gleaming in the moonlight. She caught words like, "girl," "easy," and "is this her?"

While the three Extellans stood there gawking, she spun around, stabbed one, and then raised her sword diagonally in front of her, ready for another. Their mouths dropped open and then two of the men grinned and stormed toward her.

Metal was flying and she could see her sword only when it came together against one of theirs with a deafening clang.

It turned out to be lucky for KaLeah that she had a lightweight sword, otherwise she doubted her ability to keep up against two men at the same time. It took them twice as long to heave their swords back up for another blow.

Nonetheless, her arms were already growing sore, and the reality of battle sunk in; if she tired, they would kill her.

Although KaLeah had practiced with her father almost daily, it was always one against one. This was two fully grown, fully trained soldiers with swords, against a village girl.

KaLeah reminded herself that she had killed three men alone in the woods, and two men on draggots, but it had been daylight. The second she killed one soldier, three more would appear from out of the darkness, and from any direction.

She could see the familiar faces of the Belarone soldiers around her. They cast sideways glances and double takes as they crossed paths. She assumed they wondered what she was doing here and where the princess was.

KaLeah didn't expect any of them to fight beside her or help her fend the Extellans off. She wasn't exactly their comrade, and she was a young woman. None of them had ever seen a woman fight.

She ignored their puzzled expressions, shrugging off that familiar feeling of being out of place.

The soldier she had stabbed had recovered. He joined the melee with a new sparkle of death in his eyes. KaLeah found herself in a corner, fighting off three very heavy swords. She couldn't dodge, turn, or even move. The men were closing in on her, pushing her up against the castle's curtain wall.

KaLeah kept looking around for help, but every Belarone soldier was already preoccupied with another fight. The three Extellans were sensing their victory, and KaLeah wanted to cry out.

What have I done? What have I gotten myself into? I could be curled up next to the princess, napping, and waiting it all out instead of bracing for death on a field of bloody men.

It was too late to do anything. Sweat trickled down her face, the taste of metal was in her mouth, and there was a dry pain in her throat.

Her sword fended off one blow, but the two others came down on her. She couldn't prevent their strikes. She could feel the blades slicing through her skin, and she fell to the ground.

"KaLeah, what in dragons' blood are you doing out here?"

The words were foggy and floated out in front of her, but she couldn't see who was talking. Her side hurt and so did her back. KaLeah was lifted up and she struggled to plant her feet back down on the oscillating ground.

A thousand tiny dots fuzzed in front of her eyes, and she felt dizzy. She took a deep breath and waited for the dots to vanish. When they did, she slowly focused and saw that it was Nikolat holding her steady. A soldier she didn't recognize was standing beside him.

"Why are you out here?" Nikolat asked again. "You almost got yourself killed. Where's Amirra?"

KaLeah took another deep breath and noticed the three Extellans lying in a pile just beyond the feet of the soldier. She reached an arm around to her side, brought it back to her face and saw blood on her fingers.

"I actually got stabbed," she said in disbelief, as if she was born to be indestructible.

"Of course, you could have been killed," Nikolat said.

There was no tenderness or sympathy in his voice. He

spoke like a general disappointed in one of his men for making a very stupid mistake.

"Luckily, we pulled the men back before they could injure you too badly, but that wound won't last much longer. You'll need to get bandaged up."

He lifted up her shirt to look at the cuts on both of her sides. She felt embarrassed having her shirt lifted in front of so many men.

"They are shallow, but bleeding. Now, get back inside the castle. I can't believe you left Amirra."

"No," KaLeah said, tenderly but firmly pulling her shirt back down. She tried to take a step away from him. Nikolat had a hold of her shoulders and pulled her back toward him.

"What did you say?" he asked, his face turning red.

"I said, no," KaLeah said again. "The princess is safe, and I have to fight."

Nikolat shoved her against the castle wall and the pain in her back exploded through her veins. She bit back a scream and straightened her shoulders, wincing.

She knew she was being stupid—knew she had too much pride. Why couldn't she just acquiesce and run along inside like a good girl?

Nikolat looked like he was thinking, sizing her up.

KaLeah knew he had just saved her, but it didn't really register. She was certain she did not need his help.

"I am in charge here, and I'm ordering you to keep an eye on Lamone," Nikolat said.

KaLeah squinted. Had she heard him correctly? "Lamone?" she asked.

"I don't trust him," Nikolat said. "He may try something tonight. Something traitorous. I need you to follow him around, watch him. He just went around the west side of the castle. I was following him and that's when I saw you go down. With your wound, you won't last much longer out here tonight, so do as I ask."

KaLeah had a feeling that there was more Nikolat wasn't telling her. She hated Lamone, but she didn't think Nikolat was suspicious of him. And suspicious of what?

Her curiosity was beginning to bubble up, and suddenly, she wanted Lamone to be the enemy. She wanted to catch him doing something that she could stop.

She would bring him to Nikolat and the king as a traitor. Her rebellious need to fight then getting wounded wouldn't have been for nothing.

"I will follow him," KaLeah said.

Nikolat released his hold on her, and she started running off toward the west side of the castle. The pain in her side and across her back forced her to slow to a brisk walk, but she waited until she was out of Nikolat's sight first.

She didn't know why, but she wanted him to be impressed with her, and proud. She needed his admiration and dying would not be the best way to do that, she realized, no matter how well she fought.

KaLeah walked as quickly as she could toward the west end of the castle with her sword slightly raised, ready to strike, but she soon realized that she was alone.

The battle going on behind her was so loud she couldn't hear anything except for the clanging of swords. Out in the open darkness, she knew that if she couldn't hear an attacker, she could be caught off guard.

KaLeah crept along the side of the castle, stopping every few moments to look behind her. Every step was becoming more and more painful, and a few times, she thought she might pass out from the pain. KaLeah bit her tongue harder and moved on, stiffly.

KaLeah froze at the furthest corner of the castle. Before going any further, she knew she needed to peer around the thick stone column.

She bent close, closer, and then stopped again. She could hear something. A faint whisper. Not even a whisper, but more like she would imagine shards of glass falling on stone to sound like. KaLeah knew there had to be people around the corner talking.

She started to wonder if Nikolat was sending her into a

trap.

KaLeah carefully peeked around the edge and saw two figures bathed in the shadows. If they hadn't been wearing reflective chain mail, she probably wouldn't have seen them at all.

The two men suddenly broke apart, and she could see Lamone clearly now, walking straight toward her. KaLeah jerked her head back and tried to disappear into the castle wall's shadow.

She had thought once that she may be misjudging Lamone's intelligence, but when he walked right by her and kept on walking, she knew she had not.

She looked back around the corner and noticed the other man from the shadows was feeling with his fingers along the castle wall, looking for something.

An entrance?

KaLeah focused on the man and then gasped. He was wearing the purple and black uniform of an Extellan soldier, and he was trying to get into the castle.

But why, she wondered. *And what did it have to do with Lamone?*

The man looked over his shoulder like he had discovered what he had been hunting for. Instantly, she forgot about following Lamone. This soldier was about to get into the castle unseen by everyone except her.

KaLeah took a step toward him and then fell against the wall. Her entire back began quivering and she felt deathly ill. She thought she might throw up but forcefully swallowed back the urge.

KaLeah straightened back to standing as best she could, just in time to see the man disappear into the castle. She growled and pushed herself forward. She kept her eyes on the exact spot where he'd disappeared.

The castle wall appeared to be solid stone, but she ran her fingers along the surface until she touched a bump in the stone. She pressed it in, and there was a click, followed by a door sliding open before her eyes.

KaLeah climbed through the door and saw a narrow hallway before her. She could hear the man's steps and followed the Extellan easily through the clammy darkness behind the servants' wing.

She wondered if the Extellan was another assassin and who he was after this time. She thought about Lamone. He was unarguably responsible for this man's actions and must have been behind the previous assassination attempts as well.

KaLeah followed the man to a door that was swinging on its hinges. He wasn't hard to follow; his chainmail clanked with each step. She grabbed the swinging door and listened.

He was in a small, servant kitchen, and moving toward the stairs, going up. Even though the kitchen was considered the smallest one, it wasn't small. The room was long with pantries, ovens dug into the walls, large basin sinks, tables, and chairs.

KaLeah waited for the man to reach the stairs before she crossed the kitchen to pursue him.

She made sure to stay at least a floor beneath him, as he climbed the staircase. The stairs creaked under his weight but not so much under hers. KaLeah stepped when he did so his creaking boards would muffle her own.

She wondered how Lamone had known about the entrance through the smaller kitchen, and she realized how important learning the passageways with the captain would be. She had no idea where she was or where the man was going, but he did, and that unnerved her.

KaLeah followed him up the stairs to the fourth floor and down a hallway she finally recognized. She stayed hidden in the staircase doorway and watched as the man went to Amirra's bedroom door, looked around, then threw his weight into the door, attempting to break through.

Her suspicions were confirmed; the man was an assassin, and Lamone had fed the man information on where Amirra's bedroom was.

KaLeah emerged from the shadows and ran up behind the man, who was stepping back to take another run at Amirra's door. She was glad that she hadn't stopped to put on armor, because she made no sound running up behind him.

She plunged the sword through the middle of his back without hesitation and then kicked him to the floor. She withdrew her sword and watched as he curled himself into a fetal position on the stone floor.

"Are you an Extellan?" KaLeah asked him. "Are you a man of King Sarzoe? Are you looking for the princess? Answer or I will—."

KaLeah realized she couldn't do much more to the man. He was probably going to die anyway. What would the king's men do, she wondered? Take off his fingers, toes, or worse?

Just then, she saw blood began to bubble from the man's mouth.

"Oh, for spirits' sake," she said. "Now I'm going to get into trouble again. Are you dying, really? It's not like my sword is poisoned. Did Lamone tell you how to get in here?"

It was a stupid question. She had seen Lamone show him the door.

"This torturing thing is not as easy as it sounds. Hey, are you still alive? Can you talk?"

She kicked him and he groaned, gurgled up more blood, and died.

"Perfect," she said to herself. Then to the man, "You are no help at all, you know?"

She pulled her sword back and struck him again. She made sure he was dead before dragging him away from Amirra's door and dropping him in the middle of the hall.

She hesitated for a moment, wondering if she should check in on Princess Amirra. But looking at her blood-coated clothing, she thought it would scare the little girl too much.

She inspected the doors to the princess' room as best she could, noticing they were heavily damaged now. The doors still appeared to be locked. Then she turned and headed back down the hallway to the stairs. She had to tell King Erazus about Lamone, she had to tell Nikolat, and she had to keep fighting.

KaLeah's heart pumped against her throat, and the skin around her stab wound burned as if it had been peeled off. She didn't know how much longer she could keep breathing through the pain.

But she didn't care and kept moving. She tried to ignore the agony. Her father had always told her that pain was only in the mind. It wasn't real, and only the strongest, best fighters could ignore the pain and fight through it.

"Ignore it," she told herself. "You are stronger than the pain. Be stronger than the pain. Breathe through the pain. Walk through the pain. Ignore it. There is no pain, only duty. It's all just in your head."

KaLeah walked down to the small kitchen, heading back toward the entrance that led outside. She figured it would be better to sneak back out onto the quiet side of the castle than dive straight back into the thick of the battle in front of the castle.

The kitchen seemed twice as long as it had before, and she stumbled and crashed into a chair she had not seen.

Her vision was starting to blur, and she held onto the chair to stable herself. Her body suddenly felt too heavy to support, and pain seemed to penetrate her all the way through to her bones. Her knees gave way first and her fingers couldn't stay connected to the back of the chair. She hit the floor, and everything went dark.

9 PUNISHMENT

KaLeah woke up in an unfamiliar bed. She was dizzy, and even though the pain was still there, it wasn't as bad as it had been.

Her entire abdomen was wrapped in thick, white bandages. Her blood-stained tunic was pushed up over the top of the bandages.

KaLeah groaned and looked away. There were other beds in the room, all with wounded men crying out, groaning, or silently staring blankly at nothing.

Women in long, dark gray tunics ran from bed to bed, taking water and bandages, calling out to one another with concern or orders.

She had no idea where she was within the castle, never having seen the room before. There appeared to be no windows, so she assumed she was underground. Long troughs of oil were lit all along the outer edges of the room, and lanterns dotted each bedside table down rows and rows of beds.

She tried to sit up, but the pain forced her back down quickly. With a flash, everything came rushing back—Lamone, the group of men who had cornered and stabbed her, Nikolat lifting her off the ground, and tracking the assassin to Amirra's room.

Spirits, she thought, *I need to get to Amirra.*

"Nurse," KaLeah yelled.

She tried to move again, gritting her teeth against the pain.

The nurse, Dohori, came into sight, scrambling around a nearby bed. Her short gray hair was matted down with sweat, and her tunic was covered in blood.

She crinkled up her nose and narrowed her eyes at KaLeah.

"Ah, so, you finally awake?" Dohori said, putting the back of her hand to KaLeah's forehead. "Just thought you'd sleep right through this battle, huh? Oh, but not before you go and get yourself nearly killed. Lucky that captain brought you in before you bled to death."

"Captain?" KaLeah asked, suddenly caught off guard.

"Yes, handsome young blond one. And where's the princess? Leave her to her own devices in all this mess? Or did you go and get her hurt too? Where's Amirra? We got nurses looking everywhere, but no one has dared tell the king yet. We were hoping you'd come to first."

"She's fine," KaLeah said, struggling against the pain to get out of bed. Dohori obviously wasn't going to be a lot of help. "I need to get to her."

"You're darn right you do," Dohori said.

She reached out and lifted KaLeah out of bed in one sweep with a strength that surprised KaLeah.

KaLeah's feet hurt when they thudded against the floor. Stars filtered into her sight again and she had to fight the urge to pass out. Once the room came back into focus, KaLeah used Dohori as a crutch.

"Get my sword," KaLeah said. "I need you to carry it for me."

Dohori didn't protest. She grabbed KaLeah's sword in her right hand, while supporting KaLeah with her left arm, and together, they slowly made their way out of the room.

The hallways were littered with wounded men, leaning against walls, or napping on the floor. Blood was everywhere on the lower levels. The wounded men had dragged themselves in, leaving streaks, drops, and sometimes puddles of blood along the way.

The women saw fewer and fewer injured men as they moved upwards through the castle toward the royal wing.

It was slow going, but they eventually made it to the hallway that led to Amirra's room. The assassin was still lying dead on the floor. Dohori handed the sword to KaLeah, then pushed open her bedroom door, since Amirra's was still locked. KaLeah directed her to the tapestry hanging on the wall.

"Pull that aside and you'll see a door behind it that leads to Amirra's room."

Dohori set KaLeah's sword down and did as she was told, letting out a small breath as the door came into view.

"I always assumed but never knew for sure," Dohori mumbled to herself as she started to pull the door open. "They really are everywhere, huh?"

They walked into Amirra's room and then to the princess' hidden entrance to her own secret passageway.

The women peered into the dark hallway. The blankets and pillows were piled up there, but no child princess. Dohori bent down to rummage through the bedding, just to be sure.

"Amirra?"

But the dread in KaLeah's stomach told her what she already knew; Amirra was not in the secret passageway. Her heart began to pick up speed and she hoped that her eyes were just misleading her.

Amirra must be here, she thought.

"Amirra, come out, it's KaLeah," she said again.

Dohori walked further into the passageway. She called loudly for Amirra, and both women waited without breathing.

"I don't see a princess in there, miss Favor," Dohori

said with disdain.

KaLeah let out an aggravated shout.

She didn't care if Dohori scolded her. KaLeah was livid. She could feel adrenaline begin to burn through her veins.

KaLeah turned as fast as she could, pain still stabbing both sides, and went into the passageway, using the walls to support herself. Her pain was beginning to slowly abate though, as her adrenaline and anger increased.

"I told her to stay put."

"Are you crazy?" Dohori said with a huff. "Have you ever known a child to do what it's told?"

"I always did what I was told!" KaLeah shouted in defense.

She never would have dreamed of disobeying her father. And even though she had few dealings with adults in her village, she always obeyed them as well.

"Someone could'a taken her," Dohori said in a whisper.

KaLeah didn't want to even acknowledge that thought, knowing that if that was true, it was all her fault.

She put one arm on each wall and started calling out for the princess, hoping that Amirra had just crawled off deeper into the secret hallways.

Dohori grabbed KaLeah's sword, a lantern from beside the bed, and followed her into the passageway. KaLeah was grateful for Dohori's frightened silence.

She strained to hear and see anything in the darkness.

She headed in the direction of her own room first. After checking through the wardrobe that the room was still empty, she continued in the same direction. It was the direction that the lit candles had taken her the first night she was introduced to the secret tunnels.

The two walked silently, but as quickly as they could, following the light of the lantern that Dohori held. They came to a fork. To the left, they could see nothing, but to the right, there seemed to be a faint light shining back at them.

"This way," KaLeah said, and went toward the speck of light.

When they got to the wall, Dohori held up the lantern, and KaLeah could see a small crack in the stone.

She pushed against the tunnel wall, and a secret door swung open, revealing shelves filled with books, ornately carved tables, chairs, and serving counters. They both had to squint against the sudden onslaught of candlelight.

"Amirra," KaLeah yelled, shoving through the door and into the library.

She grimaced in pain but tried to ignore it. There was no response, but KaLeah heard faint sounds and followed them to a row of windows lining the top of the library. The light flickering all around her played with her vision, but she crept closer until she confirmed that one of the windows was indeed open.

Closer now, she could hear sounds of metal swords clashing and men's voices drifting in through the window. KaLeah noted that the sounds were fewer and farther between than they had been earlier. She hoped that meant the battle was coming to an end—and even more, that they had won.

The window was too small and too high up for anyone to climb through. She wondered how it had been opened and thought about Lamone trying to smuggle in another assassin.

Dohori crept up behind KaLeah to investigate.

"You think she tried to see what was going on?" Dohori asked. KaLeah saw a chair on its side, conveniently located under the window.

"See and hear the battle, yes," KaLeah said, shaking her head. "She might be at the next closest window. Come on."

KaLeah headed to the library door, no longer using Dohori as a crutch since adrenaline was driving her forward.

"Dohori, I can take my sword now."

Dohori handed the sword over, and KaLeah felt both a sudden pain from the weight and a comfort at having the weapon ready.

"Where's the nearest window?" Dohori asked. "Not on the first floor, surely."

No, but there's a door, KaLeah thought. *Would Amirra have gone to a door?* As if in answer to her question, KaLeah reached a staircase down to the main hall. The main hall would lead to the front doors of the castle.

KaLeah bit back the pain as she ran through the castle to the main doors. She could hear Dohori panting behind her.

KaLeah reached the main hall and stopped. Amirra was lying face down on the marble floor, her tiny body bent awkwardly with her light blonde hair fanned out around her head. There was an Extellan soldier standing over Amirra. The man pulled his giant, blood-soaked sword up over his head with both arms.

"No," KaLeah screamed.

She ran at the man with her sword drawn. The Extellan was distracted for a moment.

KaLeah stopped in front of him and then spun to the side to strike him. The sword must have been too heavy for him because he had trouble moving fast enough to block her blows.

His face was hidden behind a dark beard, but she could see the frustration in his beady eyes. She had interrupted his kill. Then he started to smile, and goose bumps climbed up her spine.

Instantly, she knew Amirra was dead, and it was all her fault for leaving the child alone. KaLeah stared at the Extellan's long bearded grin, and the room began to spin.

She felt sick and weak. She couldn't lift her sword.

The man started to move toward KaLeah, ignoring the body heaped on the floor behind him. KaLeah just stared, unmoving. Everything seemed to be pushing the Extellan fighter to her, but she had no will to move.

The princess was gone. She had failed because she hadn't even tried. Protecting the princess wasn't what she wanted to do, and now, she would pay the ultimate price.

Then she heard a low moan, so low it didn't seem human, more like a vibration against the floor.

Amirra was alive, breathing, and in danger.

KaLeah snapped to attention and brought her sword up in front of her.

The soldier wasn't swayed by her sudden awakening. He grinned wider and advanced upon her quickly, raising his sword.

KaLeah met his metal with hers. She felt pure hatred for the man and walked into every blow, pushing him away from Amirra and toward the castle entrance.

KaLeah drove him through the open doors and out into the night air. The sickly sour smell of men's sweat penetrated her nostrils. The putrid smell of death and metallic blood proved to be a toxic mix, and KaLeah began to feel nauseous again.

She could hear Dohori running across the floor behind her to Amirra. KaLeah fought the urge to turn back to check on the princess. Her hesitation almost cost KaLeah her life.

The Extellan swung his sword and missed KaLeah's throat by a fingernail's width. Whatever medicine she may have been given earlier was beginning to wear off, and the pain in KaLeah's side was causing her arm to feel weak.

For a moment, she wanted to stop, to take a break, or to just let the warrior win so she could rest.

She began hearing low rumblings replacing the noise around her. The rumblings turned to growls, and the growls began to sound like whispers.

Fight.

Kill.

The words appeared in her mind, and a new energy surged through her body. The pain completely vanished as if a heavy blanket had been placed on her to block it out.

KaLeah now had a clear head and specific objective: kill the Extellan soldier before her, return to the entrance hall, and take Princess Amirra to safety.

The Extellan stood in front of her in his black and purple uniform, disheveled hair, and his face marred by blood, sweat, and dirt.

Like all the other men KaLeah had taken out, he never once looked worried.

He grinned and countered every blow, then he drove in tighter and stronger, causing her to take a step back. His false sense of confidence caused him to pause long enough for KaLeah to lunge and get her sword into a space between his armor, pushing her sword through his side.

He fell with the grin still on his face.

KaLeah quickly scanned the area. She was clear for an escape.

She turned and ran back into the castle, tucked her sword under her arm, then used both hands to close the massive wooden doors against the battle.

༄

"I don't understand why you are so angry with me, KaLeah," Amirra said in a faint whisper. They were back in Amirra's room, and the princess was sitting on a small, tufted couch.

KaLeah didn't respond. She stood by the window, clutching her sides, and watched the sun rise over the corpses.

It had been the longest night of her life, and she needed time to process. However, she wasn't going to leave the little girl's side after what had happened. At least, not until she received an all-clear message from someone in charge.

Fight.

Kill.

She had heard the words so clearly, and yet, they had not been hers. The words being proceeded by an animalistic growl made her wonder if she had thought those words at all.

She remembered the dragon from the woods and how it had seemed to speak to her through her mind… but that hadn't really happened, had it?

KaLeah had convinced herself that the entire thing had been a dream. Her father left, angry that she had not brought home a kill. He left, and she has been searching for him ever since.

Had been, she reminded herself.

With a princess like this, putting her life in danger, making herself available for assassins and murderers all the time, it was no wonder they wanted to put a guard on her.

But why does it have to be me, KaLeah wondered. *This isn't my life. I shouldn't even be here.*

"You should have stayed in your room," KaLeah mumbled, afraid to unleash her true anger. "It would have been safer. You could have been killed." She gritted her teeth together to keep from yelling.

The princess said nothing, and KaLeah refused to look at her.

"You have been up all night," KaLeah said. "Why don't you try to get some rest? The curtains in your bed chamber are closed, and I've secured the passageway door. I will stand watch here while you sleep. Go on, now."

Although only a bodyguard, she was still older and did not want to argue with a child. Luckily, the princess did not protest.

KaLeah kept watching out of the window. Nurses were checking the bodies for anyone still alive, while soldiers were carrying off anyone who was not.

She was relieved that she did not see the prince, or Hilip, among them.

She heard a soft but rapid knock against the door in her room and realized that the secret door must be cracked open. She slipped back into her room through the opening behind the tapestry.

"Who's there?"

"Captain Daven, miss."

She unbolted and opened the door. The man was brushing away bloody strands of hair, back from where they were stuck to his sweaty face. His clothing was disheveled, torn in places, but he didn't look injured. His eyes went from hers to the bulk of her bandaged abdomen.

"I wanted to make sure…" he started, then bowed slightly, catching himself. "Pardon me, Favor KaLeah, but I wanted to make sure you were alright. I received a report that you'd been injured."

"Yes, sir. Thank you for your concern. We are fine and the princess is resting now."

He shifted from one leg to the other, looking at her while she spoke, but away from her when he replied.

"I received reports of the assassination attempt, and Prince Nikolat has claimed that Lamone was the one who let the assassin into the castle."

He turned his eyes to the blood-stained carpet outside of Amirra's door.

"However, it seems that you managed to kill him before he could get to her." He sounded concerned and remorseful.

"I followed and killed the would-be assassin, yes."

"I'm so sorry that you had to do that, miss," he said, struggling to keep his eyes on hers. "I should have kept the men stationed outside these rooms. Next time, they will have those orders, I swear."

"Hopefully, there is no next time," KaLeah said, smiling at this man's chivalrous and protective gesture.

She wasn't used to interacting with men like him. Prince Nikolat reminded her of her father. He was stoic, hard to read, and cryptic about his feelings. There was a deep, brooding mystery to them that perplexed KaLeah.

This captain, however, carried his heart on his shoulder, and his concern in his eyes. She wondered, for a moment, if they could be friends.

No, he's only here checking on her because it is his job, and he's covering up for a perceived mistake, she told herself.

"We may have to go on the offensive now," Captain Daven continued. "So, yes, hopefully we can avoid a next time, of course."

She cocked her head. *Is he lingering?*

"Thank you for checking on us," she said, thinking maybe he was waiting for a dismissal.

"My pleasure," he said, bowing slightly again. "I am pleased that you are alright. I'll leave you to rest. May I?"

Hilip leaned forward in her doorway, eyes on her, with his hand extended. She looked down at his calloused fingers, confused for a moment, before realizing he meant to close her door for her. She took a small step back into the room.

"Of course," she said, feeling embarrassed.

"Rest well," he said, faintly, and closed the door.

KaLeah returned to the princess' room and sat beside her damaged door. Guards had returned to stand outside of it but promised not to repair the door until after the princess had rested.

KaLeah heard updates through the door as soldiers spread word throughout the castle. Belarone soldiers had successfully defended the castle, and the remaining Extellans had been imprisoned in the holding cells in the lowest part of the castle.

Amirra called the dungeon "the bottom," which KaLeah assumed made Amirra more comfortable. Neither of them had ever been down there, but she assumed it was filled with starving, tortured enemies whose arms were bolted to the walls, and they were forced to fight rats over the right to drink muddy water.

Exactly what those Extellans deserve, KaLeah mused.

Suddenly, a new thought entered her mind. She could not ignore the fact that word of her leaving Amirra, of Amirra almost being killed, was surely going to reach the king.

How long before I am taken down to the dungeons, she wondered. *Would the king do that to me? Would he torture me, punish me?*

Her initial justification of joining the fight as a warrior to protect the princess didn't quite hold water since the princess had almost made it all the way out into the battle.

KaLeah knew that none of this would have happened if she had just stayed in the secret passageway with Amirra. Even if the assassin had found them, she could have killed him there and not had to chance losing him through the darkness on his way to her room.

She knew she had made a mistake. Even though she had the skill and the will to fight, she had wanted to go into that battle more than she wanted to protect the princess.

She pulled her legs in under her chin and hugged her knees, feeling guilty.

"I went looking for a fight, and left her exposed to danger," KaLeah said to her knees.

She closed her eyes tightly. Tight against the realization that she had been wrong. Tight against the reality that the princess could have been killed. Tight against the impending punishment.

She opened her eyes and took a deep breath, sitting with her guilt for what felt like hours. Finally, she stood up, squirming at the pain that shot through her sides, but knowing that she deserved the pain, and slowly walked to Amirra's bed chamber.

She stood at the foot of the bed, leaning into a bedpost.

"Princess," she said. "I am sorry that I abandoned you during the attack. I should have stayed by your side. I am truly sorry."

She could not see anything within the darkness of the room, but the princess' soft voice came through.

"I forgive you, my friend. Thank you for saving me."

KaLeah bowed her head and backed out of the room as her eyes began to sting with tears.

She stood silently at the window, watching the cleanup activity below, while the sun slowly rose higher in the sky. She had grown used to the throbbing ache in her side and wondered absently if she should return to the infirmary and have Dohori re-wrap her wound with fresh bandages.

There was a knock at the door, and for a moment, she wondered if Dohori had come to do just that.

"Who's there?" KaLeah called out.

"The king requests the presence of the royal daughter and Favor KaLeah immediately," said a soldier's deep voice.

This is it, KaLeah realized.

She had fought in a battle she wasn't supposed to fight in, lost the princess, and almost gotten them both killed.

She wanted to run to the secret passageway and follow it out of the castle. She wondered how far she could run before they caught up with her. She considered briefly cutting her hair, pretending to be a boy, and hiding out in a village somewhere beyond the farmlands.

Princess Amirra emerged from her room, smoothing down the front of a light green tunic.

"Are you ready?" she asked KaLeah, who was still standing dazed and ashen faced in front of the window.

"I look… guilty," she said, motioning to her still dirty and blood-stained tunic.

"Go change and I will stall," Amirra said.

KaLeah went through the connecting door to her room and changed quickly into a clean tunic and pants. She found a new pair of boots and slipped them on, cringing at the pain when she bent over to tie them.

When she returned, she found the princess in the doorway, speaking to a soldier. She joined them and they followed him through the castle.

KaLeah assumed they were headed to the king's study. Each step was painful as she tried to keep up with the guard's fast pace.

The hallway leading to the study was lined with soldiers in their red and white uniforms. The men watched the girls quietly as they passed.

KaLeah felt no sense of camaraderie with any of them, which disappointed her. She would be reprimanded for fighting bravely, unlike these men who would be celebrated.

The girls entered the king's study. There were captains and a few soldiers in the room, and Prince Nikolat and Lamone standing in front of the king's desk. Where Nikolat's face, hands, and armor were splattered with blood, it was obvious that Bylex had only seen action from safely inside the castle.

The circles under the king's eyes were more concave than she'd ever seen them. His eyes were bloodshot, and his brows were pulled close together, driving more wrinkles across his forehead.

His uniform was similar to the others', but with a few embellishments like silver buckles and what looked like small dragon wings sewn across the tops of the shoulders.

Amirra kept walking to meet her father, but KaLeah lingered in the doorway. Nikolat and Lamone were both standing with their backs to her, Lamone's hands tied behind him and a soldier standing with one hand clamped down on the slimy man's shoulder.

Hatred bubbled up inside her at seeing him, and she wanted to run full speed at Lamone, knock him down, and hurt him.

Instead, she straightened her shoulders, bit the inside of her cheek to keep her mouth shut, and walked like a soldier to stand beside Amirra.

She noticed more captains and soldiers standing along the back of the room. One was Captain Daven. She could feel his and Nikolat's eyes on her as she crossed the room.

"Nikolat has left off the story with you, Favor KaLeah," King Erazus said, still very loud for how exhausted he appeared. "What happened when you followed Lamone around the side of the castle, as Nikolat had instructed?"

As Nikolat had instructed? What was she, Nikolat's servant?

She fought back the urge to glare at Nikolat and kept looking at King Erazus. *This is about Lamone's treachery,* she realized, *not her.* She let out the breath she had been holding.

"Lamone conversed with an Extellan assassin, Your

Majesty," KaLeah said. "Lamone showed the assassin a secret entrance. I followed the assassin to just outside the princess' chambers. Then I killed the assassin after he tried to kick in her chamber doors, Your Majesty."

"Lamone!" the king bellowed, making everyone except for the soldiers jump. "Have you any argument for your life?" His words reverberated throughout the room.

KaLeah moved her head slightly so she could look at Lamone without being noticed. He was shaking and sweating.

The cruel sneers KaLeah was used to seeing on Lamone's face had melted away, leaving him looking young and pitiful. Lamone tried to struggle against the ropes on his hands and took a step toward the king. The soldier next to him held him back.

"Nikolat showed me the passage door," Lamone said. "It was his plan. He's always helped me."

King Erazus pushed himself away from his desk and stood up. His eyes were like coal.

"How dare you," the king began.

Lamone interrupted, his voice raised louder. "How else would I have known about the entrance? How else would I have known they were on the lawns the day Amirra was kidnapped and for the second attempt?"

The king shot an angry glance at Nikolat, who looked bewildered.

"How did he know about the entrance, Nikolat?" the king asked.

Nikolat's eyes went wide, and his mouth dropped open, then he quickly recovered, narrowed his eyes at Lamone, stood up straight, and turned to address his father.

"Lamone has always been my faithful friend," Nikolat said, placing his hand on his heart as if stricken. "If he is proven to be traitorous, I never had any inclination. Perhaps he spied on me, and he must have used me when I told him I was going to invite my sister riding with me."

Nikolat put a lot of emphasis on the word "used" and

met his father's gaze straight on. KaLeah felt the hatred spilling from Nikolat and thought that he would kill Lamone right then and there if his father ordered it.

The king lowered his head and rested his palms on his desk. After a long pause, he straightened back up and looked at two of his soldiers.

"Lamone's traitorous actions will be punished," King Erazus said. "He cannot be left alive to try to harm any of my children again. He is a threat to Belarone."

Then to Lamone, he said, "King Sarzoe sent you, of course. You are his spy."

Lamone gulped but said nothing.

"Execute him immediately. And send some men to permanently seal that entrance to the castle."

The soldiers moved to grab Lamone from both sides.

They lifted his thin body off the ground and began to carry him out of the room. Lamone kicked and yelled furiously.

"Nikolat is the traitor!" Lamone screamed. "He's been working with King Sarzoe from the beginning. It was Nikolat. He set up everything. Everything! Nik!"

The soldiers pulled Lamone out of the room, but they could all hear his voice in the hall, calling out for Nikolat over and over.

The room grew quiet, and everyone turned back to the king. KaLeah noticed that he was sweating, and he rubbed the space between his uniform and his neck, as if he was being choked.

"Now," King Erazus said. "I need to speak to my children alone. KaLeah, you may stay, but everyone else must leave."

The soldiers marched out, and the king sat down in the large chair behind his desk, letting out a long sigh. He looked up at KaLeah first.

"I am glad you tracked the assassin," he said slowly and so much more quietly that KaLeah leaned slightly forward. "I am glad you discovered Lamone to be a traitor. But what were you doing out on the battlefield? I know you left Amirra alone, KaLeah. "I know she was almost killed because of you. And though she may never be a queen, her survival is important for the people of Belarone. Her survival is important to me." He jabbed his finger to his chest, and she noticed his eyes moisten ever so slightly.

Guilt spun inside her stomach and sent bile up her throat. She swallowed it down, trying not to make any facial expression as she held his eye contact.

"The only reason I do not send you to Lamone's fate is that you have saved Amirra's life in the past, and I believe that you now know how you must always be by her side to save her life, to keep her from any danger, any harm. Amirra, if anything had happened to you…" he broke off and took another breath. He pushed back in his chair and cleared his throat as if trying to clear out the fear and sadness. KaLeah saw his body stiffen as anger began to creep back in.

"Amirra, you will marry and become part of the favor families, have children, and continue the Belarone legacy. I am disappointed in both of you. I want you both to listen very carefully. Amirra, you will begin to act like a lady of the court. You will spend your days in the library reading and studying about what it means to be a wife of a favor. You will grow up and find a husband, leave the castle, and live in the community with KaLeah as your midwife and nurse. She will take care of your children while you take care of your husband. My child, you are a princess, but not a queen. Until you fulfill your duties as a wife to a member of this court, you owe your life to your king, be it me or one of your brothers. Do I make myself clear, ladies?"

KaLeah felt like her lungs hadn't received air in days. They began to hurt, and the pain blended into the aching in her sides.

She had grown up in a village where they had their customs, but she had only known her father as her leader. Nobody ruled the village, and his was the only command she obeyed.

Now, sitting in front of her king, listening to him commanding her to dedicate her life to his daughter, both confused and infuriated her.

Who was this man to tell me how to live the rest of my life?

And yet, she knew, as truly as she'd always known to obey her own father no matter what, that there was great risk in disobedience.

Her fear and her pride battled inside of her, sending bumps along her skin, standing her arm hairs on end.

"Yes, father." Princess Amirra's soft reply snapped KaLeah back to reality.

This was a king, and a king could have you killed.

Although she did not want to be a servant for the rest of her life, she wanted to stay alive. Staying alive would at least buy her time to escape. It would give her the chance to fight back.

She let the air rush back into her lungs, and a little too loudly, she said, "Yes, Your Majesty."

"You may both go," the king said.

KaLeah stood, and without looking at Prince Nikolat or Captain Daven, she followed Amirra and two guards back to the princess' chambers in a fog.

The king's words rang in her head.

KaLeah will be your midwife and nurse.

KaLeah will raise your children.

KaLeah will be your servant until the day you die.

She realized that she was lucky to still be breathing, but the feeling of relief never came. The joy of not being taken to the dungeon to sleep with rats until the day of execution seemed so dim compared to the utter weight of facing a lifetime of servitude.

It seemed like only yesterday she was waking up in her own village, hunting her own woods, and ending the days eating by her own fire.

She had never planned to marry, never planned to leave that hut or her father's side. But here she was, being handed a life she did not want, and being told she would never have her own life again.

In that moment, she wondered if her punishment was worse than death.

৵৽৻

KaLeah paced her room for hours. Her eyes burned from being open for too long. She stopped moving only when Dohori came to replace her bloody bandages and forced her to wash off in the tub.

"Neither of you are in any shape to be seen," Dohori said. "Felair and I will bring you both your dinners this evening."

KaLeah kept pacing, even after the food had arrived. She walked while eating, her body too starved to ignore the smells of baked meat, vegetables, and potatoes.

The sun had set by the time she finished, and Amirra had been washed and dressed for bed by the nurses.

Although the man in the castle foyer had knocked her down, Amirra had not been injured. The nurses still fretted over her and made sure that her bath had been extra warm, the towels soft and fresh.

Dohori tucked her in with all the loving care of a mother, and both ladies left past the guards, who closed the repaired doors behind them.

"Princess," KaLeah said quietly from the threshold of her bed chamber.

"Yes?"

"Are you alright?"

The young girl sighed. "I am. I'm very tired. I wonder who I am going to marry. Whoever it is, I'm glad that you'll be with me."

KaLeah closed her eyes tightly and clenched her fists. It isn't fair, she thought.

None of this is fair.

"I will be in my bed chamber if you need me.

Goodnight."

KaLeah turned and headed to her room without waiting for a response. Responding to the princess' needs was the last thing she wanted to do.

The castle grounds were dark. Guards, some with lanterns and some without, patrolled the courtyard outside her window. Just the other night she was looking out the same window, ready to go meet the prince, with no idea about what was going to happen.

Thoughts of the prince filled KaLeah's mind. She pictured the chiseled features of his face, and she was instantly transported back to the ballroom, feeling the nervous currents of energy flowing through her body, the rush she'd experienced when his lips had touched hers.

She wanted to see him, to talk to him, and her cheeks grew hotter just thinking of kissing him again. Her mind started to turn.

No, I hate Nikolat, she thought. *Why do I want to see him?*

But something had changed since the kiss in the ballroom. It was as if whatever wall she had been trying to build had crumbled at her feet.

He really was a beautiful man, however mysterious. Kissing him had sparked a feeling within her she'd never known before.

She hadn't been interested in any of the boys back in her village. Growing up with them, they all felt like unwanted brothers.

She wanted to be near Nikolat. She worried that she was on the verge of losing him, and that made her want to see him even more. Did he care that she would be tied to his sister for the rest of their lives?

What if my life was tied to his instead, she wondered?

Perhaps, if he decided that he loved her and wanted to marry her, then his father would release her from servitude. She was a favor, after all, and the royals married favors.

It wasn't as if she was just some poor village girl anymore.

Could this be her way out? Every woman had to get married eventually, anyway. So, at least if she were married to a prince, she could have the money and the freedom to go wherever she desired, with guards at her side.

He had told her that the king's plan was to take Extelli and put Nikolat on the throne.

She could be his queen and send her own soldiers to search for her father. She had never dreamed of being in such a position, but she hadn't dreamed of being the personal bodyguard to the princess either.

Yes, this is my solution, she decided.

It was sensible. If she had to be a servant, she would prefer being a wife over a playmate. If this was the only way to get resources to find her father, then she was willing to make the sacrifice.

She walked over to a small desk to get a pen and paper. Should she admit to needing his company? What if her letter was read by someone else? She decided to keep it brief.

Please, meet me in the ballroom tomorrow at midnight, she wrote. She signed the letter with the word "midnight" instead of her name.

KaLeah folded the letter and sealed it with candle wax. Hot wax dripped onto her finger, but the sting was nothing. She watched the wax dry and then peeled it off.

She asked one of the guards outside Amirra's door to deliver her message and was pleasantly surprised by how easily he complied.

Finding the solution and sending the note made her feel as if she had made some progress and wasn't as locked into her fate as it appeared. She relaxed and kicked off her boots, preparing to slip into a night tunic.

There was a knock at her door.

Nikolat?

She went to the door and opened it, a wide, expectant smile on her lips.

Hilip was standing there. He greeted her with a nervous

smile. He had changed into clean clothes and washed the blood from his face and hands.

"Good evening, Favor KaLeah," he said.

Her smile slipped for a moment in disappointment, but she recovered it quickly.

"Captain."

"If you are not too tired, I'd like to show you through some of the passageways."

She was exhausted, but after having to use so many of the secret corridors throughout the battle, she knew that it wasn't something she could put off.

"Alright," she said, letting him in.

10 GOODBYE

Nikolat bit the inside of his cheek, standing in his father's study. He hated the nervous habit, but was glad that to others, it just looked as if he were angry or scowling, tightening the lines of his already well-defined cheekbones.

How people perceived him, his emotions especially, was important to him. There were some people whom, for political reasons, could not know that he despised them.

He could not be sarcastic or disingenuous. He had to be careful... especially around his father.

Nikolat hadn't known that the Extellan king was planning an attack. He assumed Lamone hadn't known either, but he must have connected with someone after the battle had started to coordinate the assassination attempt on his sister.

At least, since he hadn't been involved in this instance, he didn't have to try and conceal a lie.

The longer he stood there, watching his father as he yelled at Lamone, and listening to him speaking sternly to his sister and KaLeah, the more he realized that his father wouldn't doubt his loyalty despite Lamone's accusations.

The old man had dark circles under his eyes, and the veins popped out of his hands as he leaned onto them and into his desk.

The old king waited for the girls to leave the room, and then he wiped beads of sweat off his forehead with the sleeves of his uniform.

"Father, are you feeling alright?" Nikolat asked.

King Erazus motioned for Nikolat to sit down without a word, and the prince obediently moved to the closest chair.

"I need you to know a couple things as well, Nikolat," the king said. "We had planned on having a little more time to plan our attack on Extelli, but after this, we cannot wait longer than a day. We will leave for Extelli at once, with a third of the legion. Bylex will stay behind to stand in my place while I am gone." The king nodded to the elder prince, still sitting comfortably in an oversized chair.

"Once we take Extelli, you will remain behind to rule," Erazus continued. "You shouldn't need much, but make sure to plan for an exceedingly long stay in your soon to be kingdom. Remember it is much colder there. You are dismissed to begin your preparations."

Nikolat got up, bowed, and left without glancing at his older brother.

The doors were closed by guards behind him and he finally let out the breath he'd been holding. His mind whirled with thoughts as he rushed back to his room.

Still covered in blood and mud from the battle, he washed his arms and face off in the cold-water basin. He changed into clean clothing, leaving his bloody clothing in a pile by the door.

A cold drink was next. He poured from one of the more expensive, rarer bottles, not knowing how much he would be able to take with him to his new kingdom.

It would be *his* kingdom, even though he still had to fall under the rule of Belarone. He had been planning to be in a leadership position ever since he talked the men into going to war.

Although the kidnapping attempts had failed, the war had still started, even sooner than he'd hoped. And now, he was on his way to Extelli with an entire Belarone army on his side.

He looked around his room. He had to start considering what he needed to take with him. As a traveling army, he could not take too much. He could perhaps fill one small wagon to be pulled by the rearguard, along with the additional artillery, food, water, and bandages.

But Nikolat knew he couldn't really take the things that he really wanted in a kingdom. He couldn't take the trees or the mountains, the fertile grounds, the bustling towns, or KaLeah.

He was surprised that she had popped into his mind. He shook the image of her out of his head. There were more important things to worry about.

Extelli would be a lot of work. Once taken, he'd have to be on guard for remaining Extellan loyalists. He would only be able to trust his own men.

There would be riots and chaos in the country, perhaps food shortages, while people came to terms with their new ruler.

One thing for sure, he was better equipped to handle the challenge than his brother.

And maybe once this land is behind me, he thought, *once it is out of sight, it will leave my mind, and I will be able to take on my new task whole-heartedly. Once KaLeah is out of sight…*

He tried to clear his thoughts of her again.

The sea shores of Extelli were rocky and he knew nothing of the fishing trade that the Extellan people relied so heavily on to survive. The farmland was limited, and he would have to re-instill trade between Extelli and Belarone.

He wondered if the Extellan castle had the labyrinth of secret passageways that Belarone had. He would have to be certain to send in men to seek those out so he could seal off any point of entry against potential assassins. There were so many things to plan for, and his time had been cut short.

He stood up and walked to the two large windows, put his hands on the sill, and looked out across the sky.

He would miss the view from Belarone castle. The land was lush and green, the forest beyond and the mountains were always beautiful no matter the season. He looked up at the face of the dead planet.

"At least you will still be there to keep me company," he said to himself.

His heart began to warm at the sudden memory of his childhood, growing up in his mother's care. His mother had been kind and loving when it seemed nobody else was. He could see the familiar look of love in KaLeah's eyes, but she was fiery and challenging, which enticed him.

For a second, he allowed a feeling like guilt to creep up for the way he had treated her.

In the ballroom, her lips had been as smooth as silk, and her body under his fingers… He closed his eyes and was instantly back in that room again, watching the candlelight flicker against her dress as she turned to leave him.

Nikolat tried to shake away the memory. She was just a servant. Nikolat would be the King of Extelli soon. And someday, he would return to Belarone to take the throne from his brother, once his father was safely beside his mother in the ground. He opened his eyes and stared out across the land.

"I will return to rule Belarone one day," he promised. "I will transform Extelli and then take Belarone, uniting the kingdoms under my rule. You'll be proud of me, mother."

He began packing for the journey to his new life, pausing only to eat dinner delivered up from the kitchen. He knew he could have ordered a servant to pack for him, but he wanted to take the time to choose wisely. He knew it might be years before he would be able to come back and take Belarone for himself. Bylex might turn his room into a sewing room by that point.

Nikolat worked into the night and then requested hot water for a bath. He needed to wash the battle off before he could truly settle into bed.

As the servants brought in the water, a guard approached his room behind them, stopped, then cleared his throat. "Your Majesty, a note."

Nikolat sat down at his desk and opened the note, sealed with a messy drip of wax. As he read it, a smile creased the corner of his lips.

He had won her over. She needed him, wanted him now. He had penetrated through to the heart of the country girl with just one kiss.

She's beautiful, he knew, *but perhaps dangerous.*

He leaned back in his chair and wondered if KaLeah would ever be loyal to him. If he told her everything, his deepest darkest secrets, would she reach out, touch his cheek, forgive him? Would she love him? Or would she swear to kill him?

Would she leave Belarone with me and rule Extelli beside me, even if I told her how I was the one responsible for Amirra's kidnapping, he wondered?

Of course, he never would tell her exactly that. He would tell her how Lamone had tricked him. He would say that he was manipulated and promised that no harm would come to his sister. Maybe he'd even cry a little.

His smile grew wider.

Nikolat knew he could pull KaLeah completely under his spell and make her fall in love with him if she wasn't already.

He slowly ran his fingers across the letter, across the words she had written, as if he were touching her hands.

He was interested in her; he admitted that much to himself. But he knew those feelings could very easily change. He also knew she didn't have any hope of being with him in any real, logistical sense. Being near her again would only make it harder for her, especially when he left for Extelli.

Nikolat tried to ignore the minor ache at the thought of leaving her. He was young and knew there would be plenty of other women to experience, and then there was the choosing of an actual queen someday.

KaLeah had only been a momentary infatuation. And now that she wanted to see him again, she was no longer a challenge. There was no need to drag it out any longer.

He ran his fingers across the letter again. He gripped both sides and began to slowly rip the paper. The sound of the fibers pulling and splitting comforted him in a strange way.

For some reason, he couldn't bring himself to throw the pieces into the fireplace. Instead, he slid them into a desk drawer.

Nikolat kicked off his boots and clothes, then climbed into the bath. The servant girls scampered out of the room with rosy cheeks. He closed his eyes and thought of KaLeah.

❧KaLeah❧

KaLeah woke late the next morning. She lay in bed and let thoughts of Nikolat drift across her mind.

He had saved her life out on the battlefield. Even though she had been embarrassed about having to be rescued, she was glad she had seen his face out there.

He had seemed worried, as if he wanted to protect her. Although she was injured, he still had enough trust in her to send her after that assassin bent on killing his sister. He was the good guy.

But for some reason, she couldn't shake Lamone's words out of her mind.

How had he been so lucky, she wondered? *How had Lamone known where the hidden entrance was if someone in the royal family hadn't told him?*

She supposed that he could have found out from Prince Bylex, or from a spy. But if it had been someone else, why did Lamone accuse Nikolat? The way Lamone had screamed out accusations at Nikolat, as he was being dragged to his execution, had been nerve wracking.

It wasn't just the scream of desperation, she thought. It had seemed so vengeful, so full of hate.

Don't be silly, KaLeah told herself. Lamone had made himself known to her as terrible from the moment they had met. The prince had done nothing but protect her, stare at her longingly, and kiss her in the ballroom.

Sure, he also annoyed her and made her furious, but maybe that was normal. Maybe she had just been trying to deny her feelings for him.

She smiled with the realization that she did indeed have feelings for him, and that he was going to make everything alright again. The solution was so close, so simple.

He had kissed her in the ballroom, so clearly, he wanted to be with her. He had tried to deny his feelings, at first, by trying to push her off onto Lamone, but he had apologized.

The kiss in the ballroom had wiped all of that away.

She felt an irresistible pull toward him that she just couldn't explain, like he would be the one to write the end of her story for her. The tingling excitement in her stomach told her they would be perfect together.

Will I travel with them all to Extelli, she wondered?

No, she should wait with Amirra until the army took Extelli. Once every Extellan soldier was locked away or switched to Belarone's side, then it would be safe for her to travel to be with Nikolat in Extelli… as his wife.

The word filled her with nervous excitement. It wasn't anything she had ever wanted or dreamed of, especially not with the village boys. But if her only other option was to spend the rest of her life as a playmate and nursemaid to Princess Amirra and her future children, then KaLeah was ready for marriage.

It was the lesser of two evils.

She wondered what her father would say about it. He had never discussed marriage, or even her mother as a wife.

He never talked about when people married in the village either. She had never heard him talk about being married to her mother or marriage in general.

She stretched her legs out, an aching pain surging through her wounded side. She moved slowly to the window to draw the curtains and let the dawn light in.

"Where are you, father?" she asked out into the morning mist.

For a moment, she could have sworn she saw something large moving through the mist, but then it was gone.

With a sigh, she hoped that he would find her someday.

"Alright, KaLeah," she said to herself, sternly. "Big day. You have to tell a boy how you feel about him, and hope that he wants to marry you, and take you away from this place."

She went to her wardrobe and began to plan her attire for the day. She was giddy looking at the dresses and realized that she had changed a lot since coming to Belarone castle.

Or maybe it was just that she'd never wanted to dress up for anyone before. Seeing the way Nikolat looked at her made her want to be beautiful for him.

"What are you doing, KaLeah?" Amirra asked, jarring KaLeah from her thoughts. The princess, still in her long white nightgown, walked up next to her.

"Picking out two dresses; one for the day, and one for tonight," she replied, nearly in song.

Amirra raised an eyebrow.

"You seem very happy to be picking out dresses, KaLeah," she said. "Are you feeling unwell? Maybe you have a fever from your injury. I will call Dohori for you."

KaLeah laughed nervously. "I am perfectly fine," she said. "I would just like to look nice today, that's all. At least, I'd like to dress myself nicely instead of being forced to do it. Maybe I just don't like being forced to do things."

Her mind went back to the king telling Amirra that she would marry and have children, and that KaLeah would always be there by her side to fight for her and her future family. Guilt started to swirl in her stomach and looking at dresses suddenly seemed too overwhelming for her.

"Princess, I've been thinking. If my father was in Belarone Kingdom, one of Captain Daven's or the princes' men would have found him by now. If I stay here, confined to these walls and then to a house somewhere in the kingdom, if I stay with you, I will never find out what happened to him. I have already stayed here much longer than I should have. I wish to go."

"But my father said that you cannot," Amirra said with a high-pitched squeal. "KaLeah, you cannot leave me, ever!"

KaLeah took a step back from the princess, who only stepped closer to her and grabbed her wrists.

"You are my friend, and I don't want you to ever go, but it's more than that. You are a Belarone Favor; aside from a queen or princess, that is the highest honor ever bestowed on a woman. You cannot leave Belarone without the king's permission, and he has already said that you are to guard me for the rest of your life. I'm sorry, KaLeah."

The princess did sound like she was sorry for KaLeah, but mainly sorry that she wanted to leave.

KaLeah realized that she would not be able to tell Amirra about her plan to marry Prince Nikolat and go with him to Extelli. The princess seemed more than happy that her father had ordered KaLeah to stay by her side for all time.

The princess looked to KaLeah as a friend and sister but completely disregarded her personal wishes. There were no other playmates for her, and KaLeah surmised that if the princess knew about her plan, she would run off and tell the king.

"Thank you for understanding, Your Highness."

The princess smiled, seemingly satisfied that she had won the argument.

"I will ask my father's men to keep looking for your father. I am sure that we will come across him soon."

"I hope so," KaLeah said.

"Now, what dresses will you be wearing today? Can I help?" The princess clapped her hands, excitedly.

"Of course. I would love that," KaLeah gently replied.

ဆဆ

Later that night, after the princess had fallen asleep, KaLeah changed into the creamy white dress that Amirra had helped her pick out.

She chose a dress that she could get into herself. It slipped on easily and tied together at a high waist with a braided gray cord. The high waist helped the dress hang loose over her bandaged side, without making her look too awkward.

There were long, transparent sleeves that ended a little past her wrists without completely covering her hands. She had left her hair hanging down around her shoulders.

KaLeah looked feminine and delicate, and yet it was comfortable, which made her feel relieved.

"I could get used to wearing dresses like this," she said to her reflection.

Despite feeling good, she anxiously paced her room, casting glances out at the night as if she could command the moon to move faster across the sky.

She and Amirra had not seen each other much during the day and into the evening. They had mostly stayed in their individual rooms, reading, and eating the meals delivered to them. At one point, servants brought in hot water for each of their baths, and KaLeah soaked her beaten body in her tub until the water turned cold.

She felt guilty about leaving, but justified and confident in her decision. This was best for her. She was not about to sacrifice her future, her life, just to keep a child company.

If there was any way out of this predicament, she wanted to take it.

She looked more closely at the servants who delivered food and bathwater to her throughout the day. Had they grown up knowing that this would be their lives? Were they allowed to leave the castle grounds? Did they have their own homes and families? She told herself that once she felt like talking to Amirra again, she would ask.

When it was finally time for her to go to the ballroom to meet Prince Nikolat, she grabbed a dagger and strapped it to her inner thigh. She wanted to remain careful since it was a time of a war, after all. She didn't want to be caught off-guard by another attack or assassin.

She left her room, closing the door behind her. The guard standing there didn't even look her way, but she was sure he watched her walk down the long hallway.

She walked past murals of dragons, seeming to move in the candlelight. Aside from a few guards posted in strategic locations or outside of other bedrooms, she saw no one else.

When she got to the ballroom, she took a few long, deep breaths and then walked across the marble floor, her footfalls were muffled by her soft slippers.

The room was dead silent and cold. It gave her a strange feeling and the desire to back up and blend into the nearest wall. She could see the moon in the sky through the high windows, casting an eerie light into the room and across the dead planet.

There were clocks in the castle, regularly wound by servants, but KaLeah still timed her life by the sun and the moon.

She didn't need a clock to tell her that Nikolat was late. And as the time slowly and agonizingly passed, she didn't need a clock to tell her that he wasn't coming.

The hallways seemed darker on the way back to her room. She walked slowly and close to the walls, as close as she could get without catching her clothing on fire from the sconces.

She trailed her fingers along the tapestries as she walked; feeling the tight weaving, the history, the stories of the illustrations as if she too were trapped within the fabrics.

"I hate him," she told the darkness. "I hate him, and I have always hated him, and I will always hate him."

Her words were firm. They hit the walls around her and bounced back with the same amount of force. As if in response to this echo, she whispered, "But I love him too, I think."

She stopped outside her bedroom. The guard there, never asking questions, opened the door for her. She took an awkward moment to look at the man.

Was he living a life he had chosen, she wondered? Did he wake up today excited about all the doors he would be able to open for others? Is he paid well? Does he go home to a wife, to children, to a home he built with his own hands?

He didn't meet her gaze, and she assumed that he probably didn't have the same questions about her.

Maybe we can only control so much. She had no control over this life any longer. She was no soldier, no princess, and no great love of a prince.

She was a lost daughter who failed at finding her father, forever enslaved to a responsibility she didn't ask for.

Questions burned on her tongue, but she bit them back and walked through the open door. If she were to ever escape, and if Nikolat wasn't going to be her way out, she didn't want guards or servants to start watching her. She assumed they would all be infallibly loyal to the royals.

Who was she, after all? The second she left, she would be seen as a traitor, even if she saved Amirra's life 50 more times.

The guard closed the door behind her, and she walked into the room, guided by a single candle she had left burning on the windowsill. As she started to undress, she heard a sound from her bed and crept closer to investigate. She was surprised to see Amirra lying asleep there.

"Amirra, wake up," she whispered. She put a hand lightly on the princess' shoulder and squeezed her gently. Amirra stirred, opened her eyes, and blinked up at KaLeah. "What are you doing here?" KaLeah asked, kindly.

"I was looking for you. Where did you go?" Amirra sleepily replied. "I was scared, and you weren't here."

KaLeah sat down and her eyes involuntarily began to water. She assumed it was due to her being exhausted.

"I'm sorry I wasn't here," KaLeah said. "Why were you scared?"

Amirra looked toward the window. "I had a nightmare," she said. "Huge dragons with black wings were attacking the castle."

"It's alright, I'm here now. Let's get you back to bed."

KaLeah helped the princess sit up. She slid to the edge of the bed in her white sleeping gown and then stopped.

"You didn't answer me, though," the princess said. "Where were you? You're wearing the dress I helped you pick out earlier. I thought it was for dinner, but you didn't go to dinner."

KaLeah hesitated, and after a few long moments, decided to just tell the princess a part of the story.

"I went to the ballroom to meet your brother but," she paused, "but he didn't show up. It's silly."

KaLeah shook her head and looked away, tears of self-pity edging her eyes. She wanted to live in the fantasy. She wanted to feel his hands again, his kiss, she wanted to feel something like love; the kind of love that would rescue you from an unfortunate situation.

Amirra drew her eyebrows in tight, working something out silently. She went up to KaLeah and put a gentle hand on her arm.

"KaLeah," Amirra said. "I have been sad all day long because I know that you want to leave me. You are my best friend. You are like a sister to me, and I don't ever want you to go. I don't have any friends like you. But now I think I understand. You don't want to leave me; you just want to find your father. You want to live your own life. And I guess, now I see you also want to be with Nikolat. You love him, don't you? You want to go with him to Extelli."

Instead of answering, KaLeah looked down at her shoes. They were white slippers. She was disappointed that Nikolat hadn't seen her like this, at least one last time.

Maybe she would have been able to talk him into taking her with him.

Maybe he would have realized his love for her.

She backed away from Amirra's gentle touch and inquisitive eyes, then angrily kicked off the dainty shoes.

"No," KaLeah said, heading toward her bed. "I don't love the prince, and I don't want to go to Extelli. I want to leave this place. I want to find my father. I don't want to be a guard or a babysitter or a favor. I want my life back."

She crawled into the large bed, the soft dress loose and silky enough to cocoon her body even more beneath the blankets.

Amirra stood silently by the window for a few moments and then headed back to her room. KaLeah's stomach turned at the guilt. She knew she'd made Amirra feel worse, but she had to be honest. If the girl wanted to be her friend, wanted to care about her like a sister, then she needed to know the truth.

KaLeah closed her eyes and tried to put everything out of her head. She knew that the morning would come too soon.

❧Nikolat☙

When Nikolat opened his door the next morning, he was shocked to see his little sister standing there.

177

Princess Amirra was wearing a long olive-green gown that was tied high in front with a gold ribbon. The front of the gown opened at the ribbon slightly revealing a golden layer beneath the first.

Her hair was pinned up against her head and her arms were crossed tightly over her chest. She looked more angry and older than he'd ever seen her look before.

He raised one eyebrow, crossed his arms, and looked down at Amirra.

"Are you supposed to be running around without your bodyguard, little sister?" he asked.

"I need to talk to you alone, brother," she said, putting a heavy weight behind the last word. "Why did you not meet KaLeah like you were supposed to?"

Nikolat let his jaw drop and then snapped it shut again. *How had she known? Did KaLeah tell her everything?*

The hair on the back of his neck bristled. None of his affairs were her business, or anyone else's for that matter.

He uncrossed his arms and grabbed hold of the open door.

"You are too young to understand," he said. "Now, go on to breakfast and leave me alone."

"No," she said, her voice rising in pitch. Amirra pushed past him and into his room.

"You have hurt my friend, and I demand that you apologize," Amirra ordered. "KaLeah is beautiful, and wonderful, and kind. She loves you and you love her. Even though I don't want to see her go, I think you should take her with you to Extelli. Then you can marry her, and we can be sisters."

Nikolat shot his fist out and hit the nearest wall.

"Silence!" he yelled.

Suddenly, the room was spinning.

Love? What was his sister going on about? Take her with him? The idea almost made him laugh. KaLeah was beautiful, breath-taking at times, and a torture, but a torture he could bear.

Amirra looked scared, her initial bravery wearing off, and Nikolat felt a little remorseful.

She's just a child, he told himself. She is just living out a little fantasy of hers, and he shouldn't be angry. She is cooped up in a castle all day, every day, and has no sense of reality. He unclenched his fists and put a gentler tone into his voice.

"It is time for you to leave, Amirra," he said. "I am packing to leave for Extelli with father today. I don't have time for this, for you, or her."

But Amirra wasn't ready to leave.

"Today? So soon? I didn't know…Just, please tell me why you didn't meet her, and I will go," Amirra said, cautiously.

"Why?" Nikolat began. "Because I am to be a king. Because I am being sent to rule Extelli. Because our futures lie in two different kingdoms. KaLeah must remain here with you, as your servant, not your friend. She is not your friend, and she will never be my friend. She performs her responsibility following you around like a loyal pet because she is obeying orders, and not obeying orders means death." Nikolat stalked slowly toward his sister. With every step, she seemed to shrink lower beneath him.

"And one day, she will follow you to the country, and you'll partner with a man, and she'll help you raise your children as she is helping to raise you now." He noticed that his voice shifted from irritated to defeated. Not wanting his emotions to betray him, he motioned to the door, trying to point his sister in that direction.

Amirra's eyes began filling with tears. "She *is* my friend."

Nikolat dismissed her as naïve and put his hands on her shoulders, gently steering her out of his room.

"I am leaving for Extelli today," he repeated, with just the slightest hint of remorse. "I have to conquer a kingdom, and then transform it, alone."

"Why not take KaLeah?" Amirra tried to stall in the doorway, pushing back against his hands on her shoulders. "She can help you. She can fight for you. Please brother, she loves you, and she's in pain."

"Then kill her for all I care," he yelled, finally growing impatient. He gave his sister just the slightest shove to push her into the hallway. "Put her out of her misery."

He slammed the door against Amirra, against the thought of KaLeah, and against Belarone.

He turned back toward his room and put his hands to his face. He had to believe in his own words; he had to let them sink in.

He could not care if KaLeah lived or died.

"She's a distraction," he said to no one. "From now on, she's dead to me. I have things to do."

❞KaLeah❞

Amirra returned to KaLeah's room and roused her from sleep.

"Nikolat is leaving for Extelli today," Amirra said.

"What?" KaLeah said in a barely audible whisper. She sat up slowly, feeling as if she hadn't slept at all.

"I will miss you, but I understand. If you love him, then you must talk him into letting you go with him to Extelli."

It took KaLeah's mind a few moments to register what was happening. First, the princess was telling her bad news, that the prince was leaving today. But what she was also saying was that she understood why KaLeah wanted to go with him, and that it was alright. "Amirra, thank you."

KaLeah couldn't believe the girl's change of heart. She clambered out of bed, dizzy but excited. The white dress she'd slept in was wrinkled now, but she didn't care.

"You look like a dragon chewed you up and spit you out, KaLeah," the princess said. They both looked at the crumpled white dress and frizzy hair, then laughed together. It was a good feeling.

"I'm going to miss you too, little princess," KaLeah said, wrapping the girl up in a hug.

"Come to the closet; we don't have much time." Amirra took KaLeah's hand, and together they pulled together a fresh option to win over the prince's heart.

It was another red dress, though not a ballgown like she had worn that first night. It was made more for a casual occasion, and she would be able to travel well in it, while still looking feminine. She was starting to like the way she felt in dresses.

She said goodbye and then ran down the hallways toward Nikolat's chambers. When she got there, the guards told her that he had gone to collect books from the library.

She walked quickly through the long corridors and down flights of stairs to the library, near the castle entrance where she had rescued Amirra from the Extellan soldier.

She paused, swallowing something acidic back down her throat.

Would the princess be alright without her, she wondered?

Focus on Nikolat, she told herself as she went into the library.

She quietly stalked through the long stacks, a mix of fear and hope causing her heart to beat loudly.

There was a heavy, tranquil sense of despair that seemed to be taking up more and more space in her chest, and she tried to shove it back down to her gut.

She saw his shoes first. Black boots covered in intricate lines and curves and other various designs. He was standing on the opposite side of a stack of books.

"You're leaving today for Extelli?" she asked.

"Yes," Nikolat replied. He began to move to the closest end of the stack, toward the back of the library. She watched his boots and moved with him.

"I want to go with you," she said.

"That's impossible."

"No, it isn't," KaLeah argued. "I could easily sneak into the convoy on its way to Extelli. The princess would tell your father that I had left for Erion. I can look out for myself by hiding in the outskirts of Extelli until you have taken over that kingdom."

There was no response, but they were both nearing the end of the stack and about to run into one another.

"Or you could just tell your father that you want to take me with you," she said, more defiantly.

Just around the corner, she thought. She raised her eyes. She heard him take a deep breath as they rounded the end of the stacks and came face to face.

There were those eyes, grayish blue in the dimly lit library. He wore all black, from head to toe, and looked as deadly as he was beautiful.

"Favor KaLeah," he said in a whisper.

"Prince Nikolat."

Why have we never met here before? she wondered. He could take her in his arms here and no one would see them.

"Sounds like you've thought a lot about this." There was no humor in his voice. He seemed to have no emotion, only a curious interest in the girl standing before him.

"However, my father has given his orders," Nikolat said with a firm tone. "Amirra is to solidify a partnership with one of the favor families when she comes of age, which will be in just a few years. Then you and she will go to the country. You'll help her raise a family."

KaLeah crept closer to him. She'd never dared to touch the prince. She had always waited for him to make moves, to reach out and touch her. To touch royalty without permission was forbidden, disrespectful, and dangerous. But it was more than that. She had never reached out to any boy, or any man, for comfort. Not even her own father. Affection was not something she was used to, but she yearned for it now.

She reached out her hand and brought it to his face. His cheek was cold and smooth. She brought her hand down to his neck and shoulder, then straight down across his heart and stopped there.

"Checking for my heartbeat?" he asked.

She closed her eyes for a moment and continued to feel his heart beating through her fingertips. She slowly opened her eyes and looked into his in earnest.

"I'm checking for more than that," she said, her voice pleading. A strange courage began to bubble up and words came unbidden out of her mouth.

"I can feel you, sense you like a dragon on the hunt. I know you for some strange reason and I think…" she paused, not sure how to say it, but then knew she had to. She had nothing left to lose. "I think you love me too. I can feel it through my fingertips. I can see it in your eyes."

He laughed and took a step back from her. Her hand dropped into the void between them.

"You only think you know me," he said. "You're no spirit speaker, KaLeah."

"I don't need magic to read you," she said. "I want you to know that I will always love you. That you are the man I will spend the rest of my life loving."

"Then you'll have to get used to being alone. My destiny is to do my father's bidding, to care for my kingdom, my people, and to eventually be a king. And your destiny is to guard my sister. I will not take you with me."

"That is my job, for now, not my destiny," KaLeah said, raising her voice louder now.

She felt like she was losing him. Once he left the privacy of the library, he would be surrounded by people, all congratulating him and bidding him farewell.

"I have to go now," he said. He turned and began heading toward a small pile of books on a nearby table.

"Nikolat, wait, please," she said, her eyes filling with tears.

She ran to catch up and he turned around. She didn't think about her actions, she just threw her arms up and around his neck. She tightened her arms around his neck, and he wrapped his strong arms around her back in return.

She put her lips to his and kissed him with fear and hate, love, and obsession. He slid a hand up her back and cupped the back of her neck. He squeezed and continued kissing her. Then the cupped hand pulled her neck back, away from him, and she lost her hold of his lips.

"Thank you for that," he said with a smirk. "Now goodbye."

He turned, picked up a pile of books with one quick motion, and continued walking to the doors.

"You love me," she called after him, but she didn't follow. She put her hands on the back of the closest chair to stabilize herself.

What was she doing? She was fighting to hold on to a man that she knew she couldn't be with. He had kissed her, yes, but why was he leaving without taking every piece of her first?

It didn't make sense to her. If he truly didn't love her, he would have used her up fully and completely. But he didn't. All he had gotten was a kiss from her—a kiss, and her entire heart.

She tightened her grip on the chair and then lifted it up in the air. She threw it at the closest bookshelf and then began grabbing books and throwing them against the doors that Nikolat had walked through, away from her.

She grabbed another chair and heaved it up and over, listening as it smacked and broke against another heavy bookshelf. She lifted the edge of a table and thrust it onto its side.

She had tried to convince herself that he loved her, on some deep level, but as she destroyed the furniture around her in anger, she realized that he had never shown her love, or even interest, beyond the superficial level.

She collapsed to her knees on the floor, feeling like an idiot. She had wanted him to love and accept her so much that she hadn't even considered if *he* was worthy of *her*.

"He doesn't love me," she said, tears falling, the words clutching to her dry throat.

She cried there on the floor in heavy sobs for a few minutes, then shook her head, and took a deep breath. She slowly stood back up, knowing that she would have to be her own hero. She would have to get out of here on her own and forget about her feelings for the prince.

She was a warrior—not a little girl. Not some maiden. She looked at the dress she wore in disgust. Anger rolled through her body.

"He won't help me, so I will figure this out on my own," she said out loud to the demolished library room. Then she wiped away her tears and walked out of the room with her head held high.

11 LIES

The rest of the day passed by in a blur for KaLeah. Princess Amirra was required to be present while the men prepared to invade and conquer Extelli Kingdom. The young girl had to bid her father, brother, and the Belarone soldiers farewell, and wish them a quick victory.

KaLeah was glad that she only had to stand quietly behind the princess and listen to her repeat, "Farewell and quick victory," over and over to each soldier that passed by.

KaLeah had changed into a dark gray tunic over black tights, and she had her long brown hair pulled back, hiding like a shadow behind Amirra's fluffy, bright violet and gold dress. She hoped to be as invisible as possible.

They stood beside Prince Bylex in the courtyard, overlooking the servants and soldiers preparing draggots and carriages for the seven days' journey to the coastal region. KaLeah could see Prince Nikolat and King Erazus inspecting the work nearest to the castle while doling out orders. Ranks of soldiers and their captains were gathering on the fields.

The king and Prince Nikolat were dressed in the finest of uniforms, with white long-sleeved tunics, red breast and wrist guards, white pants tucked into black boots, and the Belarone dragon emblem emblazoned on their chests. They looked regal and determined from where she stood.

Nikolat was off to rule his very own kingdom. How proud they must both be, KaLeah thought.

Prince Bylex was dressed just as splendidly in a long red cape pinned together with an elegantly carved silver dragon encircling a ball of fire on his chest. He appeared indifferent, but a few beads of sweat on his neck in the cool afternoon breeze betrayed nervousness, since the day was not yet warm.

KaLeah realized that she really knew nothing of this man who was about to be left in charge for an unknown amount of time.

Amirra smiled as she watched the activities taking place below her and received each soldier's bow kindly. KaLeah sneered though, thinking how sad that all the young princess was good for was giving birth to more favors, who may one day be bred back into the royal family.

And what of her own fate? At least she would never love again, that much was certain.

Whether she managed to escape the grasp of Belarone Kingdom or not, she would never let her heart be captured. Without a father, without a husband, KaLeah was freer than Princess Amirra would ever be.

An involuntary sigh left her lips as her glance left Princess Amirra and slid back over to Prince Nikolat.

Nik never once looked at either of them. Staring him down, her heart thundered harder in her chest.

She was angry but also embarrassed about her emotional display in the library. Her sadness about the finality of his pending departure, and how he had not seemed to care even a little bit about how she felt, tamped down her anger some.

I'm sure he's upset about having to leave his home so quickly, she thought. *I am sure that I am the least of his concerns. The young man is going to war, going to take over and rule a completely different kingdom. He could not possibly have time to think about me, or my declaration of love, or my plea to trade one form of imprisonment for another.*

KaLeah raised her palm to her forehead, hiding her eyes.

What an idiot, she said to herself as she tapped her hand to her head and squeezed her eyes shut tight.

"Good afternoon, Favor KaLeah."

The voice was a soft whisper, but KaLeah jumped at the sudden interruption to her self-loathing thoughts.

"Captain Daven, you startled me," she said. Hilip was standing beside her, and she wondered if he'd seen her tapping her forehead.

He smiled an apology, and she couldn't help but smile back at him. He emitted such a kind, peaceful presence, so much different from Nikolat, that she couldn't help but like him.

"Are you and your men prepared to leave?" she asked, making polite conversation.

"I am actually remaining here, along with one other captain and our men. Given the recent events, we do not want to leave the kingdom exposed."

"Yes, of course," she said, trying to hide her mixed emotions with a nod and smile. "I'm glad for your protection."

She *was* glad that they would have protection, but she knew that if the captain and scores of other soldiers were hanging around the grounds, KaLeah would have to plan her escape even more carefully.

She wondered if Hilip would be completely full of disappointment for her today.

"Any word of my father?" she asked him.

"I'm sorry, KaLeah," Hilip said, his smile turning to a frown. "No one in the center or surrounding villages has seen or heard of anyone named Clegg Trapper. But we will continue to look, I promise."

Her heart sank further down into her stomach. No father, no prince, no way to sneak away with so many guards and soldiers staying behind.

I should have left the princess to find her own way home after killing her kidnappers, she thought. The thought filled her with guilt, but she knew if she hadn't been so heroic, she wouldn't be trapped here now.

"Are you alright, KaLeah?"

Hilip placed his hand softly on her shoulder. Her eyes widened in surprise from the contact, and he quickly removed his hand.

"Sorry," he said, looking down as if his hand had betrayed him.

"That's fine. I'm fine."

She turned in time to see Nikolat looking up at her, a mixture of anger and possession in his eyes.

Had he seen Hilip touch me? Her eyes stung in happiness at the thought of his potential jealousy, even though it would do her no good.

Captain Daven made no more attempts to touch or speak to her. KaLeah, Amirra, Bylex, the captain, and a few favors and soldiers stood and watched the legion make its final preparations.

KaLeah hoped that Nikolat would turn around. She pictured him running to her and begging her to join him.

She stood watching with the others. They watched the legion march out of the castle gates, joining with lines of soldiers in the fields.

Nikolat never looked back.

෪෫

Days passed uneventfully in the castle.

KaLeah spent her time teaching the princess how to sword fight, and reading in the library, while Amirra received her arithmetic, history, and geography lessons. KaLeah had completed her schooling back in Erion, so she continued to educate herself simply by reading various historic books in her free time.

She found that by getting lost in the old stories, the details, visualizing the lands and events, she forgot about being locked up. She forgot about how her life had been stolen from her for a few hours. The pain and anger melted away when she was living in someone else's story.

KaLeah realized that she had seen Captain Daven more times in the last few days than she had seen him the entire time she'd been at Belarone Castle.

He was at all their meals, he came to observe during her drills with Amirra, he always seemed to be wandering the halls just outside the library or outside of their suites.

He would appear out of nowhere, as if locked onto her schedule, and politely ask to escort her.

In the evenings, after Amirra was in bed, Hilip would teach KaLeah various pathways through the secret tunnels, step by step, forcing her to remember her way around in the darkness until she began to catch onto a natural pattern.

She partly wondered if he had been ordered to keep an extra close eye on her and Amirra, to make sure they stayed indoors and stuck to the rules and schedules laid out for them. But there was something awkward in his constant presence.

His smile stayed too long on his face after they laughed about something together. His eyes seemed to linger on her own eyes when they spoke.

She told herself that he was only around because he had been ordered to keep watch over them. Although she was the princess' bodyguard, KaLeah had gotten into enough trouble to warrant an extra eye.

She shrugged off his attention as nothing more than a requirement, another form of imprisonment for her to bear.

She especially loathed when he gave her excuses about his men's inability to locate her father.

However, with the castle quieter than normal, and without her obsession with Nikolat to keep her company, she started to feel a bit of comfort knowing he was just around the corner, knowing he would be escorting them to the library after she and Amirra cleaned up after practice, and knowing that he would keep them company during mealtimes.

Late one afternoon, KaLeah was reading comfortably in an oversized chair in the front area of the library, while Amirra studied with a tutor in another area further back.

The book was an historic account of how the three kingdoms on Naldash were formed. The rulers, though ancestors of the founding families, did not all have the kingdom's names. They took the formal kingdom's name upon ordainment.

Belarone was the first kingdom founded by the Belarone family, led by a fearsome tribe warrior. Apparently merciless, Riiken Belarone made himself king and took charge of various tribes living in the area through the enforcement of other warriors loyal to him.

Two tribes refused to fall under his command, rebelled against the Belarone fighters, and after both sides suffered numerous casualties, the tribes had enough of a reprieve to escape the lands.

One escaped tribe was led by Gorgola Extelli, who took his people west until they hit rocky shores. They became fishermen and mined the cliffs for metals and jewels. When he heard that Riiken Belarone had declared himself king, Gorgola created the Extellan Kingdom and named himself king.

The second tribe was led by Lockolin Lisodanya. Similarly, he helped his people escape, but to the southeast, where the lands were more fertile, like Belarone lands.

There they spread out farms as far as the eye could see, since there were plenty of grasslands and no mountains. They enjoyed much easier winters, but harsher summers, with larger storms rolling down upon them from the north mountains.

It wasn't until Lockolin passed away many years later that one of his sons, Deckolin Lisodanya, declared himself king in order to prevent Belarone and Extelli from trying to claim their lands and people for themselves.

Deckolin established a great army to ensure a constant defensive at the ready, while opening peaceful trade with Belarone.

As the generations passed, the three kingdoms managed to keep the peace, trading marriages from time to time. If there came a time when there was a lack of an heir, a member of a favor family would be married into the royal family, but the royal name would be maintained.

KaLeah closed the book and leaned back in her chair. She had never had access to so much information, and she was glad to read and be distracted from her thoughts of Nikolat. She heard loud steps in the hallway and looked toward the door.

A young soldier burst into the library, calling out her name. She sat up so fast that the book flew down to the ground with a loud boom.

"Favor KaLeah, Captain Daven sent me. They have captured your father. He is in the throne room."

"Captured?" she asked.

Forgetting about the princess, KaLeah quickly scrambled out of the chair and followed him through the door.

They ran down the hallways and she peppered him with questions along the way.

"What do you mean, captured? Is he alright? Who captured him? What's happening?"

He didn't answer any of her questions, so she finally stopped asking.

She ran into the throne room, stopping suddenly when she saw her father. He looked so small, standing between two soldiers, with his hands tied behind his back.

Each soldier had a hand on one of his shoulders, and they stood about twenty steps away from Prince Bylex, who was sitting on his father's massive throne, his arms resting on the carved dragon heads, the red velvet oval of the chair back clashing with his informal attire.

He had clearly been pulled here from doing something relaxing, like a bath. Bylex's hair was disheveled, and he wore an oversized yellow-gold robe. KaLeah still wasn't used to seeing him on the throne. Captain Daven stood beside him.

"Father," KaLeah yelled, and everyone turned toward her.

She ran to Clegg Trapper, sidestepped a soldier, and threw her arms around her missing father's neck.

The soldiers stepped slightly back but kept firm hands on the man's shoulders.

She released him immediately, not being used to hugging her father. She was surprised by her own display of emotion and felt suddenly awkward.

She was relieved to see him but concerned about his restraints.

"KaLeah?" Clegg asked, his face scrunching in puzzlement.

"You're alive," KaLeah said. "I was so worried. Where have you been? Why are you bound?"

Then she turned to the soldiers and realizing they wouldn't answer, she turned to address Hilip. "Why is my father bound?"

Captain Daven stepped down from the dais. The captain seemed distinctly different from the young soldier who had been following her around the castle for days. He seemed more serious and sterner than she'd ever seen him before.

"Favor KaLeah, your father was found wandering the fields of Belarone and carrying a strange weapon," Captain Daven said. "He was brought in and bound as any spy or Extellan would be. We have to be extra cautious in times of war."

"Well, he isn't a spy. He is my father from Erion village." She looked back at her father and noticed how dirty he was. His face and hair were almost a shade darker, his beard was grown out longer and was unkempt. His pants below the knees were caked in mud. She bent down closer and placed her hand on his chest.

"What happened to you?" she whispered.

"I am not a spy," Clegg yelled in response to Captain David, ignoring KaLeah's question. "I wasn't even aware that there was a war going on." Clegg looked past KaLeah to speak to the captain directly.

"Don't touch that!" Clegg suddenly yelled.

KaLeah spun around to see who her father had yelled at. The young soldier who had escorted her to the throne room was now standing opposite Captain Daven in front of the dais. He was holding out a black metallic object that looked familiar.

KaLeah realized that it looked like the strange objects she had found hidden beneath their house in Erion. He glanced up slightly at her father and then back down, turning the black object over in his hand.

"That thing is a very dangerous weapon," Clegg warned, loudly. "Son, you must be careful. Please, set it down gently."

Chills trickled down her back. She had been right, they had been weapons, but like nothing she had ever known or trained with.

Why would her father train her with swords, knives, bows and arrows, but not these? Why had they been hidden?

Prince Bylex stood up and took a step down from his father's throne. He looked awkward in what she assumed was a bathrobe, but he didn't seem to care. His eyes were squinted with curious fascination.

"How is that you have come by such strange weapons and then come into Belarone Kingdom with them?" Prince Bylex asked.

"The guns..." Clegg started. He looked at KaLeah, then to the captain and back to the prince. He seemed to be hesitating.

"That weapon is not of this world, Your Majesty," Clegg finally said. "We don't have weapons like this on Naldash. I can assure you that I do not intend to do harm with it, but that it is indeed dangerous and should be handled with the utmost care."

Clegg's eyes finally rested on hers as if there was much more to say than he knew where to begin, but instead, he looked past her again to the man holding the weapon.

"The gun is made of metal and uses fire to project a bullet," Clegg exclaimed.

"Let me see this gun," Bylex said, holding out his hand toward the soldier.

"Your Majesty, I'd highly advise against…"

But Clegg's warning came too late. The man who handed the gun to Bylex set it off. The room was filled with a noise unlike anything KaLeah had ever heard. It was as if thunder had entered the room.

KaLeah watched a golden flame spread throughout the prince's skin. His eyes went wide, and he fell back. Captain Daven and a handful of soldiers ran to Bylex.

"He is still breathing!"

"Get the nurses!"

"Get something to stop the bleeding!"

"Do not touch that weapon!"

"Take the prisoners to the dungeon!"

Prisoners? KaLeah's arms were grabbed and bound in front of her, and then she and her father were dragged from the room. It took KaLeah far too long to catch her breath, draw it in, and then formulate words.

"Captain," she finally called from the threshold. "Hilip!"

But no one was paying her any mind except for the soldiers pulling her away from the chaos.

While she and her father were being hauled out into the hallway, she saw Princess Amirra run into the throne room from another entrance. Her shrill scream filled the air.

KaLeah closed her eyes tightly, knowing the scene that the young girl had just stumbled onto. She would be a changed girl after this. Her heart ached with guilt for not being there to pull Amirra away, to console her.

Her reunion with her father had turned into a nightmare for them all.

Voices crept in and out between her thoughts—voices that she was beginning to realize did not belong to her.

They were angry, undiscernible whispers, and guttural growls. She tried to shake them out of her head, causing the soldier holding her to tug her harder.

The halls seemed to get tighter and darker the further down into the castle's interior they went. KaLeah tried to count the steps between candle sconces, and sure enough, the distance even between the lights was growing, creating deeper chasms of darkness along their path.

With every step, the walls leaned in a little more and squeezed the two captives closer together. She started to wonder about the air and how she and her father would be able to breath.

At least the candles were still flickering, she thought. *If they can breathe, then so can we.*

The air in the depths of the castle was old and stale, and she imagined the putrid damp air to be thick with spirits who, with every breath she took, were trying to invade her lungs as the voices invaded her mind.

She had always enjoyed darkness and solitude, but she knew that the holding cells in the dungeon would contain a different kind of darkness and loneliness.

There she would have no control. There she would not have a way out.

KaLeah tried to remain calm, clear-headed, and silent.

Water was dripping somewhere in the dark, falling onto stone and filling up small pools of water at their feet.

They descended a narrow, uneven staircase, and then the room opened to reveal rows and rows of iron cages, the metal twinkling in the light from at least a hundred candles.

It was an underground world with a high ceiling, pools of black water, and no guards visibly attending to the war captives KaLeah could hear mumbling and yelling from within their cells.

It must have been the very bottom of the castle, exactly as Amirra had once named it.

"Put us together and far away from any other prisoners," KaLeah heard herself say without thinking. She wasn't going to allow herself to fear whatever disgusting, dying men shared her ceiling.

The soldiers led them to a holding cell without hesitation. KaLeah noticed that they obeyed her request as well. They put them into a cage, removed their bonds, and then locked them in with the turn of a key that was kept hanging on a wall near the staircase that led out of the dungeon.

KaLeah waited until the soldiers had left and then turned to her father. They both remained standing in the dirty cell, but at least they were alone and far from other prisoners.

"Where have you been?" KaLeah demanded to know. "What happened to you? What was that weapon? I found others, those guns, in our house. Why were you hiding them? What have you done? Will the prince die?"

He held up his hands, signaling her to stop her questions.

She snapped her mouth shut, feeling scolded.

He took a deep, labored breath, and then looked for a place to sit, as if settling in for a long story.

"I went looking for the ship that you found in the woods," he said.

"What ship?" she asked.

Her mind went back to that day in the woods when the ghost-like dragon with the translucent wings was digging something out of a grassy hill. Her own hands had dug and found something hard, something metal beneath the dirt.

"Are you saying that thing was a boat, buried in the woods? Why did you go looking for it?"

"Not a boat, KaLeah, a ship. A warship. A ship that travels through air and space." He sounded exhausted as he slid down to sit on the dirty floor of their cell.

"I don't understand," she said. She started pacing and biting at her nails. "There is no such thing."

"It does not float on water like a boat, or traverse land like a carriage, KaLeah. It flies through the air."

"That thing can fly through the air like a dragon?" she said a little too loudly, and then laughed, feeling ridiculous for even asking the question. She must have just misunderstood.

"Not just the air, but beyond the blue of our skies, beyond the black of space, all the way to Denlerack," Clegg said.

"The dead planet?" KaLeah said the words slowly.

"The planet is not dead, but it is dying," Clegg said. "KaLeah, please sit down. I have a lot to tell you. I was hoping that I never would need to tell you. Once your mother died, I had hoped that the past would just die with her, but it hasn't."

Her father never mentioned her mother. It was more than rare, so she stopped pacing and brought herself down to the moist dirt, not caring if the muddy floor soiled her pants and tunic. Her heart was racing so much that she thought it was going to jump up and out of her throat.

"There is a civilization on Denlerack," Clegg began. "People live there in large buildings made of metal. They have weapons such as the ones you found in our cellar, the gun that young man grabbed up there."

Clegg nodded toward the ceiling.

"Will he die?" she asked.

"Highly likely, yes. The gun contained heater bullets, designed to do irreparable damage. It is much worse than a sword. They should have left me, and the gun, alone."

"But we've been looking for you," KaLeah said. "I've been looking for you." Her voice nearly cracked but she didn't want to show emotion in front of her father. Emotion was weakness.

"Well, you shouldn't have," he said in a disappointed tone. "I was hiding from the men who are hunting us."

"Who is hunting us?" She and her father were unimportant hunters from Erion. KaLeah could see no reason why anybody would ever be after the two of them.

"Denlerack soldiers," Clegg said. "KaLeah, you were born here, on this planet, but your mother and I were born on Denlerack. We lived there. You were in your mother's belly when we landed here. She was injured and didn't survive your birth. It is not an easy way to travel, and I regret that we did not wait, but we were trying to escape."

"Why? What were you escaping from?" KaLeah asked, not able to resist interrupting him.

There was a long pause before he answered. He looked away toward a small puddle of water for a long time.

"From your father." He raised his eyes to meet hers. "I raised you, but I am not your actual father. Your mother was my friend, and she disagreed with your father's decision to invade Naldash. He wanted to conquer and enslave its people. Your mother, Huntra, came here to warn the people. Once she died, I just couldn't see how anyone here would ever believe that we were from the dead planet. Their beliefs are archaic and superstitious. They would have killed us out of fear." He shook his head and looked away from her, into the darkness of the dungeon.

"So, instead, I created a life for us here. I buried the ship in the woods where it crashed. I built the house nearby so that I could keep an eye on anyone going in and out from our village just in case I had to make up a story or move the ship. After so many years, I never... I never expected you to find it. Somehow, when you touched the ship, it activated a signal. Men, soldiers from Denlerack who have been hiding here among us, picked up the signal. When I got to the ship that night, they were there. They captured and interrogated me. I stole a gun from their camp and barely escaped with my life. I kept running. I didn't know where I was until the Belarone soldiers picked me up. I think the men from Denlerack have infiltrated the kingdoms and helped to start the war that the captain mentioned in the throne room. Creating discord, chaos, and three divided kingdoms would make it much easier for Denlerack to invade."

KaLeah's mind spun through everything he had just said. Wars. Ships. Guns. Captured. Hunted. Her mother. But the thought that stuck front and center in her mind was that Clegg Trapper was not her actual father.

What did that mean? She had another father on another planet that was not dead, but thriving and intent on war?

She stood up, looking for some window. She needed to look at the dead planet, this Denlerack. She needed something to ground her back in her own reality—the reality she knew.

There was no window in the dungeon. She closed her eyes and pictured the planet in her mind.

Her mother, Clegg, and her real father had lived on the orb that sat in the sky with the moon and sun?

It was all too much to take in at once.

She turned and looked her father over. He was a large, muscular man with a round face and brown eyes. She looked nothing like him, and yet, she just always assumed it was because she looked like her mother.

But this was the man who raised her. This was her father.

She felt as if her heart was shrinking into the shadows of the dungeon, pulling her away from him.

"Did you love my mother?" she asked.

"As a friend," Clegg answered.

"But not romantically?"

"No."

"But you left your home, your planet, for her." KaLeah wanted it to make sense. Why would a man leave an entire world with a woman he didn't love?

"Yes. I believed in her," Clegg explained. "I was part of an underground movement against Lord Keldon, your father."

"Lord?"

"Dayne Keldon. He is the lord dictator over Denlerack. There are no kingdoms."

KaLeah resumed pacing. Everything she had ever known had been a lie.

In times like this, when you feel the foundation fall out from beneath you, you turn to your family, to the ones you love for support, she thought to herself. Then a worry, a creeping suspicion and fear that she had always had but couldn't explain, rose to the surface. A question.

"Do you love me?" KaLeah asked, looking out through the cell bars.

"I do care for you greatly, KaLeah. You are like a daughter to me, and I hope that I have cared for you as your mother would have wished me to."

Like a daughter, she repeated in her head. But not a real daughter. *Like* a daughter.

"I'm so sorry about all this, KaLeah. If you just hadn't found that ship, none of this would have happened."

He said it as if all of this were her fault. If she'd just stayed on the path, not found the ship, not set off the chain of events that resulted in her finding out her true story, then it would all be fine.

"I didn't find the ship," KaLeah said, still not looking at him. She stared into the flame of a candle on a wall beyond the bars, thinking back to that day in the woods. With everything that had happened, she finally decided to admit the truth. At this point, she had nothing to lose. Even if she sounded crazy, it couldn't be crazier than the story she'd just heard.

"A dragon spirit led me to it," KaLeah said. Then she laughed, realizing how crazy that sounded.

"Do you hear their voices calling to you in times of stress or conflict?" he asked, surprising her.

She whipped around, struggling to focus on him in the dark after staring at the candlelight.

"Yes. How did you know that? I mean, I hear voices, but are you saying that I *am* hearing dragon spirits?"

He closed his eyes and leaned back against the stone wall.

"Huntra, I am so sorry," he said. "I have been a blind fool all these years." He spoke as if KaLeah wasn't there. He took a deep breath and then reopened his eyes.

"There is an ancient prophecy on Denlerack; a prophecy that the people in my rebellion believe in. They believe that a warrior will come. The dragons will call the warrior to finish the war they began and reunite the sister planets. Everyone hoped that your mother was the one. She was part of the rebellion and infiltrated the enemy, right into the heart of the dictator. But we were wrong. KaLeah, if you have seen a phantom dragon, seen the ghost of the dragons that came before us, and if you hear them calling to you, then you are the only one who can save *both* planets."

KaLeah stood there, looking down at the man who raised her, while water dripped on the stone, and men called for help and food from other cells. She blinked her eyes a few times, trying to clear her vision, trying to clear her mind.

"You do realize how crazy all of this sounds?" she said slowly.

"Oh yes," Clegg admitted. "Imagine believing in myth and magic in a land of machines and metal. Superstition and religion are not as common on Denlerack as they are here on Naldash. People get from place to place in rolling or floating machines, work to create buildings that touch the clouds. They have made the air heavy and hard to breathe. The plants don't grow above ground, and the water is polluted. That is why Keldon wants Naldash. He wants to keep it clean, but have the land worked to feed his planet. But you can change everything. You can protect this land.”

Clegg stood up and walked to KaLeah. He placed his hands on her shoulders and smiled at her in amazement for the first time in her life. She had never seen him look like a man with so much purpose before. He looked proud.

“You are the one. This is your destiny.”

KaLeah knew that she should feel proud and happy that her father was finally seeing her.

Except he wasn’t her father. He had fabricated an entire life. He had kept the true story of her mother from her. She didn’t even know what her mother looked like because she had always been afraid to ask, afraid that it would make him sad or angry because of how much she had imagined that he loved her mother.

But this man didn’t even love her until this moment when he found out she could fulfill some crazy prophecy that he believed in. Of course, he also believed that the dead planet was living, boats could fly, and dragon spirits were talking to her.

She shook him off her and stepped away. How could she believe all this now if he had lied to her for her entire life? All the trust she ever had for him, the respect and admiration, melted away.

“You were always so hard on me,” she said in a whisper.

“I’m sorry, KaLeah. I didn’t know what to do with a girl, a child that was not my own. I did the best I could. I did all I knew to do. If I failed you, then that is something you will just have to forgive me for.”

Before she could think of a response, Captain Daven came running into the dungeon.

“Favor KaLeah, Prince Bylex has died,” Hilip said. “Princess Amirra has been placed on the throne until her father can return from war. She is requesting your presence.”

Hilip grabbed the key from the wall and released KaLeah. She didn’t turn to look at her father, at Clegg

Trapper, before Hilip led her up the stairs and out of the putrid air.

204

12 GREAT WARRIOR

Once they were out of earshot of the dungeon, Hilip stopped and faced KaLeah in a candlelit stairwell. To her surprise, he reached out, gently cupped her face in his hands, and looked deeply into her eyes.

"Are you alright?" he asked intently, brows furrowed.

His empathetic touch and question brought tears to her eyes. She was so surprised by her own emotional response that she couldn't speak.

He suddenly wrapped his arms around her, pulling her to his chest. She let loose a few tears and coughed as something trickled down the back of her throat.

His arms around her were strange but welcome and comforting. She hadn't even realized how shaken she was and how she just needed someone to hold her steady for a moment.

KaLeah heard a shout from somewhere ahead and quickly came back to her senses. She pushed gently away from Hilip and furiously wiped at her tears as if they had betrayed her. She wanted to feel the anger, not the sadness.

"He isn't my father," KaLeah said, needing to say that

information out loud, to put it out in front of her, to face it as a reality.

Captain Daven looked puzzled.

"But I thought you said he was the father you were having us search for. He said he's Clegg Trapper from Erion."

"He is the same man, yes," she said. "He is the one I asked you to find. But he isn't my real father, and I had no idea. He just now told me. My real father…" she stopped herself.

What in dragon's spirits did Clegg just tell her in the dungeon? He and her mother were on Denlerack, the dead planet, but it's alive, and ruled by her actual father?

She looked up at Hilip, still peering down at her with deep concern and confusion.

"What is it, KaLeah?"

"No, it sounds crazy."

"KaLeah, Prince Bylex is dead, killed by a weapon none of us have ever seen before. It exploded at him without destroying itself. If you know something, you need to tell me."

There was a sudden air of authority to the last statement, like he was talking to a soldier. She straightened up automatically.

It was an order after all, she figured.

"He told me the weapon came from Denlerack," she started. "He and my mother came from Denlerack across the stars and skies in a flying ship. He said the ruler there is my actual father, and he wants to invade Naldash, enslave the people, and drain it of its resources."

Captain Daven made no sound, no movement, or facial expression to give away his thoughts. But he was clearly thinking, assessing the words and KaLeah, who was standing there covered in cold sweat and streaks of dried tears.

She mirrored his stoicism and stood silently with him in the stairwell for moments that dragged on.

"We have to tell Princess Amirra and counsel together with the other captain that stayed behind," Hilip said finally. "We cannot send this message to the king. We have riders sent to notify him of Bylex's death, but that is all for now. We must tread carefully with this information, or we may both end up back in that dungeon. Do you understand, KaLeah?"

She did and nodded. He clearly did not think she was crazy or that the information was incorrect. He was more concerned about others not believing the story.

"You believe it?" she asked, lowering her voice as if this would be a secret between them.

"There is no immediate reason not to, and in my position, I never take anything at face value, but I also never take new information lightly. You should never dismiss information as completely true or false because the truth always lies somewhere between the two."

Warmth started to spread from her heart and throughout her body. She found herself looking at Hilip in a whole new light. She trusted him and had a newfound faith in him, not just as a captain, but as a person and a leader.

She heard a faint humming in the back of her mind.

The dragon spirits, she realized. What her father, no, what Clegg had said to her came back in a flash.

Dragon spirits were calling to her in order to finish their ancient war. Her eyes widened as she connected the strange sounds she had been hearing to warnings of impending danger.

"What is it? Are you alright?" Hilip asked, hands on both of her arms.

She didn't want to tell him. She wasn't ready to believe it herself. She had seen the dragon in the woods so long ago that it was easy to dismiss it all as a dream.

KaLeah wasn't ready to believe that something completely outside of her control, something no one could possibly believe, was speaking to her.

"There is something else, isn't there?" Hilip asked.

Dragon's blood, he's really good at this, she thought. She took a deep breath.

"It is even crazier than Denlerack," she said.

"I can handle whatever it is, KaLeah."

She laughed nervously at that but assumed it to be true. She didn't want to be alone with this information. She wanted some guidance and especially understanding. KaLeah took a deep breath.

"Sometimes, I see and hear dragon spirits. They come to me to warn me, or in times of stress. I hear a low growling sound and what sounds like whispers in the back of my head. I can't turn it off and didn't know what it was, but Clegg just told me about a prophecy—"

"The dragon spirits will call to a great warrior to finish their war," Captain Daven finished.

"You know about this prophecy?"

"All soldiers do," he said. "Growing up, all young boys fantasize about being the great dragon warrior. We join in the service to the king hoping that it will be us someday. Men may not discuss it, but in their hearts, they are all trying to be that great warrior and hoping to hear the dragons calling to them."

KaLeah was shocked. All this time, a myth existed, something that every little boy grew up knowing, but she had never heard about it simply because she was a girl.

She was never meant to fight. She was never supposed to be a warrior. They didn't tell girls stories to encourage them to work harder, be stronger, learn how to fight and defend, so that someday they could grow up to be a great warrior. The only reason she had learned a different way of being a girl was that the man who raised her happened to be from a completely different planet.

Maybe Denlerack would be a better place for me, she mused to herself. *Maybe women are allowed to be whatever they want there.*

"Well, it isn't a man; it's me. I am the one they call to, and it's annoying." KaLeah pushed past Hilip in a huff, angry at all men and the silly traditions of Naldash as she stormed off toward the throne room.

"All boys grow up knowing this, KaLeah," she mumbled to herself as she walked. She could hear the footfalls of the captain behind her. "Men hope to be the great warrior someday, KaLeah. Ridiculous. This is all so ridiculous."

She went up a narrow staircase, into the main hall, and stopped dead in front of a tapestry. She walked closer to look at the person riding the translucent-winged dragon.

"It *is* a woman," she said.

"What is a woman?" Hilip asked, coming up behind her.

"Look here," she said, pointing at the tapestry. "I thought it was a man with long hair but look at the breast plate. The warrior on the dragon's back is a woman. A woman warrior."

A smile curled along Hilip's face.

"You think it's funny?" KaLeah asked.

"It is fascinating. An entire culture, blinded." Then he spun to face her, intimately close, but she found herself more comfortable now in his presence.

"Do you know what they are telling you?" he asked.

"Sometimes they say 'fight' or 'kill'," KaLeah said, crinkling up her nose. "They help me know when danger is near, I think."

"Fascinating," he repeated. "Listen, this is a lot of information at once," he continued. "I think it would be in our best interest not to bring too many others into this until we, you and I, fully understand what's going on. Let's go to the princess now and tell her about the potential threat that Denlerack poses, but let's keep the fact that you are hearing dragon spirits to ourselves. I am… concerned it might create more danger for you." Hilip reached his hands out and held her arms, looking deeply into her eyes.

"Some men may be jealous and think that by destroying you, they can prove that you are not the great chosen warrior." His expression was serious, and his hands on her arms felt protective. She trusted him completely and could sense the truth in the words. She had known men to fight over women, gold, egos, and just to win. Chills climbed up her spine and raised the hairs on the back of her neck.

"Agreed," she said in a whisper.

"Good. Let's go see the princess. I'm afraid that she is scared to death with everything going on right now."

"Alright," KaLeah said, quickly composing herself.

They walked side by side through the corridors to the throne room. KaLeah was fearful walking into the room.

She had been kissed and then rejected by Nikolat at the further end of the ballroom, Prince Bylex had been killed here, and her and her father had been drug down to the dungeons from this room.

Princess Amirra looked like a tiny doll sitting on the enormous throne at the end of the room. Her frail body only took up a third of the chair, as she leaned her arm on one of the dragon-carved wooden armrests. Her shimmery blonde hair hung loose around her head.

She saw KaLeah approaching and screeched very unladylike in relief. She jumped down from the throne, lifted the edges of her long, silver dress, and ran to KaLeah.

"Thank the spirits, are you alright?" she asked, throwing her arms around KaLeah.

"My brother is dead," Amirra said, without waiting for KaLeah's response to her question. "They brought me here to sit on the throne and rule the kingdom until my father can return." Amirra's eyes were filled with tears, some streaming down her cheeks. "What should I do?" she whispered.

KaLeah took account of the room. Aside from Hilip, there were only a few other soldiers clustered near the throne. There were no royal family members left, but some men from favor families, some of which she recognized from previous gatherings, were beginning to appear at the entrance of the throne room.

They looked as if they wanted to make inquiries, but they didn't know who to ask. The men lingered and nervously chatted amongst themselves.

Hilip stood protectively over the two girls. KaLeah stood up a little straighter, ready to help guide the young girl.

"First, you must look as if you are the most confident person on the planet. Do not let on that you are afraid or unsure right now," KaLeah advised, leaning in close to wipe away the princess' tears with the sleeves of her own tunic.

"This must appear to be in accordance with the king's plans. You will stand up straight, walk with your nose up, look the captains and favors in the eyes when they ask you questions, and sit up straight and proud on that throne. This is your father's land, but it is also your land. Your father is on his way back here, and you do not need to make any decisions or answer any questions if you do not want to."

Hilip cleared his throat but spoke in a soft tone. "If anyone asks how your brother died, even though rumors are spreading, you must, for the sake of KaLeah's father's life, refer to the prince's death as an accident."

"Your father, that's right. I can't believe he is finally here," Amirra said. "Had he been searching for you, too?"

KaLeah's stomach turned at their mention of and concern for the man who wasn't her true father. She tried to hide her emotions. "Not quite. Some bad men kidnaped him."

"Extellans?" Amirra guessed.

"No." KaLeah furrowed her brow, not wanting to lie.

"Bandits?"

"No, Amirra, they were from Denlerack."

Amirra paused and then started laughing. "KaLeah, is something wrong with him? Denlerack is the dead planet. No one can be from Denlerack."

"Shhhhh, please." KaLeah looked at the soldiers and men, making sure they were all keeping their distance. "My father is from Denlerack," KaLeah said, slowly, seriously.

The word father now sounded strange on her lips, as if it were a lie. But she didn't feel like this was the time to discuss her entire situation. Clegg Trapper's life may be more likely to be spared if he were thought to be the father of a favor. Besides, the first story Amirra needed to know and believe was the craziest one of all.

"Apparently, people have been living on that planet, just as they live here, but they are advanced enough to actually travel here through space. Clegg, my father, flew here with my mother on a spaceship, through the sky, and landed here. Men from Denlerack came to scout out our planet, found, and captured him. Amirra, they want to invade our planet."

The smile slowly left Amirra's lips and she furrowed her brow. She turned and slowly walked toward the throne room's entrance. She walked past the men who all stopped talking and bowed to her. KaLeah and Hilip followed her, passing silent glances between each other as they walked.

Amirra walked outside, out into the courtyard, and stopped, staring up at the large orb that she and every child on Naldash had grown up beneath. KaLeah walked up beside her.

The sun lit the face of Denlerack in the sky, making it the same color as Amirra's silver blonde hair.

"I always wondered," Amirra whispered to no one. Then louder, "Who will believe us?"

"I assume that no one will believe us," KaLeah admitted. "But there is a kingdom up there. They have scouts on this planet right now who have somehow created discord among the kingdoms in order to make us vulnerable."

"Lisodanya," Hilip said from behind the girls.

He stepped forward and KaLeah followed his line of sight out past the open fields beyond the edge of the kingdom. At least 100 men were approaching with the blue, green, and white Lisodanyan colors flying just barely above the horizon.

"Bylex has not even been dead a full day. How could they have received word so fast?" Hilip said, more to himself than to the girls.

"What do you mean, captain?" Amirra asked.

"Weakness, princess. They are here because our king is gone, our prince is dead, and they know we are weak. With your orders, I will bring the foot and field soldiers that remain to stand guard at the castle. We do not have enough time or resources to protect the entire center. I will have my men send word to the villagers to protect their abodes or come to the castle for our protection."

Amirra's eyes widened with anxiety. She recovered quickly and narrowed her eyes, then raised her chin.

"How do I give the orders?"

Hilip smiled slightly.

"You just did. Excuse me, ladies."

He gave a slight bow and then took off in a run back into the throne room to alert the soldiers. KaLeah overheard him tell the men at the entrance to gather all the field soldiers they could and bring their families to the castle.

Then all the men scurried away, no longer concerned with the princess and her bodyguard.

"Come, my lady, let's get back into the safety of the castle," KaLeah said, reaching out for the young girl caught up in a strange and frightening predicament.

"Yes, we must return to the throne room," she said, taking KaLeah's arm in hers. "I must sit on the throne and look as if there is nothing the matter, right?"

"I believe so, princess. I am no expert at these things, at royalty, but when a threat approaches, you do not run away in fear. You stand your ground. You greet the threat on your lands and on your terms."

Amirra nodded her head, her blonde hair flowing as they walked back into the castle throne room.

"I see the truth of it," she said softly.

KaLeah escorted her up onto the dais and waited until

she was seated on the gigantic throne before moving to stand beside her to wait for the Lisodanyan men.

While they waited, KaLeah's mind started to wonder. If the people on Denlerack had many more weapons and were intent on invading, what would the people of Naldash do?

Would Belarone soldiers be able to fight off these flying explosions, or whatever had come from that gun that killed Bylex so quickly and easily? She had only seen the ones in her cellar and the one in the throne room, but she saw no way of defending against them with swords.

When the king returned, there would be no way of explaining the situation to him. He would surely accuse her father, Clegg, of intentionally killing his eldest son and heir.

KaLeah's skin was suddenly covered with bumps, and her stomach was queasy. She realized, at that moment, both her and Clegg's lives were in danger. Everyone had seen the weapon. Nobody knew what it was. And a member of the royal family was dead.

Someone would have to pay.

She closed her eyes and took a deep breath.

I have to get Clegg out of here, she said to herself, realizing the weight of the responsibility to save the man who raised her fell onto her.

Opening her eyes, she set her resolve. KaLeah would break her father out while the soldiers were preoccupied with the Lisodanyan visitors. She would see Amirra safely to bed, then use the secret passageways to free Clegg. They would head off into the woods and back to Erion.

With their limited resources, the war, Lisodanya, and the mysterious threat from Denlerack, she hoped that no one would come after them.

Her and Clegg would gather what they needed in Erion and head off deeper into the protection of the woods and the mountains.

The princess sighed beside her, and she got a small knot in her chest. She did not feel good about leaving Amirra behind, but she also didn't want to stay and risk her, and Clegg's lives.

The young girl was beginning to feel like a little sister and friend, and KaLeah knew how leaving would upset her. She knew the princess would beg her to stay, or worse, sound the alarm for Hilip to prevent her from leaving.

Captain Daven, she thought to herself, and a new warmth filled her body. He was kind to her, and good, and she would miss him. That thought surprised her, as did the small smile that formed involuntarily at the thought of him.

Before she knew it, he was marching back into the throne room with a hand full of guards.

"Princess Amirra, Favor KaLeah," Hilip said, bowing slightly to them. "We believe that the Lisodanyan camp is only the first of many. They must have started coming into our lands after the bulk of the army left for Extelli with the king. With our limited remaining resources, they were able to evade our scouts."

"What are they doing here?" Amirra asked.

"News of your brother's death has spread quickly, Your Highness. I believe they have come under the guise of sympathy in order to trick you, or manipulate you in some way, since your father and brothers are not here."

Amirra sat up a little straighter.

"Do you think they can trick me?" she asked.

"Your Highness, you have never faced this situation before," he said, looking her in the eye. "Many leaders face new situations every single day with no prior experience on the matter, no advice, no guidance, or direction. Many follow their instincts and listen to more than is spoken. Sometimes good decisions are made and sometimes bad ones. The man is still a leader."

"But I am no man," Amirra said, not with disappointment, but with the blunt honesty of a child.

"No, princess," he said. "But you are more important than any of the men who will come before you today. You are the most important leader in all of Belarone Kingdom today. And because you are our leader, I believe that you know how to keep from being tricked."

KaLeah's heart fluttered at his words. She wondered who this man was, truly. Neither KaLeah nor Amirra had to do anything to earn this man's respect and trust. He bestowed it upon them, and she was beginning to feel as if he had been her friend all along, and not just a captain ordered to keep her from running off.

Hilip took a deep bow, rose, and motioned to the doorway. "On the princess' command, the Lisodanyan messengers may enter."

Princess Amirra waved her hand.

"Your Highness," Hilip said, loudly. "May I present General Atcher, Captain Kinhati, Captain Wikin, and Captain Vig of the Lisodanyan Kingdom."

General Atcher entered the room first, followed by three other men. They all wore similar uniforms, only just visible under their layers of breast, thigh, shoulder, and arm shields. They walked loudly, unable to quiet the clanking armor.

General Atcher had long, untamed blond hair streaming well past his shoulders. His face was chiseled perfection with a scar running along the left side of his jaw, only seeming to add to his appeal.

Two of the captains were dark skinned with dark hair, and the last had lighter skin with thin, light brown hair. They all had lines on their faces from wearing their helmets for a substantial amount of time.

General Atcher approached the throne, his men stopped about halfway between the door and the throne, but he kept walking until he was directly in front of the raised dais.

He looked the princess and KaLeah over from head to toe, assessing his foe, KaLeah assumed. He smiled and bowed.

"Lovely, Princess Amirra, what an honor it is to stand before you," he said. His voice was gravelly but authoritative.

"I am General Atcher of his Majesty Mikroth's royal army."

"You are welcome here, general," said the princess.

"Most gracious, Your Highness. We are deeply troubled to hear of your brother's violent death. We hope that the murderer has already been punished, and we sympathize with the grief that you must be feeling. And here, alone, with no other brother, and no father to care for you in this time of mourning, I would like to offer my condolences and the services of me and my men, should you require it."

"I am quite fine with my own soldiers, thank you," she said.

KaLeah grinned, pleased with the princess' dismissive response.

"But thank you for your condolences. Why else are you here?" Amirra pressed.

KaLeah could tell that the princess had asked the question out of sheer curiosity, not to be rude, and she was very curious herself. She doubted very much that they would receive an honest response.

"I understand that you are in great emotional pain, the loss of the royal heir to the throne is indeed tragic. Yours is a long and glorious legacy of honorable men and strong kings. It is a shame to see it end."

"It hasn't ended," Amirra said. "My father and brother Nikolat are still alive and fighting in Extelli."

"Of course, princess," the general said. "However, Extelli is resisting, and your father is beyond his warring years. It is doubtful that either of them will survive. Many of your men have been lost already and the kingdoms are suffering. King Mikroth Lisodanya believes that now is the time to step in and help facilitate peace between all the kingdoms of Naldash. I am here to arrange that peace, dear princess."

KaLeah could feel the tension rise in the room like an

electrical charge. Her hand went to her sword, as if preparing for an attack, although she knew this would not be a physical assault—not yet.

A rumbling began in the back of her head, and she knew it for what it was now. She could picture the green-scaled and translucent-winged creature in her mind from that day in the woods. It was there, warning her. Something was coming.

"Peace is a wonderful thing, general," Amirra said. She sat up straighter and closer to the edge of the throne. "My father and brother are alive. Some of my army is here and some are in Extelli. Once we defeat Extelli, most will return. I am glad that you want peace, general, because right now, there is ample peace between us, and I would hate to think you want to change that."

"Of course not, sweet princess," he said, bowing again, possibly to buy himself time. "However, if some tragedies were to befall your father and brother, we are here and ready to assist you. We would ensure your safety at all costs and will step in to ensure that Extelli will not take Belarone. King Mikroth will take it under his control smoothly and with no bloodshed. You would have our protection in his name."

"You'll take my kingdom under his control?" she asked, pointedly.

The general smiled, not unkindly, but with the confidence of a man who feels he has already won a battle.

"It would be your best, and safest option, my dear. If we do not take control, then King Sarzoe Extelli will. Under his rule, you may not fare as well. King Mikroth will protect you as if you were one of his own daughters."

KaLeah suddenly remembered that Mikroth had daughters and no sons. The kingdoms may have been united by marriage eventually, but not if both princes perished. Mikroth was trying to play various angles to ensure his eventual control of Belarone Kingdom.

"How kind of him," Amirra said. "I must consult with

my captain. Since our kingdoms are allies and you are only here to ensure my protection, I will not force you to leave our lands. You may go."

The general smiled even wider and then bowed a final time. As he and his men left the throne room, KaLeah smirked to herself, realizing how frustrated the general must be not having the child princess immediately hand over her father's kingdom. He probably expected an easy victory, but his sly smile had hidden his disappointment.

"You did very well, Princess Amirra," KaLeah said.

The princess sighed heavily and slumped back into the throne chair the moment all the men had left the room.

"You bought us time to figure out what to do." KaLeah wanted the girl to feel some victory in this dire situation.

"He wants to take the kingdom from us, right?" Amirra asked.

"Yes, he does," KaLeah responded. "They are out there waiting for an opportunity to strike. He wanted you to know that if you surrender, nobody else will die."

KaLeah thought of Captain Daven and the others fighting the Lisodanyan army on the castle grounds, while KaLeah kept Amirra safe and hidden inside. She hoped that it wouldn't come to that. She asked the dragon spirits to keep King Belarone and Nikolat alive.

"I'm hungry. Can we go to dinner now?" she asked in a tiny voice.

KaLeah smiled.

"Yes, let's go to the dining hall. You have fought enough battles for one day."

∾

After dinner, Hilip escorted KaLeah and Amirra back to their rooms. They had no more news from their own men and the Lisodanyans had returned to their camp without issue.

The captain was quieter than usual, and she could tell

that he was putting plans and contingencies in place for many eventual scenarios.

Though the number of Lisodanyans in Belarone was far less than the number of Belarone soldiers, it would not take much for Mikroth to send his full army. Would Princess Amirra hold Lisodanya off, or would she surrender?

KaLeah wasn't sure she could give the princess advice, even if she asked for it. If it were up to KaLeah, she would give up the kingdom in a moment just for the chance at freedom.

This isn't my fight or my decision, she told herself. Her next mission was to get herself and Clegg out of Belarone and back to Erion.

Once Princess Amirra was safely tucked into bed with guards on her door, KaLeah slipped through the passageways to get supplies from the kitchens.

She had her sword and had snatched an extra one from the armory for her father.

Clegg, she reminded herself. She was torn between her desire for Clegg to approve of her and love her as a father, and the knowledge that he had never actually been her father. It was too much to consider now, she thought.

At the very least, she owed him his life for raising a child that wasn't his. He trained her to fight in a culture where women were only supposed to be wives and mothers. He had never pressured her to just find a nice boy to settle down with. For all that, she knew that she owed him.

She hoped with their resources limited, and the threat from Lisodanya, the bulk of the soldiers and guards would be spread about the exterior of the castle, focused on keeping enemies from coming into the castle. She hoped they would be less concerned with people leaving.

She reached the dungeon and as she had expected there were no guards in sight. She found Clegg sitting on the ground, leaning against the stone wall of his cell.

"Are you ready to leave?" she asked, grabbing the key from the spot where it hung on the wall.

"Glad to see you," Clegg said, standing up. "Everyone seems to have left for more pressing matters. Are we clear from here to the forest, or will we need to make a plan of escape?"

KaLeah unlocked the cell.

"I have a plan. Put this on, it's a Belarone soldier's uniform. Lisodanya is on the verge of attacking the kingdom, so everyone will be preoccupied with that threat, giving us a chance of escape."

Clegg put the uniform on quickly, and then they marched through the hallways, up various sets of stairs, and toward a side entrance.

"Look straight ahead and don't say a word," she ordered. It felt strange, ordering around this man who raised her.

Who is he, she wondered? He had kept so much from her and now that she knew he wasn't her real father; everything made more sense.

He had never been warm, never supportive. He did not hug her, compliment her on anything except for successfully completing a task, and never told her he loved her. She always dismissed it as just the way he was.

He was stoic, strong, silent, proud, and had lost the woman he admired. But he had not really loved her mother either. If anything, he must have been angry at having to raise her child after she passed.

It was true that he had raised KaLeah, and she was grateful to him, but what did she realistically owe him in return? She wanted him to be proud of her, but she didn't know any more if she actually loved him.

She had felt left behind, abandoned, and had tried to find him because he was all she knew. He trained her to survive and to think for herself. Was he paramount to her survival now? The independence he helped build within her told her she no longer needed him to survive. He completed his duty in raising her.

She thought about what going back to Erion and then

up to the mountains to hide with him would look like. They would hunt and cook, as they always had, but neither one of them needed the other now.

Her life had completely changed, and after she saved his life tonight, they owed each other nothing.

"Halt, who goes there?" asked the guard at one of the side exits.

"Favor KaLeah," she responded with strength and pride at the words. "Captain Daven has sent me and this soldier to the stables on a secret mission for the princess."

The guard narrowed his eyes, looking her and Clegg over. Clegg kept his face concealed in the shadows.

"You may pass," said the guard, casting his eyes back out to watch the grounds.

She moved confidently past him and walked with Clegg behind her with a steady pace toward the stables. Once in the stables, she went to a stall to ready a black draggot for Clegg. Once ready, she moved to the stall with Maze. The tall, golden brown draggot excitedly kicked the ground and nodded in recognition of KaLeah.

"Hey girl," she said gently.

"We used to have draggots like these on Denlerack, but they went extinct. It is amazing to see them still thriving on Naldash." Clegg ran his hand down the long, scaly neck of the draggot that would carry him back to Erion.

Back to Erion, KaLeah said to herself, feeling a sense of relief.

So much had changed. The princess depended on her, although it made her a servant with no life of her own.

What kind of a life would she have hiding in the mountains? What if Denlerack really does invade Naldash? What if Lisodanya attacks tomorrow and takes the throne?

The low growls and whispers started again in the back of her mind. She felt a heavy weight on her, as if something was pushing her feet into the ground. Maze shook her head back and forth fiercely and backed away.

"What's going on?" Clegg asked.

"The dragon spirits want me to stay." KaLeah could feel the truth of it even before she heard the words pushed into her mind.

Stay. Fight.

Clegg Trapper nodded, then mounted his draggot.

"You have a higher calling, KaLeah," he said. "My calling, my work, is done. There is more for you to do here."

"But there is still so much I don't know about Denlerack, about my mother, and about the dragon spirits." KaLeah shook her head and clenched her fists in frustration.

"There is no time, now," Clegg said. "But you are the one they chose. They will not let you fail. Farewell."

She watched him turn and drive his draggot out into the night. She felt as if a hole had opened up in her chest.

The one thing she had wanted back was leaving her again. Alone.

She wanted her life back. She wanted the small, warm hut in the village. She wanted to hunt the woods.

She pictured herself sitting quietly, obediently, in front of the fireplace cleaning a kill while Clegg sat nearby. There had been so many silent nights, so many opportunities for him to tell her the truth.

KaLeah realized that she could have made so many different decisions, had she only known the truth. She turned toward Maze, looking the beautiful and powerful beast in the eye. She shook her head.

"No," she told the draggot. "I don't want to go back to Erion. I'll never go back."

13 QUEEN

The Extellan castle was carved into sea cliffs. It was cold and the stone was black and tended to sweat and grow mold.

The throne chair was constructed of the same cliffside stone. To ward off the cold, it was draped with layers of thick fur, making it more comfortable and warmer. Prince Nikolat felt pampered and rugged at the same time while sitting upon it.

His father had bestowed the Extellan Kingdom, the crown that had belonged to the now dead King Sarzoe, and part of the army upon him.

"You'll rule Extelli only as an extension of the Belarone Kingdom," his father had told him before heading back to Belarone. "Do not think this makes you king of this land, son. Though you will face many challenges bringing the people here around to our control and leadership, you may be rewarded with sovereignty of this land once your brother is on the Belarone throne. I will be watching what you do here very closely."

The words had angered Nikolat, but he'd bitten back his anger and bowed to his father. Once gone, there was nothing to stop Nik from ruling this land as his own kingdom, regardless of names or titles.

He *was* a king.

His father had returned for Belarone two days prior, and now a messenger had come from the soldiers who had been leading him home.

The messenger was thin, tall, with extraordinarily long legs, making him impressively fast. His profession as a messenger was well chosen. The man's head was bowed slightly while he conveyed his message, as if to give Nikolat some semblance of privacy to hide an emotional response.

"Your Majesty," he started. "I bring news from Belarone Kingdom."

"Out with it," Nik snapped.

"On the road, we received word that your brother, Prince Bylex, had been killed in the throne room by a mysterious weapon. The king was distraught and took off with a small squadron, not waiting for the entire legion. When we caught up to them, they had been attacked and killed on the road. We do not know if it was Lisodanya or Extelli."

"Wait," Nikolat sat up straight and looked the messenger in the eye. He wanted to make sure this wasn't some kind of trap.

"My brother and my father are dead? Both of them? Dead?"

"Yes, Your Majesty." The man didn't make eye contact but nodded vigorously.

"And my sister?"

"She sits on the throne in Belarone, surrounded by Lisodanyan army camps."

"You may go," Nikolat ordered, leaning back into the furs of the throne chair.

"Yes, Your Majesty." The man ran from the room.

His father was dead. His brother, the next in line for

the Belarone throne, was dead.

"How do you like that?" he said to the empty room.

He stood up and yelled, his voice echoing off the cavernous walls. "How do you like that, father? The youngest son is the only one left standing. Your useless heir will now rule Belarone and Extelli! Maybe you should have spent a little more time on this contingency plan," he said, pounding his chest.

"Now what, King Nikolat?" he quietly asked himself. He sat back on the throne and slouched into a more comfortable position. Nik had a lot of planning to do now.

His father was gone. Even when planning to have Bylex killed, he'd never wanted any harm to come to his father. Even if his father had lived forever, he would have rather his father given Nikolat rule of the kingdom than take it from the old man by force.

Sure, Erazus had spent more time with Bylex, but he was still a great man. He was a respectable man, Nikolat thought fondly.

He took a deep breath and looked around him. The throne room was less than half the size of the Belarone throne room. It was dark, and though he wasn't necessarily opposed to the melancholic atmosphere, he much rather preferred the idea of being in Belarone.

He had a couple options. He could stay in Extelli, fight the people who would oppose his rule, and try to turn the rock into an orchard, or he could take his men and return home.

There would be re-stabilization to be done in Belarone, but at least they already had orchards.

He stood up from the throne and stretched, feeling the cold stone permeate his boots from the floor.

Yes, he thought, *I can leave this place behind.*

He headed out to find General Array, who had stayed behind with a captain and some men, and he gave the orders to pack up and leave this land to the thieves. The land would fall to anarchy, but at least it would no longer be a threat. King Sarzoe had no heir, and most of his men had fled.

Nikolat would go claim his birthright, then send men back to rule Extelli in his name and under his command. With each step, he grew more and more excited to return to his kingdom.

❧KaLeah❧

"The Lisodanyan camps are growing, Princess Amirra," Captain Daven said.

Many days had passed since Amirra had first spoken to the Lisodanyan General. No one had noticed that Clegg Trapper had escaped, since everyone had been more preoccupied with the Lisodanyan presence.

They were in the throne room that morning after breakfast. Princess Amirra sat on the throne, KaLeah stood beside her, and Captain Daven provided his update from below the dais.

"Our armies are less than a day out, but some remained in Extelli to help your brother transition to leadership there. Once they have returned, we will still not be at full strength. We are recruiting and training more soldiers from the closest villages."

"My father will be home soon, and he can deal with the Lisodanyan General," Amirra said, looking relieved. Hilip shifted on his feet and looked away toward the windows. KaLeah knew something was wrong.

"Unfortunately, Your Highness, we just received word that your father will *not* be returning to Belarone Kingdom. He received word of Prince Bylex's death, then took off from the rest of the legion, with only a small troop to protect him. They were attacked on the road back, and everyone, including the king, was killed. I am sorry to be the one to bring you this news." He did look genuinely sorry, hanging his head and bowing before her.

Amirra stood up suddenly. "No," she whispered.

She looked at Hilip then to KaLeah, who had put her hand over her mouth in shock.

"No!" Amirra's knees buckled beneath her, and KaLeah moved quickly to catch the small girl in her arms.

Captain Daven immediately ordered the guards, soldiers, and servants away. Princess Amirra's cries reverberated throughout the grand room, and he gave the girls a gentle look before closing the doors behind him.

KaLeah led the princess back to her room, tucked her into bed and watched her cry herself to sleep.

Her mind whirled in confusion and loss. She wanted to empathize with Amirra over the loss of her father, trying to connect it to her own loss of discovering that the man who raised her wasn't her father.

She knew the king loved Amirra, and for that she felt a small bit of jealousy. But she hadn't seen him dote on her much and wondered at her pain. Would KaLeah feel the same pain if she lost the man who raised her?

KaLeah shook away the thoughts.

More importantly, what would they do now? A king and a prince dead, a prince alive in a distant kingdom, Lisodanya on their fields, and a princess on the throne.

It was all overwhelming, all too much, and for a moment, she wished she had gone with Clegg back to the mountains beyond Erion.

Oh, what peace she could have found there. But then who would have been here to catch the princess, to hold her when she cried, and to tuck her safely into her warm bed?

Maybe this is where I'm supposed to be right now, she told herself.

She stood up and went out into the hallway, nodding at the guards at the princess' door. She was grateful that at least she didn't have to stay by Amirra's side while the guards were there.

KaLeah wanted to speak to Hilip, but she needed to track him down first.

She heard men yelling and followed the voices to the

war room. Not pausing to knock, she walked into the room.

Men were standing over a long table covered in maps. They stopped talking and looked at her.

"Favor KaLeah," Captain Daven said in greeting.

"Captain, is there a plan?"

The men in the room turned their eyes to Hilip, confusion evident on their faces as to why a girl was in the room and a part of this conversation at all.

Hilip didn't appear to be fazed by their expressions.

"We have a few, depending on what we are faced with," he responded. "Right now, we are determining the best routes of escape for the princess, should the castle be taken by Lisodanya. You would, of course, be in the company of the princess during such an escape."

That seemed to put the rest of the men at ease, as if they realized, of course, she could be part of the plan since she would be protecting the princess throughout the course of an escape.

KaLeah held back the urge to roll her eyes at the men.

"Have you heard word from Prince Nikolat and General Array?" she asked.

Again, the eyes in the room darted around nervously.

"Yes, Favor KaLeah, we have. Prince Nikolat is coming back to claim the throne. The escape plan would only be put into action if he is killed in route or attacked by Lisodanya once he arrives."

KaLeah furrowed her brow in confusion. "But he just won Extelli, at the cost of lives, including his father's life. He is just going to abandon that kingdom? Who will rule over Extelli then?"

"We do not know," Hilip replied. "Some men will remain behind to try and hold it in the name of Belarone, but those men may not live very long if there is a rebellion, or if some distant relative of the dead King Sarzoe stands up to claim the throne. The decision is not ours, but Prince Nikolat's at this point. We must wait for his direction."

"But King Erazus left specific instructions for Prince

Nikolat to rule Extelli, and Bylex to rule Belarone." KaLeah placed her palms on the table. "With both the king and Prince Bylex dead, it seems to me that the next in line for Belarone Kingdom is Princess Amirra."

Then men gasped and took steps back from the table as if she'd flung fire at them.

"A princess has never ruled a kingdom," Hilip said. He was the only man who hadn't stepped back in shock at the idea. His words weren't meant to be insulting or derogatory, just a fact.

KaLeah scoffed. "If we only did things that were done before, then men never would have walked upright or ruled anything. Swords never would have been wielded. Castles never would have been built. There is a first for everything. I am a perfect example of that fact."

KaLeah turned on her heel and went back to Amirra's room. She was ready to support the princess now more than ever and was prepared to advise her.

This was no longer about survival. KaLeah knew she was the only person on the planet who could turn Amirra into what she was really meant to be... a queen.

෧෮෧

When Amirra awoke an hour later, rested but emotionally wary, KaLeah was there with a hot cup of peppermint tea and a plan.

"Who do you want to be when you grow up, Princess Amirra?"

The princess held the cup of tea, warming her hands, and took a slow sip. Her eyes were red and puffy, tissues were wadded up beside her, and streaks of dried tears lined her cheeks.

"You can run off into the woods and hide. You can let your brother become king and send you off to marry a stranger in the village. Or you can stand up proudly and take the throne for yourself as queen."

"I can't do that," Amirra whispered, not looking up from her tea.

"You can't be queen? Why not?"

"My father had two sons. One of them will be king. One of them was always meant to be king."

"What if Nikolat is killed?" KaLeah asked.

The words caught in her throat. She still missed him and the thought of him sent mixed feelings throughout her mind and body. She shook the feelings away, telling herself that she only missed the idea of him.

"Then I will *have* to be queen, but they will make me marry a man in the village first, someone from a favor family. He will be the new king."

"Who will force you to marry a man from a favor family?"

"My fa-oh." Princess Amirra had almost said her father. She lowered her head a little more toward her teacup. Fresh tears began rolling down her face.

"I suppose the generals would," Amirra said. "The men in the favor families. They will all want me to marry, so that my husband can lead the kingdom."

"If there were no men, no generals, no one to tell you what to do, what decision would you make for yourself?" KaLeah leaned in closer and pushed the teacup down, so that Amirra had to look up and meet her eyes.

"Nikolat is still alive," Amirra said in a higher pitch, looking as if she were being pushed into a corner.

"Yes, but if you were the only one giving orders, what would you allow yourself to be?"

There was an uncomfortably long silence.

"My mother was a very beautiful, brilliant woman," Amirra said, seemingly changing the subject. "The nurses told me stories of how defiant and proud she was. They told me that I look like her with my inquisitive eyes and light hair. They told me that she was a strong queen and that people listened to her. I want to be like her."

KaLeah smiled proudly. She knew that this was a hard

day for the small princess. She knew that the princess had experienced many hard days and that many more were waiting in front of her, especially if she made this decision.

But KaLeah believed that this girl could do the hard things and get through the tough days.

"Then be like her, Princess Amirra. Be the Queen of Belarone."

க்ஷ

An hour later, the nurses had bathed the princess and helped her into the finest dress from their collection. She looked like a bride in a heavily adorned white gown, with long, flowing sleeves that matched her long, light blonde hair.

She had a small amount of powder on her face, and a soft glossy sheen on her lips. She looked more regal than KaLeah had ever seen her look before.

KaLeah dressed up her tunic with a wuvat scaled vest, black pants, and laced up boots. She strapped on her sword and hid her dagger in her boots, knowing that she must be fully on-guard going forward. Anything could happen at this point.

The guards escorted the princess and her bodyguard to the throne room, where Amirra climbed up on the throne and summoned Captain Daven.

When he entered the room, he paused as if he could feel the change in the air before approaching and bowing to Amirra.

"Princess Amirra," he began. "I have some good news on this day of mourning. "Your brother, Prince Nikolat, is returning from Extelli to claim the throne. Lisodanya will surely back down their threats and leave the lands. You no longer need to worry about fleeing."

"I was never going to flee, Captain Daven," Amirra said strongly. "This is not a day of mourning. This is a day of celebration because I am committing my life to my kingdom. I will not leave this throne for my brother or for a husband. I will be the Queen of Belarone."

Hilip was silent and looked between Amirra and KaLeah, as if waiting for someone to smile or laugh. "Your Majesty, with all due respect, Prince Nikolat is coming to claim the throne for himself."

"Well, he cannot have it," Amirra said. "My father gave him Extelli Kingdom to rule. It is his sworn duty to continue ruling that kingdom. This one is mine."

Again, Hilip said nothing, clearly trying to piece everything together. "What is your plan if the prince attempts to claim this throne—to claim Belarone Kingdom as his?"

"We shall address the Belarone people," she answered, simply. "Send word that both myself and Nikolat will address the people from the forebuilding balcony in the keep at sunset. We will lay forth the decisions that my father made, and the reasons each of us wish to rule Belarone. Then we shall let the people decide."

"Princess, that has never been done before," the young captain squinted his eyes, looking stressed. "If Nikolat returns with General Array and an army, there is not much we can do to stop him from taking the throne."

Princess Amirra shifted her small body in the oversized chair. KaLeah had never seen her look more defiant. "The soldiers who support Prince Nikolat's claim may return with him to Extelli, including General Array. You will be my new general. If they support Nik, then they wage war against me, their princess, and the rightful heir."

"Princess," Hilip sighed, concern creasing his forehead. "There has never been a ruling queen. The people will not choose a woman, a girl, over a young man to rule Belarone. I am afraid of what might happen to you. I'm afraid for your safety should your brother turn against you in anger after the people choose him."

"Then I must ensure that they choose me, dear general." She smiled warmly, and KaLeah sensed a new calm confidence emanating from the young girl.

"Now go, send word to my people to gather below the balcony this evening to honor their new queen."

❦

KaLeah watched the fields beyond the castle from Queen Amirra's room. It took time for Nikolat and the men to make it to the castle. They set up camp just outside, putting their legion back together and on display for the Lisodanyan army to see.

KaLeah was surprised the Lisodanyan troops were still there, farther out, but camped as if they had no plans to leave.

She assumed they had heard word of Amirra's claim and were staying to step in to take Belarone themselves if the two siblings destroyed one another.

Belarone civilians from the city and farms were also beginning to gather outside the castle walls. Guards at the gates were letting small clusters in at a time, verifying their identities first.

Nikolat stayed out among his men and sent no word to either KaLeah or Amirra. KaLeah's nerves were on edge, and her stomach muscles were so tight that she hadn't been able to eat anything all afternoon.

She had expected Nik to storm through the gates and head for the throne as soon as he had arrived, but that hadn't happened, and the anticipation was driving her crazy.

Her mind kept playing out possible scenarios, trying to be prepared to protect the princess in each one.

KaLeah assumed that the kingdom would overwhelmingly prefer Nikolat to be the leader. Having a king was all they had ever known.

The princess was young and looked too beautiful and physically weak to fulfill their historic vision of a leader. KaLeah had little hope that the people would see the strength in her that KaLeah saw.

The young princess was feisty, independent, with real

love in her heart. She could grow into a powerful woman. With KaLeah's guidance, she could become an unshakeable leader.

But for now, the people would only see a pretty, little girl standing up against a regal prince.

Once they chose Nikolat, she envisioned herself taking the princess back to her room and keeping her under guard until she was given to some favor to marry.

Perhaps, if Nikolat were to die… no, she shook her head, *I cannot think of that. We have one chance for Amirra to sway her people to her, and if that fails, that's it. We live out the plan that King Erazus set out for us.*

Maybe someday, when the princess is married, KaLeah can slip out into the night and disappear into the woods forever. KaLeah would still have her escape plan and take the chance to live her life on her own—eventually.

Or what if Nikolat wanted to keep KaLeah for himself, marry her and make *her* the queen? She tried to imagine that plan, but for some reason, she saw Hilip's face instead of Nik's.

She sighed and dismissed the thought of either man.

"No, this is my place, beside my princess, my friend, my sister. This isn't about me anymore."

She and the princess ate an early, small dinner in the princess' chambers. The sun was at its lowest point in the sky, Denlerack was covered in shadow but looming as a constant reminder to KaLeah that something bigger than all of them existed just out of reach.

"Are you ready, Queen Amirra?"

"Yes."

The guards at her door escorted them to the front of the castle and out through two glass doors onto an expansive balcony. Princess Amirra walked to the edge; her white dress looked golden in the light of the setting sun, and she raised her hands to cheers from the people gathered below.

KaLeah was amazed by the size of the crowd, the

curious onlookers who came ready to choose a future leader.

She did not know what Amirra could say that would possibly sway all these people away from tradition, away from what they had always known. This had always been a kingdom ruled by men.

She had never heard much about the time when there was a queen, even one married to the king. The king had always ruled, even with a wife at his side.

KaLeah's own presence as a warrior and a bodyguard was odd and unwelcome, but at this point, neither one of the girls had anything left to lose.

KaLeah followed the princess onto the balcony and saw General Hilip Daven first, standing straight and proud in his stark white uniform. She went to stand beside him.

On the opposite side stood Prince Nikolat and General Array, the black man's muscles bulging in his sleeveless tunic. He was the most foreboding and intimidating person on the balcony. He had always been kind to her, but something had shifted. He seemed to be on alert.

Everyone was dressed in their finest, but KaLeah wanted to look like a warrior today, a fighter, not a handmaiden. She wore wrist guards, black boots, and had her sword at her side.

Amirra took a step back from the balcony's edge to address Nikolat. "It is good to see you safe, brother," she said.

"You as well," Nikolat replied. "It seems that the stress of the past few weeks has aged you almost beyond recognition. I understand that you were the one wanting to address our people."

"Yes, however, since you have returned, perhaps you should speak to our people first," she offered.

"It would be my pleasure," Prince Nikolat said, accepting the challenge.

He was not dressed as impressively as she was, but he still looked regal in a dark blue robe over light gray pants.

KaLeah couldn't see a sword, but assumed he was armed beneath the robe.

Nikolat walked out to the edge of the balcony to raucous applause. He raised his arms to silence everyone and then spoke loud and slowly.

KaLeah stepped into the background. She couldn't see the people below him, but the planet of Denlerack was dark in the sky beyond, reminding her again of the danger lurking there.

"People of Belarone Kingdom, I know that everyone must be feeling as sad as I to learn that we have lost King Erazus Belarone and my dear brother, Prince Bylex. But upon this dark hour of mourning, I bring news that Kingdom Extelli no longer poses a threat."

The crowd erupted at that news, and Nikolat waited for the noise to die down before continuing.

"As such, I am poised to take the throne of Belarone Kingdom." Again, he had to pause for cheers.

"I ask that you let the representatives from Lisodanya in our midst leave in peace, returning to their land. I am sure they arrived here only out of concern for the people."

The crowd did not cheer, knowing full well the threat Lisodanya had come to impose upon them.

"My sister, Princess Amirra Belarone, also wishes to address you all. She has faced many challenges since the death of our father and has borne them well. I appreciate her dedication and support of this kingdom. Princess Amirra, would you like to speak?"

Amirra stepped forward, and Nikolat stood aside, slinking closer to KaLeah.

She felt awkward with Nikolat on one side and Hilip on the other. The two did not acknowledge one another as they may have done in the past.

She wondered where Hilip's allegiances were. Would he protect the princess' claim to the throne? Or would he bow to Nikolat?

Princess Amirra looked out over the faces of the

people, her white dress, and blonde hair moving only slightly in a light breeze. She looked them over slowly, as if making eye-contact with each person in the crowd.

The world was silent.

"Dearest friends, only just a few days ago I was asked to surrender the kingdom to Lisodanya."

A collective gasp rose from the crowd. She paused to let the sound die back down.

"My father and brother had been murdered, Prince Nikolat was in another kingdom with over half our legion, and his plans to return to us were as yet unknown. You may look upon me and see a child, a girl, and yet I have protected this kingdom. I did not flee when Lisodanya came, and I did not turn over my kingdom, or my people, to them."

Amirra began increasing the volume and intensity in her voice.

"Prince Nikolat has taken and will lead the people of Extelli. It was my father's order that Prince Nikolat rule Extelli. I will not turn over my kingdom or my people to him if *you* do not wish it. I am as strong in heart, mind, and soul as any man. My brother will tell you that it is his birthright to rule Belarone, but it is my right to make sure that you are completely protected and that my father's wishes are honored."

KaLeah could feel tension building around her on the large balcony, as if the space were getting smaller.

"Stop this," Prince Nikolat said sternly, stepping forward. "What are you doing, sister?" he asked.

"You said that I may speak," Amirra stated. "I am the one who wished to address the people, to let them have a voice. Let me have mine."

A slow murmur began to build. The people were mumbling together, raising their voices together, saying let her speak.

Nikolat pushed aside his robe and put his hand on his sword, his knuckles turning white there.

Separate voices, the voices of dragon spirits long dead,

began speaking in KaLeah's mind, chanting out in unison with the human voices to let her speak.

"People of Belarone," Nikolat said, raising his voice. "Our father, your king, declared his heir to be king. I am the heir, the next in line, and it is my birthright. The Belarone people have no right to choose their leader. I am not here to defend my right to the throne. I am here to take it."

Suddenly, a sword appeared at Nikolat's throat. KaLeah was shocked to see that it was her own. She had reacted without thinking, worried for Amirra's safety. Before she knew it, General Array's sword was in line with her heart and General Daven had pulled his own on General Array. Everyone was at a standoff.

"Let her finish," KaLeah said.

Nikolat's lip lifted in a smirk, and he took one step back, but no one lowered any swords.

Amirra walked closer to the edge of the balcony, extending her arms out once again.

"I will not demand that you appoint me as your queen. I will not buy my place with promises. I only ask you to bestow upon me your faith as your now and future queen."

She then bowed her head to the people, who grew silent. Nikolat's eyes suddenly grew wide in shock. KaLeah turned her head from Nik to see what he was gawking at.

Floating behind and slightly above Princess Amirra was a large dragon with emerald scales and silver wings.

KaLeah looked back at Nikolat and then turned to each of the men surrounding them on the balcony. They had all lowered their weapons and stood back, gaping in amazement at the dragon spirit.

KaLeah lowered her own sword, realizing that everyone else could see it too. This wasn't a dream. It was the same dragon she had seen in the woods—the dragon that had changed her life forever.

"No, this is *not* happening," Nikolat yelled.

He lifted his sword again and ran past KaLeah, shoving

her aside before she could lift her sword back up. KaLeah nearly lost her balance but managed to kick her foot out in time to trip Nikolat, sending him off his aim at the last moment.

Hilip swiftly pulled Amirra away from the edge of the balcony. Nikolat jumped up, and KaLeah met his sword with hers. He fought her fiercely as he yelled, the phantom dragon still floating there above the balcony.

"This is my kingdom.," Nikolat yelled. "You are all superstitious cowards. Klackire is nothing but a ghost, a shadow of the past. This doesn't mean anything. I am your king. There is no voice to be heard, no decision to be made, and no dragon spirit to scare you all into submission. This is my kingdom!"

He was yelling loudly enough for KaLeah, for the generals, for Amirra, and for the people below to hear him.

KaLeah kept fending off his blows, but he was strong and directing all his anger at her.

He is afraid, hurt, and doesn't want to lose, she thought, not wanting to injure him but not wanting to be killed either.

She was beginning to be afraid of where this fight was leading. He had her pushed back now to the edge of the balcony. One well-placed jab and she could fall to the crowd below.

This man was one she had kissed, she had wanted to be with him always, to be his queen, but now he looked at her as nothing more than someone standing in his way. The hate stabbed at her heart, but she still couldn't bring herself to kill him.

Although she knew that one of them would have to die to end the fight.

A breeze blew across her hot cheeks, and she dared a glance back at the phantom dragon, still floating in the center of the balcony. It had begun flapping its wings and had a look of protection in its eyes.

Why would it want to protect me, KaLeah wondered? *Why was it even here?*

She heard more growls and whispers, but she couldn't tell if they were only in her mind or if others were hearing them as well.

The dragon suddenly took in a deep breath that seemed to suck the air from KaLeah's lungs. It exhaled a plume of blue flames that engulfed Nikolat.

His eyes went wide, and he screamed, dropping the sword. Within a blink of time, he was gone, leaving nothing but the sound of his sword clanking against the ground. The dragon dissipated into smoke, as if it had never been there.

"No," KaLeah said, dropping to her knees. Tears began to flood her eyes, falling down her face. "Nikolat?"

She couldn't understand why her heart cried out in pain and loss for the man who had just been trying to kill her.

She had loved him once, even if it hadn't been real or true. She had fought for him once.

And now, he was gone.

She touched the stone balcony. There was no heat and no ashes from the blue fire. She ran her hands frantically across the stone as if she could conjure him back.

Amirra and Hilip grabbed her arms and lifted her, pulling her away. As they carried her from the balcony, she could make out the chants from the people below.

"Long live the queen," they said.

⁎

KaLeah stared out of her window and up at Denlerack hanging in the afternoon sky. She had not left her chamber in days, choosing to mourn the loss of Nikolat in her solitude.

She was happy for Queen Amirra and knew that General Daven and his captains were helping her acclimate to her new role.

With Nikolat gone, General Array had agreed to go back to get Extelli under the control of Belarone. Word had spread throughout the land that a dragon spirit had ordained the new queen, and she was like a goddess now to everyone on Naldash. No one would dare touch her or speak ill of her. Amirra was safer now than she had ever been, since everyone feared her dragon protector.

The Lisodanyan king had sent livestock and jewelry as gifts to the new queen, with his loyalty, respect, and unwritten apologies.

KaLeah felt nearly useless now, so she didn't feel any guilt about hiding in her room. Even Hilip had left her alone, too busy setting up a new normal within the kingdom.

She knew that it wasn't Amirra's fault that Nikolat was dead, but KaLeah had nowhere else to direct her anger.

Me.

KaLeah heard the whispered voice in her head at the same time she saw the emerald dragon appear outside in the courtyard.

"Who are you?" KaLeah asked through the glass window. She assumed that the telepathic dragon would have no problem hearing her at a normal volume.

My name is Anissa La Alani. I am the dragon that separated the mother planet into the two sister planets Naldash and Denlerack.

"Klackire? The magical dragon?"

That is the name the humans gave me. I am the same.

"What do you want from me, Anissa La Alani? Why are you so involved in all of this?"

You already know. Your destiny is to finish the war and reunite the sister worlds. You must go to Denlerack. You must stop your true father.

"What if I refuse?" KaLeah felt a stubborn desire to push back against this phantom dragon. It had come into her life and changed everything. It had shown her the ship, gotten her father, Clegg, kidnapped, sent KaLeah on a journey that ended up with her becoming a young child's bodyguard, and then killed her first love right in front of her. How dare this dragon ghost make demands of her now.

The Denlerack ruler, your true father, will come and enslave the people of Naldash. The lands will deteriorate. Both planets, and every living thing on them, will eventually die.

"I don't care."

You will.

KaLeah considered these words. She looked away from the dragon spirit and up into the sky again. "This is crazy. It is crazy that I am even talking to you."

Nikolat was gone. The man who raised her was gone. Amirra was the new queen and would be protected by the legion she now commanded. Extelli and Lisodanya would no longer threaten Belarone, at least not for a while.

Her real father and maybe information about her mother were on Denlerack. Going to another planet seemed as unbelievable as talking to a phantom dragon.

"How would I even get there?" she asked, finally.

I can send you.

Of course, KaLeah thought, a magical dragon can divide planets, put words into my head, kill with a breath, and transport me to another planet. She rolled her eyes to herself. It wasn't as if she had anything to do or anything left to lose. Curiosity finally won and KaLeah started to pack.

She packed a small bag with supplies and a change of clothing, dressing in basic, unadorned threads, and then armed herself with daggers and her sword. She twirled the dragon favor pendant in her hands, considering whether to bring it. She quickly shoved it into the bottom of her bag then headed downstairs to the throne room.

There was now a long table in front of the throne. Amirra still looked so small, sitting on such a large seat. The captains and general were seated at the table. Everyone stopped talking when KaLeah entered.

"KaLeah," Queen Amirra said, smiling widely. She sat up straighter on her throne.

KaLeah bowed slightly and then approached.

"How good it is to see you out. Are you feeling better?"

"Yes, thank you. Queen Amirra, I must tell you something important if you have a moment."

Amirra's smile vanished and she nodded seriously, looking more closely at the pack that KaLeah was carrying.

"I will be travelling to Denlerack today to find out more about the future threat we are facing."

"Denlerack, of course," the queen said, leaning closer to KaLeah and whispering. "In all the commotion, I completely forgot." Amirra looked around the table. It was apparent that aside from Hilip, she had not yet told anyone else about Denlerack being a potential threat.

"Sirs, we have been informed that there is a kingdom on Denlerack intent on attacking us."

Captain Schar cleared his throat. "Surely, the queen is mistaken."

She turned her eyes to him sharply. "Captain, I am as serious as the dragon that stood behind me on the day my brother died. We have all been misled into believing the planet that sits in the sky is dead, devoid of human life. We must now take precautions. Favor KaLeah will go to Denlerack to gather information to help protect us against their inevitable attack. Is that clear?"

KaLeah was surprised by the changes in Amirra. It was as if the new queen's strength and courage had surpassed her own.

"General Daven, walk with us?" Amirra directed.

He stood, and the three of them walked out of the throne room and into the sunlight. Once they were on the lawn, Amirra turned and wrapped her arms around KaLeah, squeezing hard.

"Do you really have to leave today?" Amirra asked, her voice returning to that of a young girl's, thin and squeaky.

"Yes, the dragon is waiting to take me." KaLeah nodded toward the courtyard, where the phantom dragon stood.

"Wow," Hilip and Amirra both said in unison. The three of them stood in quiet awe for a few moments.

"Queen Amirra, are you pretending to be ruthless in front of those men?" KaLeah asked with a smile, lightening the mood. Amirra laughed.

"It was Hilip's suggestion," Amirra admitted. "He told me to channel the memory of my brothers and father; to act fearless and kind of mean."

"Well, it is very convincing. I'm proud of you, Amirra." KaLeah realized just how proud she felt and pulled Amirra back into an embrace. Tears filled both of their eyes, and they sniffled as they pulled apart.

"Please be safe, KaLeah," Amirra said softly. "You have become like a sister to me."

Clegg's words came back to her then, when he told her that he only cared for KaLeah *like* a daughter, but not as an actual daughter.

"You *are* my sister now, Queen Amirra," KaLeah told the child, looking deeply into her eyes. KaLeah made up her mind then and there that she would always choose Amirra to be her family. "I will come back home to you. You must be careful too. Remember, there are men from Denlerack already here. They have weapons like the one that killed Prince Bylex. They are acting as spies among us. Do not go off riding alone."

"I promise you I will not, dear KaLeah," she whispered in reply.

"Are you sure you should go alone? I could go with you," General Hilip said.

She turned and looked into his kind, light blue eyes, and was comforted by the idea of him being by her side. But she knew that taking him would be selfish. He was the only one she really trusted to keep the new queen safe.

"No, Hilip, thank you. I feel better with you here watching out for Amirra."

"I could send some of my men with you," he added.

"No. I think this is something I need to do alone."

She said farewell and gave Amirra's hand one last squeeze. Then she turned and walked toward the courtyard where the dragon Anissa La Alani waited to take her away.

"KaLeah, wait."

Hilip ran up behind her and grabbed her wrist, pulling her to a stop. He spun her around and she was so close, she could smell a sweetness on his breath.

"Take this with you." He placed a small dagger into her hand, folding her fingers softly over it.

"Hilip, I have weapons," she said, a smile curling up the corner of her lip.

"I need you to take something of mine with you," he said in a soft, gentle tone.

"Why?" she asked, puzzled although something stirred inside her looking into his eyes with his hands cradling hers.

"So, you don't forget about me." He smiled, winked, and then turned back around toward the castle.

She holstered the small blade and continued walking but with a lighter air in her step and a fluttering in her stomach.

The green dragon stood proudly with her wings spread out, looking transparent in the daylight.

"I'm here," KaLeah said reluctantly as she approached. Since the dragon had dispatched Nikolat so easily, KaLeah recognized the danger. And yet, she knew the dragon had only taken that action to save her life.

The dragon spirit had been here for thousands of years, and KaLeah was confident the dragon had no intention of harming her. She nodded respectfully to Anissa La Alani.

"So how am I going to travel to Denlerack? Are you going to fly me?"

Through the flames.

"What?"

It is painless. Do not fear.

Before KaLeah could protest, the dragon took in the familiar breath, sucking in the air from around her. KaLeah found she was breathless to speak, so she shouted at the dragon in her head.

The blue fire? The same fire that killed Nikolat?

The dragon exhaled the blue flames at her, and she felt a prickle of warmth spread along every particle of her skin.

The blue flames crawled up her fingers, arms, legs, and torso.

Her last thoughts, before the flames enveloped her head and took Naldash from view, were of Nikolat.

Was he still alive? Had the fire only transported him and not killed him?

She received no answer as she was consumed.

KINGDOM OF MACHINES
SISTER WORLDS BOOK 2

They're from different planets, with opposite lives. Will their unlikely pact take down tyranny… or lead to destruction?

Elektra is desperate to save her ravaged planet. So, strapping on leather and metal wings, she sets out to join the rebellion against the callous dictator. But she's just begun her journey when she spots a young woman under assault from violent thugs and swoops in to her defense.

Joining forces in the hope that together they can topple the tyrant, Elektra is suspicious of her new friend's claim about being from another world. And when she discovers the girl is actually the cruel despot's daughter, she fears her daring rescue may have extended her people's suffering.

Can this mismatched pair find common ground to fight back against oppression?

Kingdom of Machines is the fast-paced second book in the *Sister Worlds* YA fantasy trilogy. If you like conflicted heroes, post-apocalyptic battles, and a dash of steampunk style, then you'll love Tiffany Nicole Terry's absorbing adventure.

Buy *Kingdom of Machines* on Amazon to overthrow a vicious regime today!

ABOUT THE AUTHOR

Tiffany Nicole Terry (TNT to her friends) is a corporate communications manager by day, a novelist by night, and a mother to daughters and dogs every moment in between. A bit of a bohemian nomad, she has lived in every time zone in the continental United States but prefers to live where she can see mountains on the horizon. She is passionate about equality, diversity, and inclusion and believes the world can be a kinder and more sustainable place. Her books are full of positive empowerment messaging for girls, especially those raised through trauma, neglect, and abuse.

FROM THE AUTHOR

If you enjoyed this book, please leave a review, and spread the word. Help me reach more people who need this message. Thank you!

With love, TNT